I0640170

A
SCRAWLED NOTE
WAS
THE BEGINNING
OF
MURDER...

*My dearest dearest—I can't bear
what you said to me tonight, but
I can't bear to live without . . .*

That was all. A few simple lines. A simple suicide
note? That's what everyone thought, at first, including those two super-sleuths Colonel Primrose
and Mrs. Latham. But it turned out to be murder
—and the desperate killer returned to strike
again . . .

> *"You can't go wrong with this
> highly expert number . . . unusu-
> ally readable."*
> —New York Herald Tribune

FALSE
TO ANY MAN

". . . to thine own self be true,
And it must follow, as the night the day,
Thou canst not then be false to any man."
                    —HAMLET

By LESLIE FORD

WILDSIDE PRESS

DEDICATION
To
Janet's March Wind
who is NOT a spavined hack

False to Any Man

Published by Wildside Press LLC
www.wildsidepress.com

The fact that I'd seen Karen Lunt tripping gaily out of the polished granite façade of the Commonwealth Trust Building in K Street meant absolutely nothing to me at the time. Everybody one knows in Alexandria spends most of the time in Washington anyway, at a job or shopping or going to parties. It certainly never crossed my mind that she might be coming out of Philander Doyle's imposing suite of walnut-panelled offices that occupy the entire rear end of the second floor. For one thing, it's commonly assumed that Philander Doyle's clients never use the K Street entrance. People who don't approve of him say they come and go through the alley, and that's why the back stairs of the Commonwealth Trust Building are full of recesses and so dark that only a mole—or something used to prowling by night—could find its way there.

If I had any mental process at all, it was simply to think how enchanting Karen looked, laughing and batting her long black lashes to keep the snow out of her enormous blue eyes, and to wonder vaguely who the exceptionally good-looking young man was, leaning out holding open the door of his car for her. I saw both ideas reflected an instant later in the face of the other young man who came out of the Commonwealth Trust portals just then . . . and I thought something else too, as he saw Karen duck her high mink hat and bright corn-colored curls into the low car, followed by the rest of her, also swathed in mink. Even then I didn't connect her with Philander Doyle, largely, I suppose, because I didn't then know that Roger Doyle was in his father's office. Certainly the look on his face as he pulled his hat down against the snow wasn't one a lawyer ordinarily gives a departing client, not one who looked as enormously pleased with life as the girl in mink, anyway. Roger Doyle's face as he set out toward Connecticut Avenue was definitely what his aunt, Miss Isabel Doyle, would refer to as "a study, my dear, I assure you, a *real* study."

I went on into the bank. For a moment I couldn't get that almost savage look in Roger Doyle's lean, good-looking but rather complex face out of my mind. It was a little puzzling, too, for one heard so often, around places, that wasn't it too bad Karen hadn't had better luck with Roger. Like most marriageable girls in Washington the last five years since the Doyles had come back from New York, she'd tried and failed . . . leaving Roger, friendly but casual and definitely not interested, still loose in the sea. It would be ironical, I thought as I waited in line at the teller's window, and rather like life, if he was interested now that she wasn't.

Then I caught a glimpse of the green alarm clock on the teller's desk, and promptly forgot all about the two of them. I was already half an hour late for lunch with Colonel John Primrose, 92nd Engineers, U. S. A. (Retired), at the Army and Navy Club a block away through the snow and ice. While he wouldn't mind, his self-styled "functotum"—guard, philosopher and friend, as the Colonel puts it—Sergeant Phineas T. Buck, 92nd Engineers, U. S. A. (Retired), would mind intensely, if it isn't absurd to speak of a slab of frozen granite as being intense. I could see him—he lives with Colonel Primrose in their house on my street in Georgetown, as a kind of social, financial and spiritual manager—looking at his large gold turnip of a watch, won like most of his other very considerable worldly goods at the old Army game, his granite face, not smooth and polished like the façade of the Commonwealth Trust Building but harsh and seamed and fissured like the side of Mt. McKinley, congealing a notch lower, his viscid fishy slits of eyes in his lantern-jawed face glinting a colder grey. I've known for some time now that Sergeant Buck conceals, or rather doesn't conceal, behind that stony dead pan of his a deep-seated aversion to any potentially marriageable woman. If he could do it, I don't think he'd hesitate a minute to clap his Colonel into a monastery run on military lines and keep him there, never allowing him out to see one. —Not to lunch with one, anyway, and certainly not to be married by one when he wasn't looking. And least of all by me, Grace Latham, widow, aged thirty-eight.

So for a moment, with that gauntlet to run, I forgot Karen Lunt and Roger Doyle and the way Roger had pulled his hat down, watching her go off with the other man. It wasn't till Philander Doyle's name came up casually in the luncheon conversation, with the curried shrimps and chutney—which Colonel Primrose always orders at the Army and Navy Club and I steadily loathe—that I thought of them again.

"Do you know Karen Lunt?" I asked, apparently out of a clear sky.

6

Colonel Primrose cocked his head down and around—a bullet in the neck at the Argonne makes him do that, and he looks exactly like a parrot when he does—and looked at me with those sparkling black X-ray eyes of his, a little surprised.

"I've seen her around," he said. "She's quite fascinating, I suppose. I'm always surprised when I see her that she isn't married to somebody. However, I imagine she'd be pretty realistic about anything like love in a two-room apartment."

"Roger Doyle wouldn't present that problem," I observed.

He laughed shortly. "No, I should think not. Not with that father he's got. Is that the way it is?"

"Not that I know of," I said. "But about Karen?"

He shook his head.

"All I know is that she's Judge Candler's ward, and lives out in Alexandria in the Candlers' old carriage house."

He picked up the pack of cigarettes I'd opened carefully at one corner and tore the blue revenue stamp across its face. "If I don't, Buck will," he remarked with a smile. "He thinks laymen encourage crime."

I don't know why that came into my mind again as I passed their house on my way home that evening and saw Sergeant Buck, back from whatever fascinating thing his Colonel was doing for the F. B. I., clearing the snow off the sidewalk. I could hear his shovel ring against the uneven brick, the only sound in the street, as I let myself in my own front door. The snow had stopped, the road was still white, covered with the dry carpet that in a few more moments would be churned black by home-coming cars. I stopped for a moment on the doorstep. P Street in Georgetown looked like an old-fashioned Christmas card, and when I closed the door behind me I could hear the chains of passing cars like hollow sleighbells.

I shook the snow off my hat, listened to its sharp sizzle in the crackling fire in the living room, and drew the curtains aside to look out on the snow-covered back garden. The room, the fire, the snow-peaked frames over the dark box-wood, the patches of warm light from the window, the inside, the tea-tray on the low table in front of the chintz-covered sofa . . . all of it made the fact that a blue revenue stamp on a pack of cigarettes is worth six cents, and that racketeers steam them off and cheat the government out of a million dollars a year, seem very unreal and far-fetched, some way. I dropped the curtain in place again, thinking how remote crime is from ordinary people's lives. It seems peculiarly silly, now, that I should have stood there just then, boggling about

7

Sergeant Buck and crime. As Roger Doyle's aunt Miss Isabel said a day or so later, "You know, my dear, I think it's just as well we *don't* know what Providence has in store for us, I really do." And I dare say she's right, except for the Providence part of it. I shall personally always doubt that Providence had any hand in what happened in Chatham Street in Alexandria, Virginia, on the night of February 3rd.

Certainly I had no remotest inkling that the dark foreshadow of that night was already lengthening across the path—even less that it was creeping up my own doorstep at that moment, behind the light young feet scuffing off the snow against the old iron mud scraper. Karen Lunt and the scene in K Street were as far away as summer at April Harbor, my colored cook Lilac waddling up out of the basement kitchen, muttering darkly to herself as she answered the tinkling doorbell, was no more ominous than usual when she's interrupted starting dinner. Then I heard her voice, high-pitched whenever she's pleased, say, " 'Deed, Miss Jerry, come right in. Law, chile, you bin *wallowin'* in th' snow? Let me brush you off. There you is!—Mis' Grace, here Miss Jerry!"

And there was Miss Jerry the very next instant, glowing from the crisp cold night, her copper-colored hair red-gold in the firelight, framing her flushed pointed little face, her tortoise-shell eyes shining like stars, so radiant and alive that I positively gasped.

"Darling! What's happened? Have some tea!"

"Oh, everything's happened, Grace!" she cried. "And I'd love some. Milk and no sugar."

Jeremy Candler pushed the fraction of brown velvet hat off her bright curly head, deposited it with her bag and newspaper and woolly gloves on the chair by the door, and flopped down in the sofa beside me.

"Have you seen the evening papers?"

I shook my head.

"I just got in. Anyway, I avoid them as long as I can. My young are getting too near war age. What is it?"

She loosened her short beaver jacket and took the tea cup I held out to her and ate three hot marmalade rolls one after the other. Then she said, "Nothing, really—unless you read between the lines. Oh, Grace, it's marvelous!—Dad was at the White House today."

I looked blank. Everybody goes to the White House these days. Then I remembered, with a sudden catching of my

8

breath, what some columnist had written about Judge Candler.

"Do you mean——"

She put her fingers across her red lips.

"You mustn't breathe it, Grace! It's all an awful secret, and it's not settled, nearly. Won't be for a month, perhaps. But I had to come by, Grace! I'd have burst, or driven too fast and gone in the Potomac before I got home, or something shattering. I'm so happy I could die!"

She laughed again. "The boss thought I'd lost my mind, or had a bottle of champagne in the wash room!"

Then suddenly she became more serious than I'd ever seen her, even Thanksgiving Day when her young brother who goes to school with my younger boy—which is how I happen to know her—had such a pain that it didn't seem possible it was just an old-fashioned stomach ache and we had three doctors in to take out his appendix on the kitchen table.

"You know, Grace," she said, and stopped, her wide-set yellow-brown eyes fixed on the fire. "—But I don't suppose you do know at all, there's no reason you should."

She stopped again and smiled. Then she said quickly, "Dad's had pretty tough going."

I didn't say anything. Judge Candler had always seemed to me one of those extraordinarily untouchable people who dwell outside the common world. I'd never known him, however, except by reputation and the most occasional meeting at rather staid receptions, until the school holidays of the past winter. A fifteen-year-old boy always under foot can be an astonishing catalyst. Whatever tough going there'd been I'd more or less assumed had been on Jeremy's side of the road. It was she who took over when her mother died and raised her freckle-faced younger brother, and put up with her harum-scarum older one, Sandy, so her father could keep his head and heart in the clouds. Still, an airplane can hit bumpy patches ten thousand feet up, and I suppose men can too, even in the rarefied heights where Judge Peyton Candler lives.

"I don't mean he's ambitious," Jeremy said quickly. "I mean, not like . . . some men are."

I was a little surprised. I'd never thought of him as striving to get where he'd got.

"Not for money, I mean. I don't think he's ever thought about it. It would have made it easier, sometimes, if he had."

She smiled suddenly.

9

"I'm being a pig, and I don't mean to. And anyway, that's all over. But I mean after mother died, and he was appointed to the Court of Appeals, it seemed as if everything was—was marvelous. It was what they'd wanted, he and Mother, and all of us. Then he got sick and had to give it up."

I nodded. I remembered that from the newspapers.

"He was so frightfully conscientious, and he wouldn't stay on the Court and let the others do his work. Anyway, the doctors all said he'd die, he couldn't live six months.— That was just when the Doyles came back from New York and bought our old home across the street."

She gave a strange little laugh.

"He used to hate it so when Mr. Doyle would come and boom out about it being the drawback of Cavalier ancestry, that he was glad his ancestors were Irish navvies brought up on potatoes and peat smoke. Of course he was just trying to cheer him up, but, . . . well, you know."

"I know," I said. "I hate cheerful people when I'm sick. I'm sure I couldn't bear it if I knew I was dying."

"That's what I used to think," Jeremy said. "Then he got well. I guess the Cavalier blood was pretty good after all.— And now!"

She got up. The firelight glowed in the burnished glory of her hair. "It's too wonderful! It's just as if being poor and so tragically alone, and then being so ill, and coming back, had all made him a so much bigger person, really bigger! Oh, he's marvellous, Grace—I adore him!"

She stood there by the fire, slim and young. I thought, "It's you that's done the heaviest part of it, my lamb—you with your own Cavalier blood."

It was the Cavalier spirit burning there now in her firelit eyes and in the proud upward tilt of her thoroughbred young head. I suppose that's why I was so totally unprepared for her sudden reversion into . . . I can't think of anything to call it but just plain Salem witchcraft.

She turned to me.

"Did you ever feel, Grace, when everything was . . . perfect, that maybe it was—too perfect? That maybe it was all more than you'd any right to, and that . . . fate, or life, or something, was getting ready to give you a frightful—well, sort of kick in the pants? That something you never dreamed of when you thought you'd thought of everything would happen to send everything crashing down on top of you?"

There was a frightened look in her odd autumny eyes.

10

I nodded. It had happened to me, one cloudless summer afternoon, and to two small boys catching crabs in the shallow bay.

"That's the way I feel," she said softly. "Everything's so perfect. About Dad, and Sandy's suddenly becoming adult and working like a beaver. The stock Dad put in trust for me and Billy when they thought he was going to die is paying enough so I don't have to worry about Billy's school bills. It's all too good to be true. Billy even passed his Latin last month. It's unbelievable! I'm . . . scared. I've had my fingers crossed all day.

She stopped and looked at me.

"You know, Grace, I guess I'm crazy . . . but you know the way primitive people used to make burnt offerings, and . . . the way they put flowers at wayside shrines, to try . . . well, to try to keep on the right side of whatever gods there be?"

She stopped again, her face a little flushed, and pulled a small brown paper bag out of her jacket pocket.

"Its just raisins and suet," she said. "I thought, if you didn't mind . . . maybe I'd make a . . . well, a sort of sacrifice, to the birds in your garden. I've got to do *something*—and they'd think I was crazy, at home. Do you mind?"

I looked at her, a little startled. She was perfectly serious.

"Not at all," I said. I always wish on the evening star or a load of hay, so it didn't seem entirely crazy to me, just a little surprising that it came from someone so clear-eyed and direct as Jeremy Candler. I heard her open the garden door, felt the brief cold blast, and felt it again as she came in. She sat down beside me again.

"Don't tell Sandy."

"All right," I said. "And what about yourself, Jerry?" I asked. "Are you going to keep on with your job?"

"Of course. Unless Dad . . . well, I mean, if this *does* work out, and Dad thinks I shouldn't . . . But I don't dare think about that. I suppose if I don't need the money I oughtn't to keep it from some girl who does. And besides, Dad would need me."

I glanced at her. All the proud Cavalier and all the Salem witchcraft was gone, suddenly. She was just a twenty-year-old girl, sitting wistfully in the firelight.

"And what about getting married?" I said. "Have you ever thought of that?"

"Not lately."

11

She spoke so abruptly and with such a dead sort of voice that I was startled.

"I'm sorry," I said.

"Oh, it's all right. It's just that . . . well——"

She got up, trying desperately to get back the starch that had gone out of her.

"It's just that I guess Karen Lunt's got him instead. She had more time to work on it than I did—and more of what it takes, I guess."

She laughed, bent down and kissed me lightly on the cheek.

"I told you I was a pig.—Oh Lord, I'll be late for dinner. Goodbye, Grace."

She jammed her hat on the back of her head and dashed out, slamming the front door.

I sat there for a moment. Then I got up and pushed the little paper bag she'd brought her sacrifice in into the fire. As it flared up in a yellow flame I wondered if it wasn't her heart that she'd really thrown out there on the snow. And it was then that I began thinking about Karen Lunt and the young man holding the car door open for her, and Roger Doyle . . . though oddly enough still not of Philander Doyle, Judge Candler's oldest friend and one-time law partner.

2

If it hadn't been for all that, I doubt if I should have accepted an invitation to a party at Karen Lunt's house the night of February 3rd, the next morning when she called me up.

"I'm having a few friends in to supper, Mrs. Latham," she said over the phone. "I hope you don't mind my calling you one. The Candlers' friends have always been mine too. Jerry simply adores you! A quarter to eight. You know my place, don't you? The Candlers' sweet old carriage house in Chatham Street?"

I said I'd come and put down the phone; and all that day and evening, everywhere I went, Karen Lunt's name kept popping up. It was exactly like a new word that keeps appearing in everything you read when once you've looked it up in the dictionary or missed it dismally in a parlor game. I'd met Karen, once in a while, always, it seemed to me, the center of a little knot—ranging from two to a dozen—of men ranging from eighteen to eighty. But this day she was everywhere, or at least her name was.

At lunch the wife of a new senator from the West said, "I wonder if you know a girl named Karen Lunt."

I said, "Yes. Do you know her?"

"No, but my brother wanted me to look her up. He was at the party the night her father drove her mother and himself off a cliff into the Pacific Ocean."

"Really?" I said.

"Oh, yes. The coroner said it was accidental, but I dare say it was one of those accidents a lot of people had during Prohibition."

A girl on my right who'd been a reporter before she married said, "Somebody told me there wasn't a trace of alcohol in his brain. He was just stone broke, and she was suing for divorce, and he was mad about her and just couldn't stick it."

"I don't know about that," somebody else said, "but he couldn't have been very stone broke—Karen kept on at Briar Hill, and that costs two thousand a year, not counting clothes and extras."

"She can't have much left," a little woman across from me remarked from behind an enormous silver bowl of yellow roses. "I understand the poor child is living in the old carriage house on Judge Candler's place."

The former newspaper girl laughed. "Yes—decorated by Paravinci of 59th Street. I'd a lot rather live there than in the Candlers' old place, where your breath hangs in icicles."

She shook her head.

"It's wonderful, the way that gal's got Judge Candler buffaloed. It's a gift. He's her guardian, you know, and she's a blue-eyed orphan child. Her father was his best friend, the sworn brothers sort of thing. Philander Doyle made sort of a third wheel. They all started in old Colonel Candler's law office in Fairfax Street. Then Mr. Lunt came into a lot of money, and Philander Doyle moved to New York and—made his name."

Her eyebrows lifted a little.

"It's funny how they all come back to the old home town, isn't it.—Then Mr. Lunt married a girl he met on a boat. That would explain a lot, wouldn't you think?"

"It might very easily," I said, not having the faintest notion that anything had to be explained, or how that explained it.

"She's running around now with Geoffrey McClure," she went on. "He's a ninety-second secretary at some legation. They say he's a nice chap but has a definitely European view of marriage. Money first—love will follow.—What do you think of the new batch on the Hill? I think her husband's a lamb."

She nodded across the table at the new senator's wife and went on from there, and Karen Lunt's name dropped out.

It dropped out of my mind too, until I was coming back around six from a tea at the Belhaven Country Club on the other side of Alexandria. As I got to the light at the end of Washington Street it occurred to me that I might stop by and see Jeremy Candler, and find out how formal these little suppers in Karen's transmogrified carriage house were. And it wasn't very long before I was wishing very much that I'd had a flat tire instead.

Alexandria is a small place rather like Georgetown, except that it's eight miles along the Potomac from Washington instead of just next door. Unlike most towns, it didn't just grow. It was laid out at the end of the Rolling Road so the planters in the Northern Neck of Virginia would have a waterway to the sea and England for their tobacco, and a place where warehouses and wharves could be built. To make it completely urban, no man was allowed to buy more than two adjoining half-acre lots, at the original auction, and if he didn't build a suitable dwelling or place of business within a given period his lots were resold. And where once ships came laden with stuffs and manufactured goods from the mother country, and went back with sweet tobacco and cotton and furs from a new young land, where the tax policy that led to the Revolution was first discussed and the Bill of Rights was written, where Washington had a town house and Robert E. Lee spent his childhood, is now a sleepy town of mellow Georgian brick and new white paint, inhabited mostly by people who work by day in the capital and come back by the Memorial Highway along the Potomac to another world.

There are still old Alexandrians, of course, in spite of the Foreign Legion, living in the houses their pre-Revolutionary ancestors lived in. Chatham Street, where the Candlers have an old Georgian house with hipped roof and dormer windows, belonged, all of it, to Judge Candler's father. It's just below Lee Street, overlooking the dingy factories and wharves along the Potomac. The house across the street, however, where Philander Doyle and his sister and his son

14

now live, is the old Candler place. It was confiscated by the Northern troops during the Civil War, and when the Judge's grandfather and father returned, it wasn't, which is how the Candlers came to live in the less imposing house across the street, where Peyton Candler was born, and Sandy and Jerry and Billy. The two chestnut trees covered with wisteria were already there then, and the crape myrtles that made an arbor to the old carriage house where Karen lived. In fact very little must have changed since then, I thought as I went up the steps . . . not even the old darkey who opened the big green door and peered out through the gloom of the two old gas lamps burning in their wrought-iron standards at the corners of the iron handrail.

"Come in, Miz' Latham. Set down in th' parlor, Mis' Jerry she in th' liberry.—Ah reckon you two ladies knows each othah?"

Sitting in the crepuscular dimness of the Candler drawing room was a lady I didn't recognize for a moment . . . she seemed, like the room, so of another period altogether. Not Georgian, however, but old Edwardian, with her black velvet hat and purple feather boa around her thin shoulders. Even then I could see she'd been lovely once . . . a sort of lass with a delicate air. She rose and held out her black-gloved hand.

"How do you do, Mrs. Latham?"

"Oh, Miss Doyle—I didn't recognize you."

"No, I've been ill."

She pronounced the "been" as "bean."

"But I'm quite recovered, now," she said, with a kind of vague graciousness. "I've been sitting in this chair literally hours, waiting to see Judge Candler. He's closeted with the young people. I'm afraid he hasn't much time for an old woman, now he's becoming so famous."

She didn't say it with the least rancour, but rather charmingly, as if she were more amused than put out.

"So I really must be going. I have several things to see to. Really, my dear, I wonder one ever gets as many things done as one does. My brother laughs at me—he says I'm just a potterer. Goodbye, my dear, remember you're going to have tea with me one day soon. Goodbye! Make it *real* soon, won't you? My dear brother was speaking of you just last night at dinner. He'd be charmed to see you!"

Miss Isabel Doyle went on out, and since Philander Doyle doesn't know me from Adam, and Miss Isabel Doyle is known never to receive the people she asks to tea, I skipped that and sat down in the leather upholstered Chippendale chair she'd vacated. And I started—not violently, but definitely. That chair was cold as ice. Wherever Miss Doyle had been sitting, it was not there. And then—because I'm a natural-born busybody, I suppose—I found myself wondering why she'd bothered to say she'd been sitting in that chair literally for hours; wondering if, perhaps, it was just another patch out of the whole cloth of fantasy she always weaves.

I looked around the old room, lovely with age in spite of its dinginess. Its blue walls and white cornice and window trim and chair rail, carved but indistinct from a hundred coats of paint, and the horsehair carpet with its faded roses, all fitted so perfectly with the old furniture that generations of darkey hands had rubbed to a velvety satin patina. I doubted, some way, that Miss Doyle would have been just looking at any of this, or at the dark portraits on the wall. Then I heard the low confused murmur of voices through the closed door with the carved pineapple set in its broken pediment. It struck me instantly that that was where Miss Doyle had been: by that door, listening, deliberately, at the keyhole. That would account for the fib about the chair and her hasty departure under that barrage of nonsense about her dear brother.

I conquered an instant impulse to creep over to the door myself and find out, and it's just as well I did; for at about the time I would have got there, and probably had my ear bent down to the polished brass keyhole, the door swung open, and Karen Lunt flashed out. She wasn't in mink this time. She had on a simple black wool dress with enormous filigree silver buttons that set off her white skin and corn-colored hair as nothing else under heaven would have done. But it wasn't the dress or the hair, or even what I'd heard at lunch, that brought me to a sharp focus. It was the look on her face, perhaps in the smile on her soft red mouth, perhaps in those two wide-set eyes, as blue as lakes and almost as big. Whatever it was, it was culminated perfectly in the quick little dance step she took toward the door, flicking her open palms together at the same time as if she were washing her hands, in the most complete and triumphant satisfaction, of a matter that was in the finished business basket. She hadn't so much as seen me sitting between the two front windows in the high-backed leather chair, and I'm not small, nor is my gold wool number from Muriel King any more unobtrusive

16

than Miss Doyle's purple feather boa. Obviously Karen Lunt was so pleased with herself and whatever she'd accomplished behind the closed doors of Judge Candler's study that she hadn't eyes for anything else. Moreover, she hadn't bothered to close the door behind her, entirely, and the next instant I heard Jeremy's voice, throbbing passionately.

"I *won't*, Dad—do you hear? I *won't!* It's blackmail, I tell you! It's nothing else in the world!"

And Judge Candler's voice, quiet and slow but oh so terribly firm:

"I'm disappointed in you, Jeremy. I never thought a child of mine would be selfish and grasping."

I heard Jeremy's voice break in a hard dry sob.

"I'd never have dreamed you would turn on Karen this way. I thought you were fond of her."

"Fond of her?" Jeremy cried. "*Fond* of her? I hate her. I've always hated her—when she was going to Briar Hill and Sandy and I were wearing our cousins' made-over clothes and going to the cheapest schools in Virginia, and you working like a dog to pay for that even. I've got a right to hate her! You've always loved her better than you did us—when you were sick it was her future you were worried about, not Sandy's and Billy's and mine! Ours was accidental—you didn't know that old stock was going to be worth anything. You thought it was all right for me to get a job, but the idea of Karen getting one was unthinkable."

"I thought you *wanted* to get a job."

"I did!" Jeremy cried. "I wanted it so we could fix up the house a little, and Billy could ride, and do things other kids do, and so you wouldn't have to bother about my clothes, and his—but I didn't know you were still giving Karen her allowance every month. I didn't mind giving up the rent we got from the carriage house. I didn't mind your taking care of her when she was left without anything. But I do mind now! I won't give that stock back. It isn't hers, it's Billy's and mine, and we've got a right to it. She can't have everything that belongs to us! She'd never have dared ask for it if——"

"*Jeremy!*" Judge Candler's voice came down like the Chief Justice's gavel in a babbling court room. "That will do. I'm asking you to turn back Karen's stock. I expect you to do it. The papers will be ready tomorrow."

There was a long stunned silence. Out of it at last I heard Jeremy's voice, strangled but deadly calm.

"You're asking something I can't do, Father. It isn't right

17

—and if it were anybody else but——"

"I said that will do, Jeremy. The papers will be ready to-morrow."

For a moment I heard nothing. Then the door into the hall closed, and I heard sharp light feet on the wide pine boards and saw Jerry's plaid skirt flash by, and heard the front door slam, and in a moment the engine of a car cough violently a couple of times and start. In the next room I heard the creak of a swivel chair as Judge Candler settled down at the desk. Then, like Miss Isabel Doyle, I gathered up my bag and gloves and hurried out as quietly as I could.

3

It had started to snow again as I drove slowly back home along the Memorial Highway. Across the dark stretches of the Potomac, Washington lay like a star-spangled city in fairyland. The white dome of the Capitol and the tall shaft of the Monument with its red cyclops eye shone through the flurrying snow, fabulous beacons of light. I crossed the river under the shadow of Arlington, drove around the Lincoln Memorial with the dim heroic figure of the great emancipator seated in the lighted sanctuary, and turned down the river again toward Georgetown.

I was too troubled to notice the dirty sidings and belching smokestacks that always strike me after I leave the parkway and turn up 30th Street toward home. I couldn't get Karen's smile, and that victorious so-that's-that gesture with her open palms, and the passionate justice of Jeremy's voice, out of my mind. I unlocked the door and let myself in, and went along toward the sitting room. Downstairs I could hear Lilac banging pots and pans, and wondered what had happened now—the sounds of the kitchen being the perfect barometer of the state of our small nation. And in the living room door I stopped abruptly.

Jeremy Candler was sitting hunched together on the otto-man in front of the fire, her little pointed face as pale as old ivory under her mop of burnished hair.

"Hello," I said.

"Hello. I hope you don't mind my barging in this way. Lilac says you're not having anybody in tonight."

She turned quickly to the fire and started poking it, but not before I saw the trembling collapse around her red mouth, and the blinding flash of tears in her autumn-streaked eyes.

"I think it's swell," I said. "Let me put my things up. I'll be down directly."

I knew she wouldn't want me to see her cry, so I changed into a house coat and pottered about, as Miss Doyle said, for a few minutes. When I came down she was still pale and still hunched together on the ottoman, but quite composed.

"It's snowing again," I remarked.

"That's why I didn't want to drive out to Alexandria," she said. "My tires are frightfully smooth. I thought maybe you'd lend me some pajamas and let me stay all night. I've got to be at the office early in the morning."

It was far from me to say "My lamb, you're telling the most frightful story." I said:

"I'm delighted. I can even give you a toothbrush I got at a one-cent sale yesterday."

"You really don't mind?"

"Really."

"Then I'll call up . . . home."

She got up unsteadily, sat down in the end of the sofa and picked up the phone. After a moment she said, "William—this is me. Tell . . . my father I'm staying all night with a friend in Washington. Oh, I'm *fine*. Be sure to lock the side door, won't you? Goodbye."

She sat there staring into the fire. I picked up the paper and looked through it. Finally, as if she recognized that neither of us was acting quite normally, she said, "I've got sort of . . . of a headache, so don't mind if I'm . . . I'm stupid, will you?"

"You'd probably like to go to bed early," I said. "You'll find some non-lethal sleeping pills in the bathroom, if you'd like one."

Just then the phone on the low table at the end of the sofa rang. I picked it up. A man's voice that I didn't recognize said, "Is Miss Candler there, please?"

I glanced at Jerry. The quick fear that leaped into her eyes and the sharp panicky shake of her head really alarmed me, but I said in a quite normal voice, "Sorry. Would you like to leave a message?"

"No, thanks," the voice said. I put the phone down.

"Was it . . . my father?" Jeremy whispered.

I felt the sting of perfectly reflex tears in my own eyes—she so obviously hoped it was. I shook my head. "I'd have recognized his voice," I said, and added my younger son's

19

"And how!" to myself. I don't think I could mistake that firm utterly impersonal tone in a thousand years.

"Maybe it was Sandy," she said tentatively.

"You *do* want one of them to care where you've got to, you poor baby," I thought.

"But you'd know his voice too, wouldn't you?"

She was trying desperately to sound as if it didn't matter, and fortunately just then Lilac's black moonflower countenance appeared in the dining room door.

"Dinner's served, madam," she announced. She always goes slightly formal after she's lighted my great-aunt Deborah's Georgian candelabra, and she always drops it as instantly as she did now.

"Miss Jerry, Ah ain' goin' take that plate till you eat every las' moufful of you' dinnah. You heah what Ah'm sayin'? You'll go outa here an' get pneumonia."

I watched the child choke down the rest of her creamed spinach, blinking back tears of perfectly unreasoning gratitude for somebody to care what she did. I sat there wondering how I'd ever been deluded into believing she was grown up and enormously efficient and direct when she was nothing but a hurt heart-hungry little girl. It would take Lilac, with the mother-instinct of her race, to know and understand that.

After dinner she didn't go upstairs. She simply sat in front of the fire, staring into it. She didn't move when the doorbell rang. I don't think she even heard it, or anything—not until Lilac's voice came from the hall: "Ah don' know if she's in or not."

The voice I'd heard on the phone said, "Tell her I'd like to see her. I don't want to bother her, but——

"Ah'll see," Lilac said.

I glanced at Jerry. She'd straightened up, her lips parted a little, a faint flush that may have been from the fire or the food Lilac had made her eat on her high pale cheekbones. She looked blankly at me. Then Lilac was in the door, and just behind her, towering considerably over her grey kinky head, were the lean dark face and blue Irish eyes of young Roger Doyle.

"This gennaman wants to see Miss Jerry," Lilac said.

Since he was already in the room, I thought, there wasn't much anybody could do about it. I got up.

"Come in, Roger," I said.

Jeremy had turned away. Only the top of her burnished

head with the firelight on it was visible, but I'd seen her little
jaw tighten and the sudden smoldering embers in her eyes
as she remembered, I suppose, that there was something
about the young man in the door she didn't like. Which was
certainly not the impression I'd got when she first heard his
voice.

Roger Doyle could only see the molten-red-gold top of
her head, and then the smoldering yellow gold-flecked eyes
as she turned around. His face tightened.

"I thought I'd come and see if you wouldn't like to go
home, Jerry," he said stiffly.

"Thanks—I'm staying all night with Grace."

He stood there, baffled and rapidly secreting adrenalin—
or whatever it is people do when they start getting mad as
hops in spite of all their will to keep cool and dispassionate.

"As a matter of fact, you're just being a blasted idiot," he
blurted out angrily.

Which is a bad way to pour oil on the troubled waters,
especially if they have red hair.

Jeremy Candler straightened up, her eyes blazing.

"Oh, am I?"

Roger Doyle groaned. "Oh Lord, Jerry, can't you see what
you're doing? Why don't you let her have the filthy stock?"

I got up.

"If you two don't mind," I said, "I've got to see the man
who does dogs."

But Jerry's hand flashed out and held mine. "No, don't go,
Grace! *Somebody's* got to stick by me!"

Roger Doyle's face went a shade darker. He started to
speak, but Jerry was quicker.

"If your father had kept it, or sold it to anybody but my
father, it wouldn't have been given back!" she cried. "It's all
very well for you to say 'Let her have the filthy stock,' but
you haven't got a brother to look out for because there's nobody else to do it, and your father hasn't been paying her bills
for thirteen years the way mine has! You've never heard of
'the solemn obligation of friendship,' and if you made a
promise and found you'd drawn·a dud you wouldn't hesitate
five minutes to toss it in the river!"

She stopped just long enough to catch her breath, but not
long enough for Roger to catch his, or me mine, I'm afraid.

"You don't know what it is having bills pile up, and staying
awake all night trying to decide whether to pay for the coal
or take Billy out of school and then have your father send

21

Karen the money because the poor child's got in debt again!"

Her eyes were like shooting stars. She was really lovely—a whole blazing shaft of fire. Poor Roger Doyle stood staring at her, utterly transfixed.

"I didn't mind—not very much—when she was going to school, but I do now. She's just as able to get a job as millions of other girls. Even then she's got no right to want that stock back now. It still doesn't pay as much as she gets from Father. And why has she waited till now? She's known it was paying again for over a year. Why has she suddenly made up her mind it belongs to her? She's got no right to it, and she knows it, and you know it too! I know you're in love with her—why don't you marry her? Then she wouldn't care whether she got the filthy stock or not! Or do you want her and it too? Oh, I hate you, Roger Doyle!"

He stood there grimly for a moment, his lean jaw working, his blue eyes smoldering under his dark brows drawn together ominously. Then I put my hand over my mouth to keep from screaming as he took two swift steps toward her, and dropped it again when I saw he wasn't going to strike her. He'd caught her in his arms, her clenched little fists pinioned to her sides, and was pressing his lips passionately to hers, and to her hair, and her eyes. Then just as suddenly he held her off a little ways from him, his hands still holding her arms tight to her sides, his blue eyes looking down at her shocked upturned face.

"Don't be a fool, Jerry. It's you I love. Don't you *know* it . . . haven't you known the last five years?"

His voice sounded—and his face looked—exactly as if he were about to wring her neck.

Then he let her go abruptly.

"Only keep your shirt on, Jerry. Just a few more days—then I'll tell you about it."

He picked up his hat and was gone, without—as Lilac says—saying goodbye or good morning. I heard the front door bang and hurrying feet scrunching the dry snow.

Jeremy Candler stood there, utterly and completely demolished, and dropped onto the ottoman, her mouth and eyes wide open, staring at the door where he'd gone, her pale face crimson.

"Dear me," I said.

She moistened her lips.

"He . . . must be out of his mind!" she gasped at last.

22

"Definitely, I should say," I replied. "If you don't mind, I'm going to bed. Lilac will turn out the lights."

4

The next morning when Lilac brought my breakfast tray she put it down without a word, not even the sort of grunt that usually means that Shiela, my Irish setter, has been sick on the hall rug. She rattled up the Venetian blind behind my dressing table, banged down the window and demanded darkly, "What's they done to that chile?"

I shook my head. Lilac can't fool me. She knows more about everything that goes on than I do, and long before. I poured a cup of coffee and took a sip of orange juice.

"She done cry herself to sleep in there all by herself, las' night."

She picked up my shoes and jammed them in the rack.

"Oh dear!" I thought. I'd somehow got the sentimental notion that Jerry would go to sleep happier than she'd been for ages.

"Mus' is that devil Karen Lunt," Lilac said.

"Why, *Lilac!*" I exclaimed.

"William, he say she's a devil," she retorted. "An' he been livin' there since he was bawn. He say the Judge, she got him wrapped up in her apron, with them *blue* bat eyes."

She stressed the "blue" as if it were a strange unholy color for eyes to be.

"An' her tongue sweet as butter. He say, ain' no knowin' what devilment she up to nex'."

I don't know why I always try to defend people that Lilac doesn't like. "She seems to me a very attractive girl," I said. "I'm going to supper there tonight."

"Then you ought to be 'shamed," Lilac replied. "—An' that pore baby in there cryin' her heart out."

She went out, mumbling and muttering. I don't know why I put up with her, except that I couldn't live without her. She came before my older child was born, and he'll be seventeen before long. Sometimes her loyalties that know no shading are pretty trying . . . especially if I happen to have at the same dinner party someone she calls a saint on earth seated next to somebody who's a devil from hell. I opened my paper, wondering myself if I really ought to go to Karen's party. Then I heard Lilac coming back from the stairs.

"Is that chile comin' back tonight?"

"I don't know," I said. "Ask her."

"She's went, to th' office.—Her workin' like common trash."

"Don't be stupid, Lilac," I said sharply. "Working doesn't make people common."

"Then why don' that Karen Lunt get herself a job, 'stead of layin' in bed till noon every day?"

I realized I'd fallen headlong into a trap. She gave a kind of victorious grunt and closed the door, and I went back to my paper, thinking that after all it was a small price to pay for peace.

Then the telephone rang. If I'd really thought we were going to have any peace that day, I was wrong. I picked it up, heard the operator say "Five cents, please," heard a nickel clang at the other end and the operator say "Go ahead, please."

A man's voice said, "Is Miss Candler there?"

I said, "No, she's not. Is it you, Roger?" And before I'd got it out of my mouth I realized it wasn't Roger. It was a quite oily voice, and it said "Who?" so quickly and in such a pouncing way that I was a little disturbed.

I said, "Miss Candler is not here."

"Where can I get in touch with her?"

By this time, whether it was because Lilac had been so trying, or because I hadn't had breakfast yet, or there actually was in that voice all I seemed to feel in it, I was really worried. I said, "Who's calling, please?"

"A friend," the man answered. "It's important I get in touch with her."

"I'm sorry," I said. "Perhaps you'd better call her home."

"She stayed all night at your place, didn't she?" the voice demanded unpleasantly.

The nice thing about a telephone is that you can bang it down. Not that it did much good. An hour later he called again. Lilac answered. Not even my friends can get information out of her, so that was all right. He called again at eleven and twice during lunch. Some women came in to play bridge in the afternoon, and every half hour, it seemed to me, the phone would ring again, and Lilac would put her head—getting blacker each time—in the door and say, "That man callin' up 'bout Miss Jerry again." It got so I could almost hear that nickel clanging and hear that oily unpleasant voice.

And you can always count on your friends to be helpful,

24

especially when they're dummy. Dummy on the east said, "Jeremy Candler's a frightfully nice girl, but I do wish she'd give that old brown velvet evening dress to the Salvation Army. By the way—have you heard! Sandy's got a job, believe it or not, and they say he's working like a beaver."

She paused to fish inelegantly around in the silver dish for a chocolate that wouldn't be too fattening.

"You know, I don't see how anybody as ugly as Sandy can be so completely attractive. I suppose, though, if he'd been a Greek god he'd never have come through that crackup in the Bakers' cornfield last spring without a scratch the way he did. Just think what a good plastic surgeon could have done with that face. I know Ben Adams, who did over Lucy Dawes, is dying to have a go at him. And so far he's demolished at least three cars and the plane and nine telephone poles without so much as a sprained ankle . . ."

"I suppose now he's got a job he'll slip on the hall rug and break his neck," my partner remarked. "It's your deal, Grace."

The phone rang once more just then, and I was so jittery I exposed the only king I'd had all afternoon and then had to watch it trump the only ace I'd had for years.

Dummy on the west took up the Candlers where dummy on the east had dropped them.

"I wonder what happened between Sandy and Karen Lunt. Maybe he took it too much for granted. Maybe it's money. But in that case I can't see why Karen's wasting her time with Geoffrey McClure. He may be as handsome as sin, but the wife of one of the legation secretaries told me his family haven't anything but a mouldy old country house with thirty bedrooms and one bath and six daughters to marry off."

My partner, glowering mildly as my singleton ace dropped, said, "I should think Karen would concentrate on Roger Doyle. His father's literally rolling."

"He's not handing any of it out," Dummy said. "Do you know—I saw Miss Isabel Doyle at the auction of old Miss Fairweather's things the other day. She bought three trunks of old clothes sight unseen! If she turns up in that purple feather boa Miss Fairweather used to wear to early service at the Cathedral, I'll die—literally! That's game and rubber for us, partner. You could have taken Grace's jack if you'd finessed her eight. That's eighty-three cents you owe me, Grace."

She could have taken practically anything in my hand and

25

I could have owed her eighty-three dollars and I wouldn't have cared. Miss Isabel Doyle's purple feather boa weighted me down like the albatross, for some reason. Lilac bringing in tea was all that got me through the rest of the afternoon. If the phone had rung again, I should have died—literally.

I almost did anyway when the last one of them had gone laughing down the snowy steps, and I'd gone back to the living room to collapse a moment and the doorbell suddenly jangled as if it were being yanked off its ancient springs. My heart sank.

"If it's that man who's been phoning, Lilac," I said, "I wish you'd call Sergeant Buck."

Then my heart sank even further. I'd never thought the day would come when I'd find myself thinking of that dead pan and those fishy eyes with anything like affection. I realized suddenly that from the third time the phone had rung I'd been thinking about him—him and not his Colonel, for Colonel Primrose believes generally in law and order and Sergeant Buck, in his grim way, knows there are some things the police can't do.

I was considerably more relieved than I cared to admit, however, in spite of Sergeant Buck down the street, when it was Sandy Candler who bolted into the room, not the oily gent from some tavern pay station with a pocketful of nickels. Except that the relief didn't last very long.

He tossed his hat on the chair by the door. "Where's Jerry, Grace?" he demanded abruptly.

If my heart hadn't already been exhausted from its various sinking spells, it would have gone down to my boots with one look at his red-headed ugly face. "It's not handsome, Mrs. Latham, but it's the kind any girl's mother will trust," he'd grinned the first time I ever saw him, and I know that in five minutes I would have trusted him anywhere—even behind the wheel of a car, which was little short of suicide from everything one heard.

Now, standing in the middle of the room, his brown eyes anxious, his long lank ungainly figure lurched forward, he was even uglier and oddly enough even more comforting than I'd ever thought him.

"Where is she, Grace?" he repeated urgently.

"She left here for the office at half-past eight," I said. "Have you tried there?"

"She hasn't been there all day. They said she called up from a pay station first thing this morning. Said she wasn't

26

feeling very well, but she'd be in after lunch. She didn't come in, and didn't phone."

He started to stick his hand in his pocket, and reached down instead to the silver box on the mantel for a cigarette. I noticed that the knuckles of his big red hairy hands were crisscrossed with fresh clean adhesive tape. I took a deep breath and counted ten. After all, Jerry was a pretty intelligent young person and there was no sense getting alarmed. There are lots of times, I told myself, when one wants to get off alone. But I could have counted ten hundred without stilling the sickening dread in the pit of my stomach. Jerry might be intelligent, but she certainly wasn't herself, and one look at Sandy and no one would have called him an alarmist—especially about his own sister.

"If she's out driving around the country in that collapsible crate she's probably lying in a ditch somewhere," he groaned. "The roads are like glass, and those tires of hers should have been boiled down for erasers fifteen thousand miles ago."

"There are worse places than ditches," I said. "Especially nice snow-filled ones."

He threw the half-smoked cigarette into the fire. "Look, Grace—did she say whether she was going to show up for Karen's party?"

"So that's what you're chucking your weight about for?" I asked. I was a little annoyed that it was Karen he was thinking about, not Jerry at all.

"And it's plenty," he said shortly.

"I suppose what really matters is her getting home in time to sign the papers your father's——" I remarked, and stopped as Sandy jerked up as if I'd struck him full in his ungainly face. "Oh, Lord," I thought; "you *complete* idiot!"

"You mean, he's——"

He picked up another cigarette, turned his back to me and lighted it. "So that's it," he said after a moment. "The poor little devil."

"Look," I said. "I don't know what all this is about, and very likely it's none of my business. But why is it Jerry that's on this spot?"

"Because she was twenty-one three weeks ago," he said. His big elastic mouth twitched ironically. "Up to that time she wouldn't have mattered. Dad and Mr. Doyle could have done it instead."

It still didn't make sense to me.

"Does she *have* to give Karen this stock everybody's jittering about?"

Sandy bit his lips. "I guess she does. Unless she wants to sink the ship with all hands aboard."

"Legally?"

"Not legally."

"Morally?"

"Nor morally either."

"Then why——" I began.

"To keep Dad's name out of the headlines, in case this . . . business in Washington goes through," he answered quietly. "That's why. Don't try to make it make sense. It doesn't, and it didn't, and it never will."

"Sandy—do you want her to give it back?" I asked.

"I didn't, this noon." He looked down rather grimly at his plastered knuckles. "My guess now is it'll be the . . . well, the easy way out."

I nodded at his hand. "What happened?"

He shrugged his big angular shoulders.

"I don't exactly know. A cop was picking the rat up out of the gutter in front of the Treasury Building, the last I saw. I was running like hell."

"To keep 'Judge's Son Arrested in Street Brawl' out of the headlines?"

"Something of the sort. The guy collared me as I was coming out of the office. Said he was an attorney looking into the management of Miss Lunt's estate, and we'd better do something about a certain stock, or else. I didn't catch the rest of it—a fireman's parade was going by."

My hand against my cheek was as cold as ice. Sandy looked at me.

"What's the matter, Grace?"

His brown eyes—all brown, not flecked with sun like his sister's—tightened apprehensively.

"Just that I'm wondering if that's the man who's been calling here for Jerry all day—sort of oily-voiced."

His face went a shade grimmer. "The dirty bastard," he said softly. He got up. Somehow I had the idea that it would take more than a telephone pole to stop him when he got going. He picked up his hat from the chair. "I'll see you at Karen's," he said.

I shook my head. "I don't think so."

"You've got to," he said quietly. "The family may need a friend."

28

5

I don't think I ever dressed for a party with less enthusiasm. I put my hair up and put a bunch of flowers in it, and promptly took them out and put it down again. There was no use adding an extra hurdle to the evening. The same was true of driving the eight icy miles to Alexandria. I called a taxi, and was glad I had. The roads were foul, but they were the driver's problem, not mine, and at that he made it faster than I'd have believed possible. It wasn't quite half-past seven as he skidded to a stop in the cobblestoned gutter in Chatham Street and said immediately, "Jeez, I guess it's that little white house all lighted up like a Christmas tree you want to go to, not this graveyard."

I looked out. He'd stopped in front of the Candlers'. The two yellow gas jets burned feebly in their delicate standards on the high stoop railing. The fanlight glowed dimly over the door. Otherwise the house was dark as pitch.

"No, this is fine," I said.

He got out and opened the door. "Okay, Miss. Don't slip in them fancy heels."

I made my way across the glassy hillocks where the roots of the old maple tree had disrupted the brick sidewalk, and went up the stone steps. As I started to pull the bell I glanced back, attracted, I suppose, by the fact that the taxi hadn't started off. Or perhaps it was the sound of approaching feet scrunching in the dry snow. The driver had stopped in front of his cab and was waiting. A man came into the narrow yellow circle of the headlights and stood talking to him. I couldn't hear his voice, but I heard the driver say "Okay, buddy, I'll stick around—gotta light?"

The other man struck a match and held it out. For one instant it illuminated his own face. I caught my breath sharply. It was swaddled in bandages, with one particularly big white patch strapped across his nose. Before I could recover myself sufficiently to take hold of the brass bell knob he'd turned and disappeared into the dark, in the direction of the big house across the street.

It flashed suddenly into my mind that he'd made a mistake. He'd probably asked for the Candler house and had been directed to the old mansion, still known by that name but now owned and occupied by Philander Doyle. I waited a moment. I could see his dark figure go up the steps and stand silhouetted against the big white door. And then the door opened and he went in immediately, as if he was not only known there but was expected at that moment.

I heard myself say, "Well, for goodness' sake!" The taxi driver cut off his motor and switched down his lights. The cab stood as a dark island against the curb. Another car pulled in a few yards ahead of him, toward Karen Lunt's gleaming little jewel of a house, some people got out, laughing. I pulled the Candlers' bell and waited, with a strange conflict in what writers of a more reserved age would call my breast, but which involved, it seemed to me, my entire viscera.

For a moment nothing happened. I was just on the point of giving up and going on to Karen's when I heard a big booming voice on the other side of the door. "I'll answer it," it said, and in a second there stood before me, the dim light from the old brass lantern in the hall framing his fine leonine head, the gas jets on the stoop illuminating the broad immaculate expanse of white shirt front with its gleaming black pearl studs and the diamond and platinum chain cabled across his magnificent embonpoint, the noted if not actually notorious figure of the owner of the house across the street.

"Good evening—is it Miss or Madam?" Philander Doyle boomed, with vast cordiality. "The party's next door."

"I know," I said quickly. "But I stopped to see if Jeremy'd gone. I'm Mrs. Latham."

He put out a warm welcoming paw.

"My *dear* young lady! I must be losing my grip. The prosecutor said so last week, but I thought he was a fool. Come in, come in!"

Except for that big rich Irish voice—I'd seen a dozen of the women feature writers who cover trials refer to it as a siren's song wooing the jury to destruction on the rocks and shoals of injustice—there was no sound in that cold dark house. "Jerry, Jerry, where are you?" I thought desperately.

"Come in, Mrs. Latham." Philander Doyle drew me across the threshold into the frigid hall. Then out of the library came a sudden little cry. "It's Grace! Oh, come in!" and Jeremy Candler came running out into the hall. "Oh, I'm *so* glad you've come!"

The hands she seized mine with were cold as blocks of ice, the cheek she pressed against mine was scalding hot. I was so relieved to see her—even to see her in the familiar brown velvet evening dress that Dummy had wished she'd give the Salvation Army—that I didn't think of what icy hands and feverish cheeks must mean. Not until she'd led me into the library, and then I knew.

A green glass-shaded reading lamp cast a white glow on the tooled leather top of the old mahogany desk, on a single legal-looking paper at one end, on the black penholder, its shiny nib wet with ink, that lay beside it. In the soft emerald light above it stood Judge Candler, tall and slender, as distinguished and courtly in dinner dress as he is in the pictures you see of him in his robes. Between the two high windows, their heavy blue worsted curtains drawn against the night, a fine old copy of the St. Memnon of Mr. Justice Taney framed his own splendid white head. He bowed to me, but there was no friendliness in his greeting. The fire his once red hair had indicated burned sombrely in the depths of his fine brown eyes set deeply under his bushy greying eyebrows. He looked past me at his daughter.

I saw Philander Doyle look at her too, at the end of the desk, at her proud little head with burnished shadows from the coal fire behind her playing on her copper hair. Whether it was admiration in the brilliant blue eyes of her father's one-time law partner and long-time friend I wouldn't know. For a moment I thought it was more than that . . . pity, even. But I can sometimes be amazingly wrong.

Then the strained silence in the emerald-shaded room was broken abruptly—not by Judge Candler's firm gavel tones, or the fabulous voice of Philander Doyle, or Jerry's passionate voice, bell-clear, but by a respectful and at the same time oddly admonitory throat-clearing from the corner. I glanced quickly around, and blinked my eyes.

In the green dusk I saw something that, if it hadn't cleared its throat, I should have thought was a smaller-than-life-sized figure of a law clerk from a Dickens novel. He was sitting bolt-upright, clutching a green baize bag across his knees. He had a wisp of grey hair combed like a Jacob's ladder across his bald egg-shaped head, which was rather too large for the rest of him. And he cleared his throat again, with less respect this time and more admonition.

Judge Candler turned to his daughter.

"It's getting on, sir," he said, in a high-pitched and rather querulous voice that couldn't have been more perfect.

Judge Candler turned to his daughter.

"If you'll sign, please, Jeremy. Mr. Pepperday goes to bed

at eight o'clock."

Jeremy drew a deep breath, standing there silently for an instant, her sun-flecked eyes fixed on her father. In the emerald light he looked so extraordinarily like the Wizard of Oz that I knew she'd have to sign. The silence in the room was so overpowering that I could hear the blood throb in my own throat. Then a strange thing happened. So quickly that it was almost legerdemain, and yet with no suggestion of anything but the utmost calm, Philander Doyle's hand reached forward and picked up the black penholder, snapped it between powerful fingers like a matchstick and tossed it across the hearth rug into the blazing fire.

It was all the stranger, and the more astonishing to me, because in some way I'd definitely got the idea that Philander Doyle was in favor of her giving the stock up to Karen. But I was certainly wrong.

"Listen, my friend," he said, his mellow voice vibrating through the emerald shadows in the still room like firelight through old wine. "You can't do this. It's Billy the girl's thinking of, not herself. Billy and you and Sandy. If you force her to do this, you'll lose a daughter's love, and faith, and everything that's made you what you are tonight. Believe me, Peyton, I, who have never had a daughter, know."

He stopped for an instant, frowning a little, as that absurd tiny figure in the corner, looking at a vast silver watch that came out of its checked waistcoat pocket, cleared its throat again.

"If it's Karen you're concerned about, you may ease your mind. She and Roger have come to an understanding. I'm not a rich man, but my son's wife will never want. Roger loves Jeremy as I love my dear sister—he would never allow his wife to accept such a sacrifice from her."

I wasn't looking at Jeremy when he started to speak; I didn't dare look at her now. Outside in the hall I could hear the grandfather clock girding its ancient loins to the hour. It struck . . . "Boom, boom, boom . . ."

"And furthermore," Philander Doyle said, his great voice positively lathering with concern,— "it's Mr. Pepperday's bed time."

That's when I looked at Jerry. She was like a frail shaft of burning ice. Her pointed tongue crept out to moisten her paralyzed lips. She put out her hand. "Give me your pen, Father," she said—each word a drop of scathing fire. "Karen may have the stock—with pleasure."

Judge Candler opened the drawer in front of him, took out a pen, dipped it into the silver inkstand under the reading lamp and held it out to her. As her fingers touched it Philander Doyle's hand shot out again, grasped the paper in front of her, crumpled it and tossed it into the fire. Before Jerry could flash across the hearth rug to retrieve it the flames had licked it up, leaving one feather of grey and black curling on the poker. I turned around, my heart beating rapidly. Mr. Pepperday was putting on his overcoat. He bowed to the Judge and scurried out. Judge Candler stood motionless for an instant, a curious light flickering in his dark sombre eyes. Then, without a word, he pushed the desk drawer shut, came out into the room, picked up his daughter's wrap and stood quietly holding it for her. Jeremy stood there a moment, a hot flush burning on her high cheekbones, her eyes smoldering embers. She stepped forward, her father put the coat around her slim bare shoulders.

Philander Doyle wrapped his white scarf around his neck and struggled into his overcoat.

"I hope we have something fit to eat," he said heartily. "But we won't. My sister's been in charge of the kitchen. Allow me, Mrs. Latham."

The front door burst open just as we started into the hall and Sandy burst in. "Hey!" he shouted. "Karen's fit to be tied, everything's getting cold!"

He darted a swift look at his sister, then at his father.

"Coming, my boy, coming," Mr. Doyle said.

"Okay. You go ahead. I'll lock the door. Don't slip."

Philander Doyle's warm hand on my elbow squired me down the steps. I glanced back. Jerry was waiting for Sandy.

"Watch out, Mrs. Latham."

Mr. Doyle's grip tightened, steadying my precarious balance. But it wasn't what he thought that had upset me. It was the sudden sight of my taxi still at the curb, and the sudden thought that came to me: what was the attorney looking into the management of Karen's estate doing in the Doyle house with its master not there?

I wondered about that as we made our way along the slippery bricks toward the carriage house. Several cars were lined up in front of it now, and from inside came the warm laughter of people having a very good time.

"You go ahead," I said. "I don't want to spoil an entrance. I'll wait for Jerry."

His big voice gurgled joyously. "All right, Judge, I'll be

the bailiff." He stepped forward and opened the door. I heard his jovial "Oyez, Oyez!" and the burst of laughter from inside, and I heard another door close across the street.

I went back to join the others. They had stopped and were looking back. I heard footsteps in the snow as the headlights of the taxi leaped up. Two men came into the lighted path, one with a heavily bandaged face, the other bareheaded in evening clothes. I saw Jerry's hand shoot out and clutch Sandy's arm as he swung around after one incredulous stare, and heard her voice: "Don't, Sandy—please!"

The motor of the taxi raced violently, the door slammed.

"Come along, you two—I'm freezing!" I called, trying frantically to sound gay and normal.

They came toward me, and behind them, whistling, along the icy street came Roger Doyle.

6

We stepped from the dark street into a warm softly-lighted room all white and cherry-red and turquoise blue. It was gay and lovely, but so enormous that it took my breath away. For an instant I stood completely bewildered. Then I understood. The whole of one side and the entire end of the carriage house were one immense sheet of beautiful mirror glass, so that the small room with its cleverly concealed lighting looked twice as long and twice as wide as it actually was. The image of one side of the room, with its two windows draped in an Empire turquoise blue chintz with magenta flowers on a yellow stripe, and its pair of deep cherry red love seats, perfectly balanced the real side; the long glass-legged table against the mirrored wall was only half a table made whole by its own reflection. The floor was completely covered with the palest eggshell carpet, the chairs were chromium with white leather seats and backs. The garden end of the room was only the reflection of the entrance door and the two narrow chintz-draped windows full of flowers. It sounds fantastic, and it was actually exquisite and completely convincing.

Karen Lunt, her shining hair piled in a coronet of corn-colored curls, ravishingly slim in a black velvet frock that entirely covered her until she turned her totally bare back, came forward to meet us.

"It's done with mirrors!" she laughed gaily. "Don't you love it?"

"It's enchanting!" I cried.

She dropped my hand. "Jerry!" She kissed her affectionately on the cheek. "Darling, you don't look a bit well. It's so sweet of you to come when you'd probably much rather be in bed. Hello, Sandy. Oh, *here's* Roger! We've been out of our minds—I *told* everybody you were coming!—See?"

She took Roger Doyle's arm in both hands and pulled him forward.

"Look, everybody! He's really not horrid at all, he has a *beautiful* soul! Jerry, do take Mrs. Latham upstairs."

We went up through a gay barrage of greeting. I knew everybody there, it seemed, except the handsome young man pouring a cocktail out of an enormous crystal shaker for Philander Doyle. "It's an odd gathering," I thought as I followed Jeremy up a tiny real staircase panelled in mirrors. There was one nationally syndicated columnist, a Northern senator and his charming wife, a woman whose name one constantly heard connected with all sorts of political intrigue and whose father had once been a power in the diplomatic game, the Doyles, the Candlers, myself and the young man with the cocktail shaker. As we reached the second floor I saw Miss Isabel Doyle emerge from what I suppose was the kitchen—she was licking her lips, anyway. She had on a fantastic violet lace gown studded with purple velvet bows that would have looked divine on an Edwardian debutante.

"Did I hear my dear brother?" she was asking, in that odd vague manner of hers, and everybody broke into gales of laughter, especially Philander Doyle.

Jerry looked at me. She was perilously near tears.

"Buck up, my sweet—it's just beginning," I said. I laid my wrap across a glamorous shell-pink ivory-satin divan. It was a practical enough bed, I suppose, fundamentally. I looked around at the mirrored walls, and at the tiny shell-pink bathroom beyond. Except for it there was nothing, really, to indicate a bedroom.

"It seems funny that . . . that this is the hayloft where the rats used to eat March Wind's oats, doesn't it?" Jerry said, with a strangled attempt to laugh. Suddenly she buried her head against my shoulder. "Oh, don't let me be a fool tonight, will you, Grace!"

She broke away quickly and patted at her eyes with the puff I handed her from my vanity. "Ready?" she asked, and we went down stairs.

"You know everybody but Geoffrey, don't you, Mrs.

Latham?—This is Geoffrey McClure."

Geoffrey McClure bowed and handed me a beautiful dry Martini. "How do you do, Mrs. Latham?" he said. Somehow, even when he spoke he seemed to be looking at Karen; in fact, he hardly took his eyes off her at any time, and in a room that was mostly mirrors that was almost embarrassingly magnified. Nobody, however, seemed concerned about it, except Miss Isabel Doyle. When we were settled in various spots with enormous white and gold plates of country ham and fat broiled oysters, with crisp browned sweet potato balls, and celery braised with almonds and beaten biscuit, she was beside me.

"Mr. McClure is an unusually attractive man, isn't he, my dear?"

I glanced at Mr. McClure. His blond rather wavy hair, his Bond Street dinner jacket, his blue Nordic eyes and little blond mustache, made Sandy, who was visible in the mirror beside him, look like nothing holy.

"Very, I should say."

"Should you say he was interested in Karen?" Miss Isabel inquired. I don't see how he could have helped hearing her.

I laughed.

"I do hope Roger isn't jealous," she said. "My dear, you wouldn't believe it, but Roger has the most abominable temper. He's not a bit like my dear brother—his father, you know."

I nodded.

"I'm sure Karen will make him a perfect wife," she went on. That was fortunately drowned in a burst of laughter from the group that surrounded Philander Doyle. Judge Candler and the Senator glanced over from the other end of the room.

"I was just saying, Senator, that it's the Judge who ought to live in a glass house, not Karen. Inviolable integrity is wasted in a woman."

It didn't really sound funny enough for the peal of laughter it had brought forth. Somebody remarked that fortunately Judge Candler never threw stones, and Miss Isabel said, "You know, my dear brother has always been opposed to Roger's passion for Karen. Isn't it too marvellous he's finally consented? I've been so afraid Roger would simply drift into a marriage with Jeremy."

I looked at her, rather more savagely than I'd intended, I suppose.

"Oh, my dear, don't misunderstand me. Jerry's a lovely child, but I mean . . . really, they're *so* like brother and sister."

I glanced at the two of them, seated as far apart as the constricted actual space allowed. Jerry was very lovely, talking to the Senator's wife, and Roger Doyle was being distressingly aloof, his eyes, like Geoffrey McClure's, following his hostess from one small group to the other. When she came at last to Jerry and perched on the fragile arm of her chair, I saw Jerry stiffen for an instant. Then I heard her say, in her beautiful bell-clear voice, so that everyone in the room could hear:

"Karen, the bank is turning all your aircraft stock over to you in the morning, with all the back dividends."

Karen's voice pealed out joyously. "Darling! Aren't you wonderful!"

"It's Dad, not me. He couldn't bear to think of your starving in this appalling squalor!"

If there was anything but the utmost and most engaging friendliness in any of that, it certainly wasn't apparent to the naked ear. If it hadn't been that Miss Isabel dropped her fork on the pale soft rug, the infinitesimal silence that met it would hardly have been noticeable at all. In the rush of male helpers I glanced in the mirror at Roger Doyle. His face had darkened alarmingly. Geoffrey McClure glanced very casually at Karen and away, and the moment was over. A kind of too gay tension had suddenly relaxed, and for the next hour a group, civilized and *au courant* in the affairs of the world, chatted pleasantly.

In my sudden jerk forward to catch the sweet potato ball that lodged in one of Miss Isabel's purple bows I'd wrecked a shoulder strap. When the first guest rose to depart and there was the usual instant following of everybody who had to get back to town, I slipped upstairs to the shell-pink bathroom. But Karen's house had nothing visible that held anything as utilitarian as a pin, and before I had the strap anchored it was too late. Outside the door I could hear the clipped Oxford speech of Geoffrey McClure.

"But it's dishonorable, Karen, don't you see? That sort of thing isn't done."

I could hear her soft voice, but not her words. And then his answer:

"Oh my dear, I love you too—madly, insanely—but we can't, not that way. It would ruin everything—my family, our future. No, my dearest, I'd rather be dead—I'd rather see you dead."

There was a pause then with the passionate undercurrent of Karen's voice, and Geoffrey McClure's again:

"No, you shan't. It isn't cricket, old girl—it just isn't."

I waited—and after a long, long time I peeked out. The gay little room was empty. From downstairs I could hear Karen's voice, too high and too bright. I slipped down unnoticed—I hoped; certainly by Karen, who was saying goodbye at the door to Geoffrey McClure. Judge Candler and the Washingtonians had gone; only the Doyles and Jerry and Sandy were still there. Karen came back from the door.

"You haven't seen my house, have you, Mrs. Latham? Not the business end, anyway."

She took my arm. "This is the kitchen."

She pushed a crystal rosette, a glass panel slid smoothly to one side.

"I'm frightfully proud of it, it's my own idea. Oilburner, hot water." She waved at the small green oil heating unit and the gas hot water coil and storage tank compactly installed above it. The pilot light was a pencil point of blue flame at the bottom.

"Aren't they wonderful? I'm one of those people they advertise about—you know, that buy their fittings at a junk shop and call in the plumber to put them in. Only I didn't buy them, a friend who's modernizing gave them to me instead of the junk man, and I got another friend to install them. He says they're obsolete, but they work. Not the oil burner, it's the latest. I mean the rest of them. You'd be surprised if you knew how little it cost.—Here are the cupboards."

She displayed stacks of neatly arranged dishes, all washed and put away.

"Jerry loaned me William, and Miss Isabel sent her maid over," she went on.

I looked at her. She was chattering like a magpie, but her heart was not in it.

"Oh, here's my tonic," she said. She picked up a glass of milk from a silver tray on the neat little metal sink and drank it, making a charming face, and put it down again, smiling brighty.

"It's all marvellous," I said.

We went back into the white room. The others had gone upstairs for their wraps; I could hear them talking and laughing. Then I heard another and quite different sound, closer by, a definite and very plaintive "Meow, meow!" I turned around. Karen broke into a peal of laughter.

"Come in, Mrs. Harris," she called.

A small Siamese cat of a lovely *café-au-lait* shade stalked in from the kitchen, rubbing her back against the panel edge, purring heavily.

"I had to hide her tonight," Karen said. "Miss Isabel hates cats. Come to Karen, beautiful."

She picked the cat up just as everybody came down the narrow stairs of the old hay loft and pressed her face against its head. It struggled out of her arms, jumped down and made a dash for the kitchen, and just in time too. Miss Isabel said, "I thought I heard a cat."

"No, indeed," Karen laughed. She opened the front door. Miss Isabel peered into the kitchen.

"Karen, it *is* a cat!"

I could hear her poking around among the pots and pans. Suddenly she gave a wild screech and flew back into the room, pulling at the glass panel. Mrs. Harris, even more terrified, made a leap for the narrow opening and streaked, hair on end, through the room, practically upsetting Philander Doyle, and out into the night. Miss Isabel Doyle leaned against the half-closed panel, her bloodstream pounding in the veins of her thin throat.

"You know, I'm terrified of cats," she gasped, looking at her brother as if it were his fault, not Karen's. "I do hope it won't go over to our house."

"It won't," Karen laughed. "Good night, everybody!"

She stood in the doorway for a while as we went out, calling "Kitty, kitty!" and finally closed the door.

"I'll phone for a cab from your house, Jerry," I said. Then I noticed that Roger Doyle was still with us. Jerry and Sandy —who'd been quieter all evening than I'd ever seen him— moved ahead. Roger walked with me.

At the steps Jerry turned.

"Good night, Roger," she said quietly. "We won't ask you in, it's so awfully late."

Roger Doyle stopped abruptly with one foot on the step.

"Oh, of course," he said stiffly. "Good night. Good night, Sandy."

I hoped my own too cheery good night covered Sandy's silence. He opened the door. I heard Roger's retreating steps crunch the dry snow.

"You shouldn't have done that," I said when we got inside.

Neither of them spoke for a minute. Then Jerry said, "Stay all night, Grace. It really is late. Lilac can bring you something in the morning."

I hesitated, and then, perhaps because some primitive instinct stirred inside me, perhaps only because it was the easiest thing to do, I said, "All right, if it isn't a lot of trouble."

"Just be careful not to wake Dad when you go up, is all," Jerry said. She glanced at her brother.

"I'm turning in," he said. "Hurry up."

He stood with his forefinger on the switch. I noticed then something I'd been vaguely unaware of all evening. He had at last taken the hand with the taped knuckles out of the pocket of his dinner jacket.

"Scram, pals," he said.

Then at last, when Jerry had said good night, I lay slowly overcoming the frigid linen sheets. Neither of us had mentioned Karen or her party, absorbed, it would seem, in the mechanics of my staying all night—as if I'd never borrowed a pair of outing flannel pajamas before or Jerry hadn't spent half her life coping with unexpected guests. There was no visible sign of what the pale enigmatic mask of her face concealed. No one else would have guessed that the subdued fire in her dark gold-flecked eyes was dying ember, on her heart's altar, of a sacrifice that made the suet and raisins she'd offered up to the birds on the snow so pitifully inadequate.

7

If Capitol Hill were being demolished in an air raid, I'd still get my sleep. Unless, of course, the neighbors had left a cat out; and this night one of them had. I woke up gradually in the pitch dark, a faint "Meow, meow, meow" seeping through into my conscious mind. I turned over and resolutely closed my eyes. It still went on. Mrs. Harris didn't yowl, she merely moaned.

I muttered savagely, for all the world like Lilac, "Why doesn't that blasted Karen take her cat in?" I don't know what it is about a low pitiful noise that makes it so unbearable. At last I sat up in Stygian darkness, thinking that of course the animal must be half frozen, and turned on the light. Then I thought it must be entirely frozen. It was after five o'clock. Mrs. Harris still mewed, so close as to sound almost under my window.

I thought, "Why doesn't it go home and wake its mistress?" but I got up, put on Sandy's bathrobe and woolly slippers and went to the window. The sound must at last have waked Karen too, I thought; there was a light in her house, both upstairs and down. I waited a moment, expecting to see her open the door and call her cat, but she didn't. Mrs. Harris's cry rose again. She'd seen my lights go on, I supposed. Then I saw two little balls of fire raised from the Candlers' garden doorstep.

"If I liked cats, Mrs. Harris," I said, "I'd come down and get you"; and then I added, "—with more pleasure," knowing very well that I couldn't let a rat lie there and freeze to death. I opened the door and stepped out into the hall. The house was as silent as the grave. I crept down the wide old staircase, and stopped abruptly. Someone else was awake too. I could hear quiet footsteps behind me. I turned around. In the faint light from the window I could see no one.

"I must have imagined it," I thought, and started on down. The soft footsteps behind me started too. I whispered, "Who's that?" There was no answer, nothing but the utter silence, and Mrs. Harris's faint wail still sounding outside. My heart, never too brave, crawled up to my mouth. My fingers were like icicles on the old pine stair rail as I realized that I couldn't go back, I had to go on. "If I can reach the switch," I thought, and started quickly. The soft thump-thump-thump sounded again, closer now. I dashed across the hall, fumbled with shaky fingers at the switch, clicked it on and whirled around . . . and saw the long heavy tassel of Sandy's bathrobe flying around after me.

I said "Fool!" and tied it up, but I stood there for a moment, my heart still pounding. Then I made my way back through the door beside the stairs and into the garden entry. I felt around for the light there, found it at last, and started to reach for the big old-fashioned key in the polished brass lock. Then I stopped abruptly, staring down at the worn old drugget on the pine floor in front of the door.

A piece of caked snow lay in the middle of it. It was dry and perfectly firm. Someone had come in that way, and not very long before.

My lips were so parched that I moistened them without relief. Mrs. Harris's low wail on the other side of the door was the only sound in the world except my own heart pounding dully. I turned the key in the lock and drew the door open. Mrs. Harris slithered inside instantly and rubbed against me with a grateful "Meow!", her icy fur electric against my bare ankle.

I looked down at her, and I looked down, through the bare branches of the crape myrtles, icy black above the snow-white garden, at that little gem of a house. I don't know what it was that made me just stand there, for a moment, staring down at it with some kind of a nameless dread catching at my heart. I'd certainly never pretend I'm psychic . . . and yet there was something about that gay lighted little building that wasn't gay at all—like a brilliant ballroom quite empty of dancers. Maybe it wasn't that; maybe it was just my bloodhound's sense of smell communicating something strangely unfamiliar in the clean night to my subconscious. Or perhaps it was some curious foreboding that had been plucking at the muted strings of fear in my mind all that evening. I don't know. I only know that as I stood there the tiny house seemed unreal and frightening to me, like brilliant rouge on cheeks drained of life.

It must have been sharper and more compelling, too, than I was aware of, or I'd never have ventured down the icy path in Sandy's sheepskin slippers, hugging his bathrobe around my frozen limbs, until I came almost to the end of the path. And then I knew—for the foul acrid smell of gas was unmistakable.

I ran those last few steps, and banged frantically on the door.

"Karen!" I called. "Karen!"

The lights from the little windows shone brightly still, but no longer gaily . . . like wide staring grimaces, utterly horrible. I dashed to the nearest one. Through the chinks in the Venetian blind I could see into the living room. Karen Lunt, still in her black velvet evening dress, the bright corn-colored curls still piled on top of her head, was sitting motionless in the cherry-red love seat.

I banged at the window, and cried out desperately. She didn't move. Then, almost beside myself, I searched frantically around on the snow-covered walk until I found a loose brick, pried it out, dashed back to the window, and then—I shall never forget that crash as long as I live—hurled it through the pane. A flood of gas poured out, choking me as I tried to get closer to tear down the blind.

I vaguely realized that the lights were going on in the

Doyle house across the street, and behind me in the Candlers', as I scooped up a handful of snow, held it over my nose, reached through the broken glass and seized Karen by her black velvet shoulder. She swayed there for just an instant, toppled over and lay, quite inert in a huddle on the eggshell rug.

My head reeled then, and I had just enough consciousness left to bury my face in the snow as I fell, and to hear voices all around me then and the crashing of window glass. The next thing I knew I was in Judge Candler's study. And then for a brief instant I was alone, the smell of gas making a roller coaster of my stomach. I pulled myself together with a dreadful effort, reached for the telephone on Judge Candler's desk, and whispered to the operator:

"Get Colonel Primrose at District 0091 and tell him to come to Alexandria, to Judge Candler's house, at once! Tell him Mrs. Latham wants him."

8

Nothing, of course, not even battle, murder or sudden death, will ever keep me from acting on the impulse of the moment . . . or from sitting afterwards just stewing in the consequences. That was what I did now, the instant the telephone was back in place and the operator was going efficiently about the intricate simple business of transmitting my message.

"Why on *earth* did I do that?" I thought, staring blankly at the pool of brilliant light on the leather-topped desk in front of me. It occurred to me then that I must really be losing my mind. For what if Karen *was* dead? It simply meant that infinite trouble and heartache for the girl whose outing flannel pajamas I had on and the boy whose bathrobe was all that was keeping me from freezing to death was at an end. What right had I to jump to perfectly preposterous conclusions just because I'd found a bit of caked snow in the garden entry? Thinking that, and because so many people would be happier with her dead, and there was really nothing you could do about it anyway, I reached out and picked up the phone again.

It tinkled lightly at just the same moment. The operator's voice, cool and businesslike, said, "I've delivered your message, madam. Colonel Primrose said to tell you he'd be down immediately."

In any other country I'd have had time to change my mind a dozen times.

I said, "Thank you." If I called him then and said not to come, I knew he'd come anyway. He's always had more confidence in my intuitions than in my reasoned processes. I had, to the best of my ability, tossed the fat into the fire, and all I could do now was think, wretchedly, "If I'd *only* learn to mind my own business!"

Outside I could hear the clanging of the fire department and excited voices, and one muffled shout: "Put that cigarette out! Do you want to blow us all to hell?" I sat there, wrapped in icy misery. My head ached, my arm where the window glass had scratched it hurt like poison. Suddenly I just couldn't sit there any longer. I ran upstairs, got my white caracul evening coat, slipped it on and came back downstairs. In the garden entry I stopped and looked down at the drugget. A dozen people had tracked snow and ice across it since I'd let Mrs. Harris in. My head didn't seem to pound so badly then.

Down the crape myrtle path I could see dark clusters of people gathered around the little carriage house. The lights had been cut off, but the powerful searchlights trained on it from the fire engine made it a white island in a sea of darkness, lighting every nook in it like an X-ray. I hurried down. Old William, the Candlers' butler and man-of-all-work, was standing at the end, huddled up in an old pink chintz quilt. His eyes were rolling eggs.

"Twah'nt me, miss," he whispered as I stopped beside him. " 'Deed an it wasn't. Ah only used th' ee-lectric stove, Ah nevah touched no gas. Mus' was somebody else, miss. You tell Miss Jerry tell that man."

For a minute I couldn't see Jerry. When I did, she was standing by a tall light-haired man about forty, with a lean intelligent face and a sharp but controlled manner, who seemed to be in charge. I made my way toward them through the broken glass. The firemen had put a rope around the house, and two of them, wearing masks, were standing by for orders. The man with Jerry went over to them. One of them shouted back to the engine, someone dashed up with another mask that Jerry's friend put over his face. The three of them stepped across the rope, and in another moment I saw them lunge against the door with their shoulders. It gave

44

in, the firemen stayed there while the tall man went inside. Through the window, its Venetian blinds ripped down now, I saw him go up to Karen Lunt, stoop and lift her, and carry her quickly out. He laid her on a tarpaulin on the snow. I turned away as the pulmotor from the fire engine went into action.

Jeremy's fingers clutching my scratched arm made me suddenly quite sick again.

"Oh, don't, Grace, don't!" she whispered frantically. "Oh, *poor* Karen!"

I heard someone say, "What's Fox doing?"

The man who'd carried Karen out was back in the little mirrored room. I saw him bend down by the cherry love seat, pick up a piece of note paper from the floor, look at it and look around—his head with that mask horribly grotesque in the white light. He folded the paper, put it in his pocket and made his way toward the kitchen. He struggled for a moment with the crystal rosette and the glass panel, opened it at last and went inside. I saw him put out his hand toward the hot water coil. He came back into the glass room, stood looking around a moment and came out.

Someone at the edge of the silent group around the pulmotor said, "She's a goner."

Jerry's grip tightened again on my aching arm.

"It's all my fault, Grace," she whispered. "I'm a beast, a hideous selfish beast!"

"Hush," I said softly. The man called Fox was coming toward us again through the dreary little crowd.

"Where is the lady who gave the alarm, Miss Candler?" he asked.

Jerry nodded toward me. "This is Captain Fox, Grace. He's the Captain of Police. This is Mrs. Latham. She . . . she found her."

Captain Fox's grey eyes fastened on my face.

"You look as if you needed the pulmotor on you," he said, not unkindly. "You'd better go back to the house—both of you."

Just then the long yellow headlights of a car stretched along the dark street. A patrolman in uniform stepped out and held up his hand. The car stopped. I saw two familiar figures scramble out. The shorter one spoke to the officer, and they came quickly toward us. Captain Fox turned, stiffening for an instant. Then he stepped forward and held out his hand.

"Glad to see you, Colonel—howdy, Sergeant. I guess it's all over here but the shouting."

My knees seemed suddenly just plain fluid. Sergeant Buck, who can spot me as a buzzard can spot a carrion sheep—not that I'd dream of thinking of Sergeant Buck as a buzzard, but I'm not sure he doesn't think worse than that of me—nudged the Colonel's elbow.

"How *am* I going to explain to Jerry?" I thought unhappily; but I'd forgotten for a moment that Colonel Primrose, whose grey hair and snapping black eyes and anything but military bearing wouldn't indicate it at all, has an extraordinary sense of atmosphere. I don't think it took him two seconds to see the spot I was in. Except for a quick flash of concern in his eyes, he mightn't have known I was on earth.

"We're on our way south," he said quietly. "Got the radio call in the car. Knowing it was your bailiwick I thought we'd drop in."

"Stick around, sir, if you aren't in a hurry," Captain Fox said. He turned to Jeremy. "This is Colonel Primrose, Miss Candler. And Mrs. Latham. She was the first on the scene. I was just telling her she looks too rocky to be standing around here."

"She does," Colonel Primrose said. "You go inside at once, Mrs. Latham."

He nodded to the huge figure at his side, and Sergeant Buck stepped forward smartly the way he does, as if he were clicking his heels together and saluting before executing some very complicated manœuvre.

"Come along now, ma'am," he said. It was exactly as if he was speaking to a rookie who'd got a sunstroke and was running amok in an arsenal and had to be handled carefully.

"You'd better go, Grace," Jerry whispered. "I've got to find . . . Dad, and Sandy."

I could feel myself swaying. I was quite faint all of a sudden. Colonel Primrose's sparkling parrot eyes rested on me.

"I thought the radio report said gas," he said shortly.

Captain Fox nodded. "Couldn't you smell it a mile off?"

"Then what's that?"

Colonel Primrose pointed to my coat. I looked down. I was a lurid mess.

"It's blood," Sergeant Buck said, out of the corner of his mouth. The menacing way he spoke, exactly as if it was somebody else's, not my own, was all that kept me from keeling over in a dead faint. But oddly enough it was Sergeant

46

Buck, back in Judge Candler's study, who slit the sleeve of Sandy's bathrobe and mopped off my arm, which was practically in ribbons, while the coroner gave me a tetanus shot. William, who'd discarded his eiderdown sari, made a blazing fire, and I was warm and alone at last.

I don't know how long it was that I sat there before the rest of them came back in. The winter dawn was seeping up from the west. William had made coffee and put it on a great old silver waiter on the desk. Sergeant Buck handed me a cup. It was the first time in my life that I didn't have the feeling he'd gladly have choked me with it. Then the rest of them came in, Captain Fox and Colonel Primrose, and Jerry and Sandy, both looking as if they'd been through the fires of hell. I heard the heavy tread of the firemen bearing Karen up to the room she'd spent all her school vacations in. Philander Doyle came, and Roger. For once Mr. Doyle was silent. He sat heavily down in a chair beside the door, his great head bent forward on his chest, the folds of his collarless neck lapping under his chin. Roger Doyle stood beside him, his hand on his shoulder. Philander Doyle put his big hand up, patted his son's briefly and dropped it again. His face had a heavy flush. If and when he died, it would be apoplexy, I thought suddenly.

Colonel Primrose, moving over to the fireplace, picked up my bandaged arm as he passed and looked at it.

"It's amazing," he said, and I suppose only Sergeant Buck and I who knew him attached any meaning to his casual remark, "how severely one can be hurt and not notice it, under stress."

He put my arm gently back on the arm of my chair and stood by the fireplace, his eyes moving from one to another of us. Captain Fox, who'd gone upstairs, came slowly back into the silent room. He looked like a man who never had entirely got used to this aspect of his job. It made it easier, in some way, to sit there, waiting for I dreaded to think what.

He spoke to Colonel Primrose and came over to Jerry.

"Your father's upstairs, Miss Candler. He'll be down directly. I'd like to wait for him."

He poured himself a cup of coffee, and put it down as the front door opened. I heard Miss Isabel Doyle's voice, and old William answering her.

"It isn't true . . . about Miss Karen?"

"Yas, ma'am, Miss Isabel, it's true a'right," the old darkey said. "Ain' no way gettin' round it."

I couldn't hear what she said then.

"Yes, *ma'am*. But ain' lef' no gas on. 'Twarn't me. Ah don' have nothin' do with this here *gas* people usin' nowadays."

Miss Doyle came in. She was swaddled in the most outlandish assortment of old shawls topped by a sealskin tippet brown with age. She stood in the doorway an instant, looking at her brother; then she went quickly up to Roger Doyle and gave him a shy, strangely touching embrace.

"Oh, my dear boy!" she said. "I know how much this means to you—but you mustn't give way, you mustn't Roger!"

Roger Doyle, who looked less like giving way at that moment than anyone else in the room, released her arms, not unkindly but with some embarrassment. "Sit down quietly, Aunt Isabel," he said.

Jerry pushed a chair over by her brother and she sat down, huddled in her shawls, looking older, without her sometimes almost startling makeup, than I'd ever seen her. I noticed Colonel Primrose's black eyes sharpen with interest. Whether Miss Isabel herself was the cause, or the obvious relation she'd indicated between her nephew and the dead girl, I wouldn't know. I do know that Captain Fox—who did know Miss Isabel—pricked up his ears too, and studied Roger with more interest than he'd shown in him before.

It must be hard, I thought, for anyone like Colonel Primrose, coming completely cold into a group that contained Miss Isabel Doyle, not to think she was something made up out of a piece of whole cloth. She was certainly fantastic; her getup, for one thing, and the startling way she had, for another, of uttering a plain truth at precisely the moment when it was the one thing that had best remain unsaid. I was thinking that just then, hoping she'd forbear this once at least. I suppose the vague, sort of aloof way she looked about was what made me think of it. Even then I wasn't prepared for what did come.

"You know, my dear," she said, not to anybody in particular, just to the room generally, "*I* never liked Karen Lunt."

Her voice was so gentle that I don't think any of us was aware for a full second or two of what she'd said. Then I thought her brother would stop her, of course; but Philander Doyle sat there quite motionless, as if he hadn't heard her.

"Nevertheless, I'm very sorry she's dead. I wouldn't want anyone to think I was unfeeling.—Oh, Peyton!"

She got to her feet quickly and took a step towards the door. It was the first any of us had noticed that Judge Candler was standing there, his tall lean figure, distinguished even in his old mulberry wool dressing gown, towering over us in the doorway. His face was grey as death, the dark sombre eyes under his thick thatch of snow-white hair burning fiercely.

Miss Isabel stood there, hesitating.

"I'm afraid I was very unkind. Please forgive me, Peyton," she said quietly, and sat down again, huddled in those shawls.

Judge Candler crossed the room slowly, without speaking, and stood behind his desk, his face ghastly in the emerald light of the reading lamp, his lean jaw gripped tightly to keep it from working in sharp spasms. Neither his son nor his daughter moved from where they were standing, rigidly controlled, at opposite ends of the book-lined room. Whatever kinship there was between them and their father was powerless to affect them now. I saw Colonel Primrose's quiet gaze move from one to the other of them. I knew, because he'd told me so, that he admired Judge Candler intensely, though he knew him only in the most formal way. No one could have stayed unmoved by the emotion in every rigid unemotional line of his body as he stood there now, plainly not trusting himself to speak too quickly after Miss Isabel's casual heartless observation.

At last he turned to the head of the Alexandria police.

"Have you anything to say to us, Captain Fox?"

His voice was quiet and controlled.

"Nothing positive, sir," Captain Fox said simply. "But from a superficial examination, I think I'm safe in saying it looks as if Miss Lunt took her own life."

There was no sound in the room except the hard impersonal crackling of the pine log in the fire and the deep personal tones of the old clock in the hall, booming the seven hours it had stored up since midnight. Miss Isabel Doyle's cool vague voice flowed across it.

"I think that's *most* unlikely, Captain Fox," she said.

Judge Candler spoke quickly but almost gently.

"Hush, Isabel. Captain Fox would hardly make such a statement if he hadn't reasons for believing it to be true."

Captain Fox's hand in his grey tweed pocket brought out the piece of note paper I'd seen him pick up in front of the love seat where Karen had been sitting.

"She was writing this letter," he said. He glanced at Roger.

Doyle. "Perhaps . . . one of you can help me explain it."

He unfolded the small double sheet of delicate blue.

"No one from the press is here?"

Judge Candler shook his head.

"I've assumed she was writing this as she was overcome by the gas fumes. The last word trails unevenly, the 't's' are not crossed."

Captain Fox spoke slowly and soberly, as if trying, I thought, to soften what he must think would be a terrible blow to Roger Doyle.

"It says, 'My dearest—I can't bear what you said tonight, but I can't bear to live without . . .' That's as far as she got."

He folded the paper again and put it back in his pocket, his eyes resting quietly on Roger.

I realized suddenly that I'd quite unconsciously sat bolt upright in my chair, my lips opened to speak. It wasn't fair to Roger for me not to. And then I could hear that clipped pleading voice: ". . . My family, our future, everything. . . ." If Karen had taken her own life, why should his—his family's, his six unmarried sisters'—be ruined too? I settled back against the worn dark-green leather and held my peace.

Then, being guilty as I was, I glanced quickly at Colonel Primrose. He was looking at me, of course, and there was an ever so faint smile on his lips as he turned back toward Roger Doyle.

"Well, Roger," Judge Candler said patiently. I realized that of course it would never have occurred to him that Karen would address any but the man she had an "understanding" with in such terms.

"I'm sorry, sir," Roger Doyle said quietly. "It means nothing to me. I didn't have more than a dozen words with Karen . . . all last evening."

"You must be *quite* sure, Roger," Miss Isabel Doyle said quickly. "Mustn't he, Captain Fox?"

"I am quite sure, Aunt Isabel," Roger said. His voice was cool, but his blue eyes kindled and his jaw tightened. I saw that he was looking across the room at Jerry, and she was looking at him. As their eyes met I couldn't fathom his, but hers were burning with resentment, and anger, and doubt. She turned away, leaving him angry and resentful too.

50

9

Captain Fox got up. "I will probably want to talk to you later, Roger," he said. He turned to Colonel Primrose. "Are you coming?"

Colonel Primrose moved out from his post at the end of the mantel.

"You'll want to talk to Mrs. Latham, later, I suppose?" he asked.

I'm sure Captain Fox had entirely forgotten me for the moment. He glanced at me in my informal and anything but glamorous attire—it flashed into my mind that that explained Sergeant Buck's sudden tolerance—and said, "Do you live around here, Mrs. Latham?"

"She's staying with me," Jerry put in quickly.

"Then I'll see you later, Mrs. Latham."

He went out with Colonel Primrose, the sergeant executing a sharp movement to close files behind. The front door opened, and closed, and silence fell on the house again. It was only for a moment. Philander Doyle got heavily from his chair.

"Come, Isabel," he said. "I'll be at home today, Peyton, if there's anything I can do. Coming, son?"

Roger Doyle, looking at the burnished swirl of the back of Jerry's copper head, hesitated. Sandy took a step so that he stood between them—whether intentionally or not I wouldn't know.

"Goodbye," he said shortly.

The two stood facing each other for a moment like strange bull dogs.

"Goodbye," Roger said. He followed his father and his aunt out into the hall.

Miss Isabel's voice came back through the open door.

"What *is* the matter? Has something happened?"

I heard Philander Doyle's great voice:

"Only that Karen Lunt has been murdered, Isabel.—Try not to act like a damned fool for just once, will you?"

Miss Isabel's low cry of protest was drowned by the opening door. I looked quickly at Judge Candler, erect and motionless still behind the old mahogany table desk. If he had heard what I heard, and what I knew Jerry had heard, from the wild startled light in her tearless eyes, he gave no sign of

51

it. Her reaction had been purely reflexive. The old business of breeding had clamped itself down instantly, she stood there shaken but controlled.

Judge Candler sat motionless for a few moments.

"I think we'd all better get dressed," he said then.

The door bell rang while he was speaking. We all waited while William padded out. He came back with a suitcase and my other fur coat.

"There's a colored man brought your car an' some clothes, Miz' Latham," he said. "Say to let th' cook know when you comin' home."

"Thank you," I said. It seemed to me I recognized the fine Italian hand of my friend Sergeant Buck in this, but I was glad to have them. I couldn't go around all day looking like Miss Isabel wrapped up in blankets.

"Breakfas' is ready, Miss Jerry, when you all is," William said.

We might have been so many ghosts seated around that gleaming old Sheraton banquet table in the Candler dining room, William's bunion-filled shoes creaking as he padded from place to place serving bacon and eggs and delicate golden-brown hominy grits fried in bacon fat. Nevertheless, I felt my own spirits rising in a still slightly nauseating aroma of gas. My lungs and every one of my hundred sinus cavities must have been filled with it. Mrs. Harris, purring happily, rubbed in and out among our feet. I could tell when she touched Jerry, even when she touched Sandy, by the slight movement of their eyes. Whether she skipped the judge or his nerves were under better control or he was impervious to cats, I wouldn't know. Only once did Jerry slip her a crisp bit of bacon. I didn't dare to. The presence of old mahogany, the silver urn and candelabra and the portraits of five generations of Candlers on the white panelled walls deterred me as much as the silent old gentleman at the foot of the long table.

Then William came in with my coat in his hand. "Cap'n Fox say if you don' min', Miz Latham, would you come ovah to Miss Karen's house?"

There was a sudden flash of alarm in Jerry's eyes. I pushed back my chair, recognizing the not-so-fine hand of my friend Colonel Primrose in this move to get me away from the frightened girl whose guest I was.

"You'll come back, Mrs. Latham?" Judge Candler said. "I think Jerry would appreciate your staying with her a day or so."

52

"I'll be glad to," I said.

Sandy held my coat.

"Don't shoot till you see the whites of their eyes, lady," he whispered to the back of my head. Food was telling on him too. In spite of that I recognized the earnestness of his entreaty as he glanced at his sister, her eyes fixed on her scarcely-touched plate.

As I passed through the hall on my way out the garden entry I saw the front door open and the odd little figure of Mr. Pepperday come in. He put his green baize bag on the table and began to unwind the wool muffler that stood out around his neck like a small overblown tire.

I went out. The little white brick carriage house looked different now that the pale sun was up. Only the trampled snow and the picture of that searchlight from the fire engine engraved on my mind remained of the night, until I got halfway down the leafless crape myrtle path and saw the broken panes of glass strewed about. A sound at my back made me turn quickly. Mrs. Harris was coming with me, lifting her paws gingerly on the cold ground. Across the street through the iron palings the Doyles' house stood out stark and lovely against the winter scene, its old mauve brick and freshly painted white trim and green shutters making it obviously a munificently restored job compared with its lovely but shabby and time-beaten neighbours.

I went around the brick walk to Karen's front door. The smell of gas still filled the room. Except for that and the broken windows, and the sense of appalling emptiness that death leaves in a house, nothing was changed. Captain Fox had seen to that. Two patrolmen at the ends of the street diverted curious traffic, and the people who lived in the block had decently gone about their business. How many eyes watched from behind window curtains of course I didn't know. It seemed to me I saw a figure move behind the neat Venetian blinds in the Doyles' house, but it may have been a colored servant.

Captain Fox and Colonel Primrose were standing in the middle of Karen's eggshell velvet carpet. They both had on their overcoats and hats, and their reflection in the mirrored walls made the room seem pretty full of overcoats and hats. Sergeant Buck coming down the narrow stairway added still more.

I hesitated on the threshold. There was something in their faces that made the muscles of my heart contract as if a new dread had gripped it.

Captain Fox pushed a chair toward me. "Come in, Mrs. Latham," he said. "Tell us about it." His voice was crisp and staccato but not unfriendly.

"There isn't much to tell," I said. "Miss Lunt's cat woke me up, crying under my window. I looked out and saw that the lights here were on. I thought she'd got up to let the cat in, but when there wasn't any sign of life"—I hadn't meant to say it so literally—"I thought then that she'd probably gone to sleep without putting out the lights."

"She had a party," Captain Fox said tentatively. "Was she . . . ?"

"She certainly wasn't," I replied promptly. "We had a cocktail before dinner, and the men had whiskey and soda afterwards. I don't recall any of the women having any. I don't remember seeing Miss Lunt have even a cocktail, for that matter. It was definitely not a drinking party."

"Go on, then, please. You heard the cat."

"And went down to let it in. It was half frozen."

"Is that it there?"

He nodded toward the door. Mrs. Harris, one foot daintily balanced on the sill, the other raised tentatively, was casting her queer eyes round the room. As Captain Fox bent over and snapped his fingers she backed away and was gone like a shot.

"She did that just as the last people were leaving," I said. "I suppose Karen was waiting for her to come in. She's a rather valuable cat. She has a lot of points, or whatever cats have. If you *like* cats."

Captain Fox was chewing his lower lip, frowning a little. "When did she wake you, Mrs. Latham?"

"It was twenty-five past five," I said. "I don't know how long she'd been crying outside my window. Not long, I imagine."

I wondered then: *how long had the caked patch of snow been on the drugget inside the garden door?* I looked over carefully at Colonel Primrose. He was watching me, of course.

"What time did the party end, Mrs. Latham?" Captain Fox asked.

"It was twelve-thirty when we got back to the Candlers'."

"Did you go directly there?"

I nodded.

"Were you the last to go?"

54

"Always," I said.

Sergeant Buck's granite visage congealed visibly. He thinks life is grim and should be treated so. I suppose he was right, just then.

"Who was here, Mrs. Latham?" Colonel Primrose asked.

I told him, pairing Geoffrey McClure's name in the middle with the lady wirepuller so that it sounded as if they'd come together. As a matter of fact they hadn't even left together, because she was going with the Senator and his wife before I went upstairs.

"The Doyles and the young Candlers and I left together. Judge Candler went earlier with the others."

"Did Miss Lunt seem particularly disturbed or excited, Mrs. Latham?"

"I shouldn't have thought so," I replied. "But then I don't know her very well. She was . . . vivacious, but whether abnormally so or not I haven't an idea."

"Go on with your story, please, Mrs. Latham," Captain Fox said. "You heard the cat at five-thirty or so?"

I nodded. It was a little disconcerting, the way he marked my progress.

"I can't tell you why I felt there was something wrong," I said. "Except that it was so quiet here, and all the lights were on and everybody had gone a long time before. I don't think I could possibly have smelled the gas that far . . . though it was cold, of course, and maybe there was a little breeze that way. I don't know. I don't even remember thinking she might be ill. It just seemed odd and unnatural. Every other house was completely dark. If she was waiting up for the cat, why didn't she let it in?—I suppose that was part of it. Anyway, I came down, and I smelled gas as soon as I came to the end of the path. It seemed to be seeping out everywhere. I called Miss Lunt, but she didn't answer. Then I saw her through the blinds. She was sitting in that little sofa, perfectly upright. She didn't seem to hear me when I banged on the window and called. That's when I picked up the loose brick out of the walk and broke the pane. I reached in and caught her shoulder. I'm afraid I knew she was dead. She just fell over on the floor, the way you found her."

"But you pushed her over?"

I nodded. I could still feel the touch of her velvet dress on my hand, and see her slowly toppling over.

"Then she hadn't got up to . . ."

Captain Fox's voice trailed off.

55

Colonel Primrose waited for him to go on. Then he said, in a moment, "You didn't hear her call the cat again, Mrs. Latham?"

"No. But I was inside, so I wouldn't have."

Captain Fox moved about the room.

"It looks to me as if she let everybody out," he said, "went upstairs and turned on the water, came down and turned off the pilot light, disconnected the icebox, and just sat and waited."

I looked blankly at him, and at Colonel Primrose.

"The type of gas-hot-water heater she has comes on automatically when the water in the tank gets below a certain temperature," Colonel Primrose explained. "The pilot light ignites it. The gas burns then until the water reaches the set temperature again. The pilot light was off here and the tap upstairs was running. The tank would cool off pretty quickly. The oilburner was switched off too, so the gas wouldn't ignite."

I said, "Oh."

"I must say, Colonel, it looks pretty straightforward to me," Captain Fox said.

I felt Colonel Primrose's eyes resting on me.

"And I'd like to have as little stink about it as we can."

"I think you're right, probably," Colonel Primrose said.

I went out. I knew he was coming after me, and I would have given my soul to avoid it. As I turned up between the crape myrtles, their bare icy branches glistening in the pale sun, he caught up with me and took my whole elbow.

"Now tell me all about it," he said, as if he was speaking to a child who'd just been telling a frightful whopper to avoid punishment for breaking the basement window.

"I've told you," I said.

"Look, my dear," he said gently. "If you'd only made an abortive attempt to rescue that girl, you wouldn't have called me—and you wouldn't have gone around not even noticing that arm for an hour and a half. If you hadn't had some kind of background of fear, you wouldn't have come flying out in that astonishing costume you had on this morning."

"You've dealt with crime too long, Colonel Primrose," I said, as coolly as I could. "You ought to go to Florida for the winter."

He nodded.

"I've dealt with crime—or maybe just people—too long

56

not to recognize that every one in Judge Candler's study was waiting for some kind of a blow to fall, Mrs. Latham . . . and that Fox's suicide note wasn't it."

I stopped and faced him in the middle of the path.

"Look, Colonel Primrose," I said earnestly. "I'm frightfully sorry I called you this morning. Can't you just go back to Georgetown and forget it?"

"Do you want me to?"

"Oh, terribly!" I cried. And I saw instantly, from the little sardonic glint in his sparkling black eyes, that whatever possible doubt he might have had that I hadn't been—shall I say—entirely straightforward with him was gone. It disappeared instantly, however, leaving him just looking at me soberly, not even very critically.

"I'm just naturally an alarmist," I said. "It was probably only my arm hurting that made me jittery, don't you think?"

"No," he said with a smile.

"But you can see that I'm a guest here, and that guests can't send the roof crashing down on people's heads this way. I can't go on and say, 'Look, everybody—if it hadn't been for me and my friend Colonel Primrose, you wouldn't have made the headlines in every paper in the country—every move you take and every bite you eat is subway fare and dinner table gossip throughout the country, all because of me and my little hatchet'—don't you see?"

"I do see, my dear," he said quietly. "I also see that a successful murderer is the most dangerous enemy society has."

"Rot," I said rudely.

"And that's not all.—Whoever did this knows by now, probably, that you did call me . . . and knowing my profession, and making the natural error of thinking you're rational and intelligent, not completely impulsive, must therefore assume that you had logical grounds for suspecting something. Every night that goes by, he's going to lie awake wondering just how much you know—until at last he just can't stand that hideous uncertainty. And because it was so easy once . . . some morning Lilac's going to call me up and say, 'Mis' Grace, she daid.' I don't want to alarm you—unduly—and I know it's foolish of me to care about it. But I——"

Behind us at the end of the path Sergeant Buck, a vast cast-iron repetition of Mr. Pepperday, cleared his throat violently.

"I'm serious about this, Mrs. Latham," Colonel Primrose

said. "But . . . I'm going to go, if you say so. I don't want to embarrass you. I see your point—I just know it's completely wrong."

He smiled at me, and lifted his hat.

"I'm pleased you thought of me, in any case. Goodbye."

10

He went back down the walk. Sergeant Buck, waiting, in effect, at attention, saluted in effect and fell in. I stood there, watching them go along the side of the house to the street, shivering, not so much from the external cold as from some kind of a numbness inside my own brain. Then Sandy opened the garden door.

"Playing statues?" he asked. "I guess 'Niobe Weeping For Her Children.' "

I blinked. I hadn't realized I had tears in my eyes. It was the first time, for one thing, that I'd ever seen Colonel Primrose stop at the threshold of his duty. That he'd done it to keep from embarrassing me somehow made it worse.

"Wrong," I said. "It's 'The Thinker.' "

"Then quit it, Grace," he said. "It's been the ruin of your whole sex. Don't you know?"

He closed the door behind me and helped me off with my coat. "How's the old arm?"

"Swell. How are the knuckles?"

He grinned.

"Your friend Colonel Primrose doesn't miss much, does he?"

My heart sank.

"Where is he, by the way?" he went on.

"He's gone back home. Captain Fox says there's no doubt she turned on the gas herself."

"What do you think?"

I met his dark eyes as candidly as I could.

"What do *you* think?"

He underlined each word so lightly that if I hadn't known him I wouldn't have been conscious of it. "I think it was suicide," he said, his steady gaze unwavering.

"Then that makes it unanimous," I replied, as airily as I could.

He followed me into the Judge's library.

"Do you know Mr. Pepperday, Grace?—This is Mrs. Latham, Mr. Pepperday."

The little man got up and bowed. He wasn't so grotesque —quite—as he'd appeared in the emerald light the night before. His seedy black coat and trousers looked too big for him, if anything: His hair combed over his bald egg-shaped dome seemed to cover it more adequately, hence to be quite reasonable. His voice, however, was still high and reedy as he said, "How d'ye do, Mrs. Latham?"

He settled himself down again on a chair by Judge Candler's desk.

"I imagine you don't need to transfer the stock now, Miss Jeremy," he said, sorting the papers he'd taken out of his green baize bag.

Jerry's hand tightened sharply on the arm of her chair.

"I'd rather have done it a hundred times than have this happen, Mr. Pepperday," she said quickly.

The little man nodded rather sourly. "The Candlers would have been rich now, if they hadn't been quixotes."

His emphasis on the last word gave me, in some way, a curious picture of long lines of Candlers trailing generously to a drunkard's grave.

"Oh, please, Mr. Pepperday!" Jerry began, and stopped short as her father appeared in the doorway. Mr. Pepperday screwed his face together to shift his spectacles into position on his small nose.

When Judge Candler had crossed to his desk I said, "Captain Fox asked me to tell you he'd be around this afternoon."

He nodded, looking at me with a rather odd intentness. "Has he . . ."

"He only repeated what he said before," I answered.

"Thank you, Mrs. Latham."

He turned to the little man. "That's all this morning, Mr. Pepperday. I shan't be down for several days."

Mr. Pepperday gathered up his papers. He went as far as the door, and turned back.

"I told Miss Karen that hot-water heater was an obsolete type, and that was a dangerous place to scrimp on money," he said, irritably.

Judge Candler looked up. "What do you mean, Mr. Pepperday?"

"She got me to put it in for her, to save money," the little man replied. His high-pitched voice made him sound more excited than he was, I thought, for he added, with a sort of treble dignity, "I was glad to accommodate her, during my spare time. But I told her it hadn't the safety device the modern type has. She said she knew it, the people who gave it to her had explained that, but she had to save money somewhere. I told her she had to be careful, in such a small place, that the wind didn't blow out the pilot light if the gas was low or the air valves needed tightening."

Judge Candler's eyes were burning. "Do you mean," he said slowly, "that it . . . may have been accidental?"

Something behind the lines of his stern face seemed to crumple like tissue paper. For a moment he sat there, his head bent again. Then he raised it and said, with deeper feeling than I ever believed a voice could hold, "I'd give anything to believe she didn't purposely destroy herself. I can't endure that."

I stared at him. Of the two alternatives that had occurred to me, suicide had seemed infinitely the preferable. I must say I hadn't thought of the possibility of accident.

"You must wait and see Fox, Mr. Pepperday," Judge Candler said. "I want you to tell him what you've told me."

Mr. Pepperday's face screwed into a series of contortions.

"No, indeed, sir," he said promptly, to my surprise. "I couldn't consider doing any such thing, I assure you I could not."

His shrill voice rose almost to a squeal. I gazed at him dumbfounded. He was like an irascible little terrier. If he'd jumped up and down on the floor he couldn't have been more astonishing. And it wasn't so much that he was annoyed, I thought, as that he was alarmed.

"He probably made the whole thing up and doesn't want to get caught out," I thought, with unbecoming cynicism.

"I don't understand you, Mr. Pepperday," Judge Candler said.

"Possibly not, sir. But I beg you to forget everything. And I wish you good morning."

Mr. Pepperday hurried out, more like the March Hare than the White Rabbit, except that he was consulting his big watch as he went.

Judge Candler looked after him for a moment. Then he sat back in his chair.

"I'd like to be alone, if you please," he said to Jerry. As we all moved to the door he added, "Would you mind staying a moment, Mrs. Latham?"

I said, "Not at all." When the others had gone and I'd sat

down in the chair by the fire, he sat there, tapping the tooled old leather on the table desk with his long slender fingers. They looked so fragile that I glanced at his face uneasily. He had never been particularly robust, I imagine, but now he looked nearly ill.

After a long time he said, "You're fond of my daughter, I believe, Mrs. Latham?"

"Oh, very," I said.

He paused again. Then he said, "You know, I presume, that she was very much upset about transferring certain stock back to Karen."

"Yes, I know," I said.

"Mrs. Latham, I believe it was you who called in Colonel Primrose this morning."

I thought dismally, "How things *do* get about." I nodded. "Why?"

"Because I was . . . frightened," I said. "I'd hurt my arm pretty badly. I suppose I was . . . overwrought. He's a very good friend of mine. I just naturally thought of him. He's extraordinary in emergencies."

The sound of his fingers tapping made me as nervous as a cat.

"It wasn't because you felt that . . . Karen had been killed?"

Since it obviously wasn't Judge Candler who'd done it, even if she had been killed, and those sombre burning eyes of his could see through any dissimulation of mine, there was no use of my bothering.

"I suppose that must have occurred to me, Judge Candler," I answered, as stoutly as I could; "just as it apparently occurred to Philander Doyle. Or I shouldn't have called him."

I couldn't tell him that it had seemed, some way, the logical resolution for all that had gone before, like spontaneous combustion in a lot of oily trash in the cellar closet; nor could I tell him about the caked snow on the drugget in the garden entry.

"Your reasons?" he asked quietly.

"I have none."

He looked straight ahead of him for a long time.

"Thank you, Mrs. Latham," he said at last.

I got up. As I got to the door he said, "You'll stay on with Jeremy a few days, won't you?"

I expect I'm no worse coward than most women, but my knees were a little wobbly just then. He was looking at me

61

with those extraordinary steady Candler eyes.

"Jeremy's counting heavily on you, Mrs. Latham," he said. "I should be most grateful to you."

I thought, "Oh, *dear!*" but I said, "Thank you, Judge Candler," and got out and hurried up to my room. Then I sat there in the window seat looking out at Karen's house, more disturbed than I'd yet been.

William had made a coal fire in the grate. The high four-poster with the three steps going up to it, covered with faded worn old gros point, the old-fashioned basin and pitcher in the corner stand, the stiff high-backed fireside chair, the bow front satinwood chest with the mildewed girandole above it, all seemed friendly enough . . . but I could close my eyes and remember the pitch black and cold they'd been the night before. The heavy tassel of Sandy's bathrobe cord plump-plumping in the dark on the steps behind me made me uneasy just remembering how utterly terrified I'd been. And some one *had* been in the hall, watching me. I was perfectly sure of that, now that I thought of it again. Some one who had come from Karen's house—or why hadn't that cat stayed huddled up in her window, protected from the cold wind? Or why wouldn't she have come at two, or four, if she didn't want to stay there? It was perfectly obvious that she'd followed some one to the garden door.

I sat there in the little room, thinking; and the more I thought the more the prospect of spending another night in that house became a complete nightmare. What, for instance, if Colonel Primrose was right? I hadn't the slightest interest in being numbered among the unvalorous dead. How had it become known that I called him in? How had they guessed I'd thought Karen had been murdered?

A knock at the door startled me practically out of my wits. I had to moisten my lips before I could say "Come in." And when I'd said it, I just sat there practically petrified, watching the door open. Who or what I thought it would be I don't know; I only know I was absurdly relieved to see it was only Jerry.

She smiled just a bare fraction of a smile, came in, and sat down beside me. Then, seeing Karen's house from the window, I suppose, she got up and moved to the wing chair by the fire. She sat there a few moments, poking the dead coals back from the black painted bricks on the hearth with the toe of her shoe.

"You don't think Karen killed herself, do you?" she asked

62

abruptly, not moving her eyes from the grate.

"Why do you say that?" I said.

"Because I don't either," she replied quietly.

I didn't say anything. There seemed so precious little I could say. I had the awful feeling that any minute now she'd ask if it wasn't I who . . . and before I'd got the words out of my mind she'd said them:

"Was it you that called Colonel Primrose?"

"Look," I said. "—How did you know?"

"Because Mr. Doyle called up and told Father he thought we'd better get you out of the house before you had us all hanged."

"Oh," I said weakly.

"He said Colonel Primrose only dabbled in high-class murder," she added, with an odd little sound that could hardly be called a laugh.

"I'm sorry I called him, Jerry," I said.

Her wide yellow-flecked eyes met mine directly for the first time since she'd come in.

"Oh, I'm *glad* you called him!" she cried. "It would be horrible, to think she was . . . murdered and nobody knew who did it!"

I looked at her in astonishment.

"Grace!" she said suddenly. "You don't think I did it . . . or Sandy?"

I shook my head.

She got up abruptly, moved across to the front window and stood there looking out into Chatham Street. I knew, in some way, that she was making a tremendous decision—making it all by herself. I sat and waited. She turned around in a moment.

"Grace," she said slowly, "—I want you to call him back. I know you sent him away because you thought it would . . . embarrass us. It won't, Grace . . . believe me, it won't. It'll embarrass us a lot more if it . . . goes as suicide and Miss Isabel says at a tea some day, 'You know, they *murdered* Karen, my dear, they *really* did.' "

She spoke so precisely with Miss Isabel's vague aloof inflection that I could see a dozen unnerved dowagers dropping tea cups and saying, "—How *awful*, Isabel! Are you *sure?*"

"You know what she's like, and now that Mr. Doyle has told her Karen was murdered, she'll stow it away like she does all those old clothes and bring it out the way she does them, at the worst possible moment."

I just stared at her.

"Oh, Grace, don't you see?" she implored. "I like Miss Isabel, I really do. I don't mean she'd hurt us, but she's always been very odd. You know, it wasn't till a few months ago that she ever put her foot in this house. She lived just across the street, Mr. Doyle was an old friend—but she wouldn't ever come with him. Once Sandy and I were talking about it at table and father said, "I dare say she has her own reasons," the way he does that finishes things. But she never did, not till she thought I wanted to marry Roger. I don't know why that appalled her so. It's just that that's the way she is. Don't you see?"

"I'm not sure I do," I said. "—And I'm very sure I don't understand about your father and Karen and you, at all."

She sat down wearily in the window seat and leaned her head back against the trim.

"You just don't know him, Grace. Listen. Mr. Lunt was his dearest friend . . . and friendship is more sacred to him than anything else of the sort—love, or his family, or anything. It's hard for anybody to understand, nowadays. He made a solemn promise to Karen's father, and the business of his death, and his wife's ruining him financially, and all the rest of it, just made the obligation greater in his own mind. Then there's another thing."

She smiled as if she realized the tragi-comic irony of it.

"You see, we're Candlers. We're Colonel Candler's grandchildren and Judge Avery Candler's great-grandchildren. And Karen's father's father wasn't anybody. That makes it important for Karen to go to a fashionable school and marry well . . . but we Candlers, we don't need any gilding the lily. We don't need a lot of money. We don't need to make a show. It's only people who haven't got family and background and what have you that have to make one.

"You see, father was brought up by people who'd lost everything in the Civil War. Poverty was distinction, to them —having money meant you'd sold out to the enemy. It doesn't make sense, Grace, but he feels it genuinely. Oh, it's Sandy's fault as much as his. We've been too proud to tell him how we felt about it. We pretended we wanted to go to the schools we went to, and were proud of our shabby house and the things in it, because they'd all belonged to us always, and hadn't been bought at an auction because somebody like us had had to part with them. Of course, we're really tarred with the same brush—we're as bad as he is, really—except that we can see the waste of it. He never has. We've kept him locked in his ivory tower. We've never told him how wasteful and extravagant Karen was. When he said Karen needed fifty dollars to pay her throat specialist, we never said a word, even if we knew her throat was O. K. and it was a new hat she wanted.

"But you see the point is, Grace, that father believed in people. He believes in the sacred obligation of friendship. He believed an orphan girl whose father killed himself because he was broke and his wife was leaving him for fairer fields, needs more to meet the world than his children—they have family and a home and decent cultured backgrounds as far back as William the Conqueror. We've got protoplasm—we don't need tinsel. And of course, money means nothing to him, really."

"Was he . . . in love with Karen's mother?" I asked.

Jerry shook her head.

"No—that's one of the reasons for his attitude toward Karen. Her mother hadn't any background for anything . . . except a pretty face. Whenever Karen did anything that even father thought was a bit thick, he'd say, 'I know, my dear, but you must remember her mother's background.' We were silk purses. Karen wasn't precisely the opposite, but —well . . ."

She shrugged unhappily.

"You see. And the sickening thing is that I thought by giving Karen back the stock, now, I could avoid . . . the kind of publicity that would hurt father."

She closed her eyes and sat there, rocking her head from side to side against the shutter panel.

"—Who'd ever have thought anything so horrible as this could happen!" she whispered wretchedly.

"It's ghastly," I said. Downstairs I heard the front door close. Jerry moved her head to look out, and caught her breath sharply. I saw her eyes move along the street, following slow steps crunching in the snow.

"It's Dad," she said. "—What's he going to the Doyles' for?"

The alarm in her voice almost frightened me.

"Jerry!" I said. "Why shouldn't he?"

"Because he mustn't!" she said desperately. She twisted around, her knees on the window seat, and tugged at the heavy window. It was too late. I'd gone over to her, and I could see the Doyles' beautiful white front door open and

65

the Judge's tall figure disappear inside before it closed again.

Jerry flew out into the hall.

"Sandy!" she called. *"Sandy!"*

Old William came up the stairs in a minute.

"He done gone out, Miss Jer'my. He say to tell you he gone to th' nation's capital. He didn't say *wheah* he was goin'."

Jerry came back, her face quite pale. I saw her slim body in the dark-brown wool frock that fitted tightly up to the base of her slender throat stiffen abruptly and draw back from the window. I looked out just as she pulled the glass curtain across it and saw Roger Doyle come out of the house across the street. He ran down the pointed steps, hesitated, and crossed the street.

I looked at Jerry. The golden streaks in her eyes were almost obliterated. I heard Roger's quick steps on the stones, and the doorbell ring.

"Go down, please, Grace, and tell him no one's home," Jerry said. Her voice was so calm and deadly that I started in spite of myself.

"Why, darling?" I asked.

"Don't ask why, Grace—please! Just go and tell him, if you don't mind."

William's voice came up the stairs.

" 'Deed, Mr. Roger, come in. Miss Jer'my'll be mighty glad t' see you. Mr. Sandy, he's done went."

Jerry looked at me. *"Please,* Grace! I can't see him, really!"

I went downstairs. Roger was standing in the hall, looking up eagerly. His face changed instantly when he saw it was only me. A look of complete despair came over it.

"I've got to see Jerry, Grace," he said.

He followed me into the parlor where I'd met his aunt that day. "Won't you tell her?"

"Look, Roger," I said. "Jerry doesn't want to see you. She hasn't told me why, but I think I know. You must know too. So go away. If you have any explanations—and I hope a lot you've got one—write her a letter. I'll see she gets it."

He stared at me so blankly that I could hardly believe my eyes. I knew by now, of course, that his father and his aunt would have been marvellous on the stage, but I hadn't realized he took after them. Then I thought perhaps I ought to have known it last night, when I saw him come whistling down from the taxi, and talking so cordially to Judge Candler after supper. I found my blood pressure rising a little. And Roger, who after all has more Irish in him than I have,

66

flushed hotly.

"Look here, Grace," he blurted out angrily; "Jerry knows I didn't give a damn about Karen!"

I must admit that while that wouldn't have surprised me the day before, it did now. After all, and in spite of his racked avowal to Jerry in my sitting room, his father had at least said in effect that he was engaged to Karen. I suppose too that Sandy and Jerry's interpretation of his interview with the man with the plastered face had probably colored my belief in his sincerity.

"I . . . thought," I began.

"Whatever you thought, Grace," he interrupted, "Jerry knows better. My God, I spent most of yesterday morning telling her so."

"Oh," I said. "Then why did your father practically announce your engagement to Karen here last night?"

I was telling myself all this time that I must be careful. A girl had been murdered half a block away less than twelve hours ago. I was telling myself also that Jerry's instincts were better than mine here: she knew more of what had gone on than I did, and it was her life that was involved, not mine.

"If he did, he was cockeyed," Roger said coolly.

"I wouldn't know anything about that," I said. "I only know that Jerry's terribly upset and fearfully distressed by something that I do know happened, and that you're concerned with. That's probably more than I ought to say. You can take it or leave it."

His face hardened.

"You wouldn't be accusing me of murdering Karen, would you, Grace?"

"*Murdering?*" I said. "I thought Captain Fox said she'd committed suicide."

He flushed darkly.

"You didn't think that when you called Colonel Primrose in."

"Colonel Primrose has gone home hours ago," I said.

"Then what's he doing down at the police station in Fairfax Street right now?" he demanded curtly.

11

I didn't go back upstairs immediately. I was suffering from an acute attack of the common female malady of pique . . . or perhaps it should simply be called deflated ego. After Roger had gone, hurt apparently, certainly very angry—and chiefly at me—I wandered about the shabby lovely old drawing room. The blue walls were hung with Candlers—British in red with powdered hair, Colonial in a blue and buff without. I kept seeing bits of Sandy in their dim ageless faces, and in the lovely lady with Titian hair piled high in shining curls, her liquid eyes flecked with gold, her low-cut Empire gown revealing the swelling curves of her bosom, I could see the girl upstairs twenty pounds plumper. It was the curled definitely Mona Lisa smile tucked away in the corner of her ripe mouth that fascinated me. Whether nature or the long-forgotten painter had given her that Borgia look I had no way of knowing. I probably wouldn't even have noticed it if everybody hadn't been whispering "Murder!"

Of course nobody was, actually. The house was like a frozen tomb. I moved away and examined the little pair of water colors hanging beside the door. One was the ruins of Washington's grist mill, now restored, near Mt. Vernon. The other was a catboat, the *Isabel D.* They were both signed "P.C." I'd never, somehow, thought of Judge Candler as a water colorist, and I'm sure he's a much better jurist—at least I hope so. I glanced back at the lady over the mantel, and started violently. Mrs. Harris was rubbing against my ankles.

"Look, cat," I said. "Somebody's got to put a bell on you—you'll have us all, including me, in the madhouse."

She apparently understood, because she raised her tail like an offended banner and stalked back toward the kitchen. I stalked upstairs. There was one thing at least, I thought: I wouldn't have to give Colonel Primrose the minor satisfaction of calling him back. He was still there . . . like a cockle burr in a spaniel's tail feathers.

I opened my bedroom door and started to tell Jerry as much, somewhat sugar-coated, and stopped short. She was lying across the high old fourposter, her head buried in a pillow. For an instant I thought she was crying. Then I saw she wasn't, not any longer. She was fast asleep, her smooth ivory cheeks streaked with tears, a great wet patch on the linen slip, her breath coming in uneven little sobs. Her long dark lashes clung to her pale cheeks. Her red mouth drooped at the corners like an unhappy child's, not in the least like a sleeping Borgia's.

I spread the faded chintz eiderdown from the foot of the

68

bed over her, picked up my hat and coat and slipped out, closing the door softly behind me.

Old William came padding out from the kitchen as I came down the stairs. He must, I thought, have the ears of a lynx. I was tiptoeing as quietly as I could.

"If you's goin' by th' store, an' if you don' min', Miss Grace," he said, "will you see if they's any nice vegetables for dinner? Ah don' like leave th' house with people traipsin' in an' out."

I nodded. "Miss Jerry's asleep in my room."

"Pore baby," he said. "—But this here's goin' take a right heavy load off'n her little shoulders. Miss Karen, pore soul, she wasn' no help to *nobody*, not 'ceptin' herself."

In view of his previous comment to my Lilac, it seemed a studied understatement of his true opinion.

"She's daid now." He shook his woolly old head. "They done took her away, pore soul."

I could see as I started out that he was relieved that they had. At the door he called after me.

"Miss Grace, would you leave this here at Jedge's office on you' way?"

He handed me a large old-fashioned key. I nodded and put it in my pocket.

I drove to the corner of Prince's and Chatham Streets, turned up from the leaden strip of the Potomac to Royal Street and turned right, looking first for a grocery store and second a place to park in, glad to have something useful to do. There were markets enough, with piles of golden grapefruit, jade-green and white cabbages and dun-colored potatoes, but no parking places that I could see. I crossed King Street with the strange Masonic Memorial towering on the hill at the end of it and went on. At the City Hall across from old Gatsby's Tavern, where Washington spent so many of the crucial hours of his military life, I spotted a place and a market, and drove in.

I don't remember about the vegetables now, but I do remember the pear-shaped bags of Smithfield hams that decorated the posts of the old market like grotesque maypoles. Then I heard a familiar voice say, "*You* may call them chinee apples, *I* call them pomegranates.—Oh, good morning, my dear!"

Miss Isabel Doyle bowed to me across the sawdust aisle.

"Isn't it a lovely day?"

I finished my marketing and she finished hers, so we came

69

out on the street together. I don't know why, but there was something about Miss Isabel's aloof detachment that irritated me. After all, a girl she'd known for years, whom she'd wanted her nephew to marry, was dead—murdered, if she was to believe her brother. It didn't seem human not to discard her purple feather boa at least, and have some film of awareness in her faded eyes.

I suppose it was all too human for me to set myself up as Miss Isabel's moral censor. Nevertheless I said, "Poor, Jerry. This has knocked her into a frightful heap."

Miss Isabel paused and looked at me as if she hadn't an idea in the world what I was talking about.

"About Karen," I said.

She touched my arm lightly and glanced around at the motley little assortment of marketing wives and colored people moving along the street.

"Oh, my dear," she said softly. "My brother's being very firm. I've been forbidden even to *think* about it. My brother assures me it's the only course to follow."

She moved her light fingers from my arm.

"Goodbye, my dear. Remember you're having tea with me. Goodbye."

She was gone, and I stood in the cobblestone trough by my car, looking after her, feeling like an ill-bred gossip-monger. I reached in my pocket for my car keys and felt the old key William had given me. I remembered then I'd told him I'd leave it at Judge Candler's office. I looked around, and stopped an old colored man.

"Where is Judge Candler's office, do you know?" I asked.

"Yes, *ma'am*. You go right through here."

He pointed to a nearby alley.

"—An' down thataway." He moved his horny old hand toward King Street. "Mah pappy work fo' ol' Colonel," he added with a snag-toothed grin. I suppose that's why I gave him a quarter instead of a dime.

I went through the alley into the old market place, empty except for a couple of colored men lounging in front of a fish stall, and gave an involuntary start of surprise. The iron-barred windows at the opposite side of the paved courtyard made a little chill run down my spine . . . and the fact that Colonel Primrose and his Sergeant were in there now with the Captain of Police didn't make the place at all less alarming. I glanced around. An ancient unlovely alley with several cars parked in it half-way across the market place led into

70

King Street. I picked my way along its icy uneven cobbles and turned left into Fairfax Street. Then I kept on, back around toward the police station again, until I came to a tiny red-brick house with "Peyton R. Candler, Counsellor-at-Law" in black and scaled gold-leaf letters on one of the windows.

I glanced in. The brown mesh screen over the lower half of the window just cleared the top of my head, concealing the inside of the front room from the street. I opened the white door and stepped in . . . and drew back, unfortunately too late. Through the door into the book-lined back room I could see not only the egg-shaped head and Jacob's-ladder of grey hair of the tiny Mr. Pepperday, but the lantern-jawed dead pan of the concrete-visaged Sergeant Phineas T. Buck; and I knew that the file-covered wall of the outer office was all that kept me from seeing my friend Colonel John Primrose, 92nd Engineers, U. S. A., Retired. Moreover, they'd seen me—Colonel Primrose if only by reflection in the viscid depths of his sergeant's fish eyes and in his quietly congealing façade.

I don't know why—except that instinct is a property of all the lower animals—I thrust the anonymous iron key I held in my hand back into my pocket, and pretended I'd come for the Judge's mail.

For a moment I thought Mr. Pepperday was going to un-mask me with a shrill announcement that he'd taken the mail over already and that I knew it. But he didn't. Instead, after one surreptitious glance, he scrabbled about in the old walnut desk drawers, fished out a couple of unopened circu-lars from a legal publishing company dated June 3rd of the preceding year, and handed them to me with what I believe is called old-world courtesy, except that here and now it was ludicrously absurd. I put them in my pocket and backed to-ward the door.

Colonel Primrose smiled almost as if he'd quite expected me to turn up and that was why he was there.

"Sit down, Mrs. Latham," he said. He indicated an old worn leather chair in front of the iron safe in the corner. I couldn't tell if he did it because he knew I'd be facing a rusty white board hanging on the wall behind him. On it were three rows of substantial hooks, each labelled. Only one hadn't a key of some kind hanging on it, some old-fashioned and enormous like the one in my pocket, others small and modern.

The black letters under the empty hook said "Carriage House" . . . and I knew then that that was the key I had.

But more bewildering still—how had Mr. Pepperday known it? And what did he know about it that I didn't? I glanced at him balanced back in Judge Candler's chair, the tips of his ink-stained fingers—they looked more like a steam-fitter's than a law clerk's, in their small way—barely touching as his elbows rested on the worn leather-padded chair arms. His feet, I knew, couldn't possibly be touching the floor, which was no doubt why the chair wobbled dangerously under him.

"I was just asking Mr. Pepperday a few questions, Mrs. Latham," Colonel Primrose said politely. My heart sank as I recognized his very blandest tones.

"I hope he's got more sense than to answer them," I retorted, waspishly.

"I'm naturally *most* reluctant to discuss the Judge's family affairs," Mr. Pepperday said in his cracked treble. He screwed his face together so that his spectacles returned to their niche on the bridge of his nose.

"Naturally, Mr. Pepperday," Colonel Primrose agreed, with a suavity that I found infuriating beyond words but that Mr. Pepperday swallowed as easily as if it had been a juicy fat oyster personally shucked for him . . . as indeed it was, in a sense. "—My only thought was to save the Judge and Miss Candler as much . . . pain as possible under the circumstances."

I looked angrily at him.

"I understand Miss Lunt was the Judge's ward," he went on pleasantly.

"And a very lucky girl," Mr. Pepperday remarked. "No one else would have kept her in an expensive school when her parents went over a cliff in the ocean. And nobody can tell me her father hadn't figured on that, or he wouldn't have kept writing to the Judge forcing promises out of him that no mortal had a right to demand."

I looked helplessly at Mr. Pepperday. He was like an irascible little fly determined to get to the flypaper. In his excitement his spectacles had worked off the bridge of his nose again. He screwed them back with his series of amazing facial contortions. Colonel Primrose waited blandly.

"Why!" The little man's voice rose half an octave. "He's spent more money on one year's schooling for that girl than he did on six of his own daughter's!"

I thought helplessly, "If he only keeps off the aircraft stock!"

"Sacred obligation!" Mr. Pepperday snorted. "Sacred obligations begin at home in my opinion. I think the good Lord holds that too."

He looked angrily at all of us, and went rushing on to everybody's destruction.

"I regret that I should have been an unwitting instrument in the Divine Plan, but it certainly was not a situation in which I can consider myself at fault."

I couldn't help looking at Colonel Primrose. Even his overpowering composure was shattered a bit. I could see him mentally struggling to unravel the butterfly of sense out of Mr. Pepperday's elaborate cocoon of verbiage.

"I don't quite understand you, Mr. Pepperday," he said affably. Nothing in his voice would have indicated a sudden intense interest, but his black parrot's eyes were sparkling and his cigar ash splattered down his grey vest and stayed there.

Mr. Pepperday was tapping his fingers on the desk exactly as Judge Candler did, only rapidly, like a hungry little baldheaded woodpecker tattooing on a flagpole.

"It's simply that when Miss Karen was doing over the old stable she ran out of money before she got the plumber in," he said. I settled back, not so obviously relieved—I hoped—that Colonel Primrose would notice it, but very much relieved indeed.

"She begged me very prettily to install the various oddments she'd scavenged, I may say, from friends who were remodelling and modernizing and from junk shops. My father and grandfather were plumbers, and I personally prefer plumbing to the law. Both professions are concerned with drainage. I take pride in both, but if I may say so, I am a better plumber than lawyer. I told Miss Karen it was the one place in the house where she ought not to economize, but she said she had to somewhere and she wasn't a baby. I pointed out the danger of installing a model without the safety improvements that present-day heaters are equipped with, and that if the pilot light were turned off, or blown out, and the temperature of the tank went down, the gas would go on nevertheless. She said I needn't worry, she could smell. She'd get a modern one some day, and she'd be very careful.—It's my opinion that she slammed the door and the pilot light went out. Though I admit that's difficult, because the local gas pressure is remarkably steady."

Colonel Primrose sat for a moment looking absently at him. "Why have you not already told the police about that,

Mr. Pepperday?"

Mr. Pepperday drew a circle on the blotter, enclosed it in a square, and bisected both.

"Because I am not a licensed gas fitter," he said at last. "I've never appeared before the Board. I am entirely, may I say, an amateur—I had no right doing it for her. Not that I didn't do it as well as a professional, but you see my dilemma. In fact, I should never have accommodated her except that I wanted to save the Candlers' money. The judge had no idea how much had already gone into remodelling the stable. I knew they couldn't very well afford any more."

Colonel Primrose nodded, still looking at him. Then he got up abruptly. "Thank you, Mr. Pepperday," he said. He held out his hand. "Now if you will do one other thing for me?—Phone the house and tell Miss Candler that Mrs. Latham won't be in to lunch. Thank you. Good day."

12

I am not having lunch with you," I said, when we'd got outside the tiny building.

"Oh yes, you are," he said. "I'll see you at two, Buck."

I suppose Sergeant Buck gave the usual effect of saluting. I didn't dare look at him.

"My car's in Royal Street," I said coldly. We walked through the market square. Colonel Primrose opened the car door and got in after me.

"I think the Anchorage in Queen Street is the best place," he said. It wasn't till he'd ordered that he relaxed in his chair and said, "Well?"

"Who have you decided to hang?" I inquired, acidly.

"No decision so far, my dear."

He couldn't have been more suavely affable.

"I'd almost decided not to bother. If anything happened to you, I could spend the winters in Honolulu. But I'm not going to let a murderer go scot-free.—My social conscience got the better of my personal comfort."

"Have you got one?" I asked. "—A murderer, I mean?"

He reached in his inside coat pocket and took out a piece of paper.

"Read that."

I took it. It was an ordinary sheet of scratch paper. On it, copied very carefully, was:

"My dearest dearest—I can't bear what you said to me tonight, but I can't bear to live without . . ."

Even the trailing off of the last letters was copied, and the "t's" of the last word were uncrossed.

I handed it back without comment.

"It doesn't look like a suicide note, does it?" he said quietly. "If she'd said '*And* I can't live without you' it would have been a horse of a different color."

He waited until the trim maid put down our food.

"That letter was written by a woman who was determined to do something in spite of what somebody she was in love with had to say."

I ate my chicken to the bone. I knew if I spoke I'd say whatever the most wrong thing happened to be at the moment.

He looked at me oddly for an instant.

"Mrs. Latham, there's an old bit of doggerel about criminal investigation that you've probably heard. It goes,

> "What was the crime and who did it,
> When was it done and where,
> How done and with what motive,
> Who in the crime did share?"

Tentatively applying that to Karen Lunt's death I think we can say the crime was murder, done by a person or persons unknown. 'When' is a large X at the moment, but we know the place. We think we know how it was done. If we go further into it after this afternoon, we'll send the viscera to the F. B. I. to make sure. With what motive we had no idea, nor do we know who in the deed did share—if anybody."

I stirred my coffee slowly.

"From all I've heard about Karen Lunt, suicide is the last thing she'd have dreamed of. And from the list of guests at that party, I think it's further evident that it hadn't even crossed her mind. Because you know, Mrs. Latham, as well as I do that it wasn't the kind of group that Karen ordinarily enjoyed. There were seven men and six women there.— Look at me, please."

I looked up.

"You know Washington well enough to know that guest lists at small parties are made up either for pleasure, in which case congenial people are asked, or for a purpose, in which case you ask useful people. Now, I can't see what a single person at that party had in common with any other one."

"We had a lovely time," I said.

He nodded ironically.

"—Ending with that letter and a dead hostess."

I was silent for a moment. "Mightn't Mr. Pepperday be right?" I asked then. It seemed to me that my voice sounded nauseatingly meek.

"All that Mr. Pepperday's remarks indicated to me, Mrs. Latham," he said, with exasperating calm, "was that he is astonishingly familiar with the mechanics of Karen Lunt's plumbing system."

"Oh, that's absurd, and unworthy of you!" I said hotly. "He wasn't within miles of the party!"

I was astonished to hear myself add, "Anyway, Mr. Pepperday retires at eight o'clock."

"I'm not accusing Mr. Pepperday of murder, my dear," he said peaceably.

"I certainly hope you never will."

"All right, then, I never shall," he replied.

He settled himself to a large piece of deepdish apple pie and heavy cream. When he'd finished he looked up with a faint smile.

"I needn't tell you, I suppose, that it doesn't seem to me you've been entirely frank, need I?"

"Is there any reason why I should be?" I asked coolly.

"Not at all, my dear."

I flushed to the roots of my hair.

"I'm not really trying to be an obstructionist," I said. "It's just that . . ." I stopped on the very verge of saying all the things Jerry and Sandy had said about the future of their father's career.

"It's just that murder's a foul mess and you don't want any part of it," he finished for me, with a smile. I noticed, however, that there was a gleam in his black eyes for an instant. He paid the bill and helped me on with my coat.

"I think it's only fair to you," he said as we went down the stairs and across the brick walk to the street, "to let you know there are a number of things in connection with Karen's death, none of them conclusive in itself, that point away from suicide. Would you like to hear them?"

I nodded.

"First, then," he said slowly. "If Karen wanted to kill herself, it's almost inconceivable she wouldn't have just simply opened a fresh bottle of sleeping tablets that she had in the

76

medicine chest upstairs. A handful of them would kill a horse."

I sat behind the wheel, making no move to turn on the ignition.

"Second. Assuming she did decide on the method that was used—why didn't she turn on the tap in the kitchen sink? Why choose the bathtub tap, and why pull the shower curtain across to hide it? And third: why did she leave an order under her milk bottle on the front step for an extra quart of milk? And fourth: why did she leave a note for the maid saying not to wake her till noon, and make cream of mushroom soup with part of that extra quart of milk, for lunch for two?"

I stared straight ahead up the street. Piles of blackened snow lay in the gutters. The brick walls were as clean as if they'd been scoured.

"And there's another point I'd like to know about," he went on. "If you won't think I'm accusing Mr. Pepperday of murder, I'd like to know why the only key missing on the board on the office wall is the one to the carriage house—which in spite of Mr. Pepperday's calling it the stable is the house Karen lived in."

My hand, thrust deep in my pocket, closed mechanically on the hard shaft of the old key.

"If you can answer those questions, Mrs. Latham, I'll go back home and forget it," he said quietly.

"Where do you want to go—back to the police station?" I asked. I couldn't answer any one of them, much less all.

"I'm really sorry!" he said. We were both silent for a moment. Then he said, "I'm meeting Fox at Karen's house. If you'll drop me there . . ."

I'd liked to have dropped him in an ice hole in the river, but since I had only myself to blame I merely started the car and turned back. We got to Chatham Street. The patrolman on duty recognized Colonel Primrose and let us through. I stopped in front of the Candlers' house and switched off my motor.

"By the way," I said, "Jeremy Candler asked me to call you back. She very sensibly feels that there ought to be no possible doubt to rise up later . . . if the verdict is suicide."

He looked at me with a quick smile.

"I can see it might be important—if what I hear around Washington is true."

He nodded to the little oblong plate that said "Press" above the District license of the coupé in front of us. "That's the

77

problem at the moment, not the police."

He opened the door and held it while I slid out across the seat. "Will you come along?"

I hesitated. My duty as a guest waged an internal tug-of-war in conflict with my curiosity as a woman.

"Might as well be hanged for a sheep as a lamb," he said with a smile. I saw his sharp black eyes come back from the upper window of the house across the street.

"Just so I'm not hanged for anything else," I remarked. I went along with him, leaving my duty as guest to crawl from the field as best it could.

Captain Fox was in the mirrored room, talking to a couple of men who may not have had eyes like ferrets at all, though it looked to me as if there wasn't a crack or cranny they weren't creeping into. A young man in a brown suit and soft hat came down from upstairs, following in the large square wake of Sergeant Buck, who had to stoop to clear the ceiling as he came.

"Nothing doing in the bathroom, Captain," the young man said. He crossed the room, knelt down and opened up a black case. He looked around the mirrored walls. "This is going to be a honey," he added tersely.

Colonel Primrose pushed a chair over to the door, I sat down.

"I think I'd begin in the kitchen," he said to Captain Fox. The young man looked at his chief and said, "Okay." He started back.

"The panel first," Captain Fox said.

Sergeant Buck gripped the sliding glass section gingerly and moved it out. From my place at the door I saw a fine dusty cloud rise like grey smoke. I tried to think whose fingerprints they were going to find there. Karen's, Miss Isabel's and mine, I knew for sure. The servants, of course, who'd helped out the evening before . . . William, Miss Isabel's maid, Karen's own girl. Sandy's and Roger's, probably, since they'd dispensed whiskey and soda to the men after dinner.

"That won't help much," Colonel Primrose said. "It's the pilot light and the oil-burner switch I'm interested in. And the plug to the icebox."

The young man in the brown suit edged through the narrow opening into the kitchen, Sergeant Buck following with considerable difficulty. Captain Fox stayed behind. He was apparently his own camera man. I watched him and Colonel Primrose at the job of recording the elaborate smudges in the film of grey powder that covered the glass like a summer's mildew. Even before they were through I heard the detective's voice from the kitchen.

"Nothing on the pilot, Captain."

I saw Captain Fox look at Colonel Primrose, his face more troubled and grimmer than I'd seen it even in the white glare of the searchlights from the fire engine the night before. He put down his camera and edged into the little kitchen. Colonel Primrose looked around at me. In the mirrored wall I could see my own reflection, grinning like a slightly sick Cheshire cat.

"It's the *absence* of prints that's so damning, Mrs. Latham," he said quietly.

I heard the detective from the kitchen again. "Here we are, sir. On the power switch. It's a honey!"

Colonel Primrose crowded in through the panel. There was a moment's silence, then Captain Fox's voice. "That'll be mine, I had to feel around to cut the oil burner off."

Silence again; and then I heard Colonel Primrose's voice, as suavely polite and quiet as ever but so charged with intent and dramatic meaning that I caught my breath sharply.

"Where is the chronometer, Buck?"

Without knowing why, I felt my breath coming rapidly through my startled lips.

"Right here by the cupboard, sir."

"Read it."

"Off at twelve, on at six, sir."

There was another silence in the kitchen, almost electric. I sat there. Colonel Primrose came back, Captain Fox and the others following. No one so much as glanced at me.

"Well," Colonel Primrose said, his voice so deadly calm that my blood froze, "That's plain enough. The idea was that no one would ever find Karen Lunt dead of gas. The burner was to go on at six . . . when there was enough gas in the house to blow it all to hell."

Captain Fox didn't move or speak, but his eyes were cold and hard as blue steel.

"If it hadn't been for the cat's waking Mrs. Latham, and her waking up the neighborhood, you'd have entered an accidental explosion on your books—one life lost. And if you hadn't been on the job, and cut off that power switch when you came in, you'd have had the same thing with the loss of fifty lives . . . your own, and Mrs. Latham's, and all the people standing around here. You're dealing with somebody as shrewd as sin, Fox—somebody too dangerous to have loose."

Captain Fox nodded grimly. "It was three minutes to six when I cut that oil burner off," he said shortly. "—And all those people out there."

"And all very simple," Colonel Primrose added.

Captain Fox nodded again.

"We'd better get going," he said.

I'm not sure how I got going back to the Candlers'. My knees shook so that I had to lean against the iron porch rail a moment for support before I could open the door and go inside the cold hall.

13

Somewhere in the back of my mind I had the idea that the kindest—perhaps even the most important—thing for me to do was go at once to Judge Candler and tell him what I'd just learned. I even had a vague conviction that that was what Colonel Primrose meant me to do, so that when the official juggernaut started moving he'd be unofficially prepared for it. There was definitely no doubt in my mind that Colonel Primrose was official, and that any consideration he might give the Candlers as friends of mine would be by way of casual suggestion through me.

I glanced at the closed library door and hesitated as I noticed a man's neatly folded overcoat and a black derby hat lying on the old needlepoint bench against the wall between the white door frames of the library and drawing room. The grandfather clock on the landing struck three as I stood there. The low murmuring of voices from the library went steadily on, with no sign that the conversation in there was drawing to a close. As I obviously couldn't stand around waiting, I went upstairs. I hadn't meant to go quietly at all, but there's something about a very quiet house, I suppose, that makes ordinary movements sound as if a herd of buffaloes were clattering about, and sort of forces one to creep involuntarily. I got to my room and closed the door behind me.

The fire was still burning in the grate, the quilt I'd laid over Jerry was pushed aside, the impression of her slim body still on the old-fashioned fringed counterpane. I took off my coat and moved across the big black and red and faded yellow rag rug to the shallow closet to hang it up. I opened the flimsy door and stopped. From the next room I heard, quite plainly,

"It just didn't work. It was all set. Something went haywire."

And it was Sandy Candler speaking.

I stood utterly petrified, too appalled, too completely horrified, to move or close the door and put my frozen hands over my ears so I couldn't hear Jerry's calm dead voice reply:

"So now we have a murder on our hands instead."

In the silence that beat through the flimsy wall board— I think even at that moment I realized it had been put there to make a closet by blocking up what had been a deep door between the two front rooms—I struggled back across the room, suddenly too ill to think, and sank down on the pine blanket chest at the end of the high bed, out of range of the quiet voices of Judge Candler's son and daughter. In the dark silvered mirror of the Adam girandole over the bow-front chest of drawers I could see my face, drawn and grey-green, my lipstick a grotesque red line that had no relation to my mouth. I sat there a little longer and got up. As I picked up my coat to put it back on, the pocket struck against the blanket chest with a subdued knock. My heart sank again. It was the key to the old door of March Wind's stall that was now Karen's converted kitchen. In it, at this moment, stood all the simple domestic equipment that had been arranged to blow Karen, the house and every scrap of evidence that could conceivably have pointed to murder to the sky at six o'clock in the morning.

Sandy's voice was saying, "It just didn't work. It was all set. Something went haywire," stood out in my numbed brain like the after image of a flash of ghastly light on the retina. Then I remembered: "So now we have a murder on our hands instead"; and I saw again the cake of ice and snow on the drugget inside the garden door, and the cat that had followed the footsteps that had left it there. I closed my eyes. The face I could see wasn't Jerry's face. It hadn't her delicate piquant loveliness, ivory-toned under her copper hair. It was the face of the woman over the mantel in the shabby beautiful room downstairs, with the Borgia smile tucked away in the corner of her full ripe mouth.

I put on my coat, my icy fingers touching the key deep in my pocket and drawing back as quickly as if it were white-hot. I didn't take it out. What could I do with it, I thought desperately, if I did? I couldn't take it to Mr. Pepperday— Colonel Primrose had seen the empty space where it had been. If he saw it returned . . . Still, I thought, Mr. Pepperday knew I had it. William knew; probably, by this time, Sandy and Jerry knew too. As I stood there, my loyalties seemed suddenly to get all mixed up. I tried to think of Jerry, and all I could think of was the face over the mantel. I tried to think of Sandy, cheerful and grinning, and all I could see was his hard eyes fixed steadily on mine as he said, "*I think it's suicide*," and all I could hear was his grim voice through the flimsy wallboard of the makeshift closet. — Against that was Colonel Primrose, saying, more grimly than I'd ever heard him speak, "You're dealing with somebody as shrewd as sin—somebody too dangerous to have loose."

I tiptoed to the door, slipped out into the hall and down the first step, my hand clinging to the stair rail. I suppose I stepped on a weak old board. A loud creak rent the air and my nerves. I heard a door open behind me, and whirled around as Sandy came out in the upper hall. His face underwent a lightning change, but not to a smile—far from it.

He said, "Oh, it's you. Just coming in?"

My voice sounded choked and ghastly to me as I said, "Yes," and forced my protesting feet back up the stairs as normally as I could.

"Come on in," he said. He hadn't taken his dark eyes off my face, and he didn't as he held the door open for me to pass him.

I'm not sure, quite, how I did it, and I'm not sure whether I really expected him to fell me with a crack across the skull. He didn't, anyway, and I stepped into a room very like my own, with a higher fourposter with fringed and balled tester curtains and needlepoint steps. It was a more comfortable room than mine, with a deep leather chair by the empty fireplace with its heavy unpolished brass andirons, and its simple pine mantel crowded with signed portraits of half the Hall of Fame. In the recessed seat in the front window Jerry was sitting, shielded from outside view by the long snowy muslin curtains.

She looked up as I came in, and I started in spite of myself. It wasn't the woman downstairs in the over-mantel at all. It was the pale pointed-faced girl with frank wide autumn-hued eyes and burnished copper curls and sweet serious mouth, young and fresh, and there was definitely no Borgia smile tucked in its slightly drooping corners. Her eyes raised to mine were full of questioning anxiety.

"Did you see Colonel Primrose?" she asked.

I nodded. "Apparently Captain Fox has drafted him in the present emergency," I said, trying to be as casual as I could.

"What does he think?" Sandy asked. I thought he was trying to be the same.

I shrugged. "I wouldn't know, entirely. They all looked pretty grim."

"Oh, please, Grace!" Jerry cried. "Don't try to . . . to save us anything. Tell us what's happened. It's so horrible, just sitting here, waiting . . ."

"What's the use of having an amateur gumshoer in the house if we have to wait for the evening papers?" Sandy said sardonically. "Let's have it. We can take it."

As I looked at Jerry, all the last few days came crowding back to me. Her distress, the way they'd bludgeoned her to give up the first security she'd felt for years, for her father and for her younger brother, probably playing basketball that very minute with my own kids; the awful blow to her proud little spirit when Philander Doyle said Roger wouldn't let his wife accept a sacrifice from her, the poignant little sacrifice she had made—to the half-frozen sparrows in my back garden; her hopes for her father, her fears that she'd hoped too high. Karen had been the stumbling block then. I wondered suddenly if now that she was dead, the stumbling block hadn't become a mountain instead of a molehill.

Anyway, looking at her pale upturned face, her lips parted a little, her gold-tinted eyes wide with unspoken alarm, I felt all the old desire to save her if I could . . . even from the consequences of murder. I sat down in the deep window seat beside her. Outside, the dirty soot-streaked streets and clean-washed brick walls were empty except for my car and a large limousine waiting in front of the Doyles'.

"Well, here it is, then," I said. "It seems Karen made elaborate preparations for today—notes to the milkman and the maid. She was expecting somebody for lunch, and was having mushroom soup and mixed grill for two. They can't see why she did all that if she didn't expect to wake up; or why she went to the rather involved business of gassing herself when she had enough sleeping pills upstairs to do it much more pleasantly and neatly. Colonel Primrose doesn't think that note sounds like despair and suicide; he thinks it sounds like a woman still determined to do what a man she was in love with had told her was a dishonorable thing to do."

I realized instantly that I'd given Colonel Primrose the dubious benefit of my own special knowledge, in saying much more than he'd said.

Jerry's eyes dropped to her folded hands.

"*Not* Roger," I said. She looked at me quickly.

"How do you know?"

"Because Roger didn't give a damn about Karen," I answered, thinking with a kind of mild amusement that first I'd put my own words in Colonel Primrose's mouth, and now I was quoting what Roger had said as if it were my own.

"How do you know?" she asked, softly.

"What do you care, precious, anyhow?" Sandy demanded grimly.

"I don't."

"Then let's skip it."

I looked around at him. His face was set, and his eyes were burning with a kind of smoldering resentment that was definitely disquieting.

"I'm sorry," Jerry murmured. She turned away and stared out the window.

"You wouldn't think, you two," I said, "that maybe you're being a little hard on Roger?"

"I said let's skip it," Sandy replied shortly.

"Don't be an ass, Sandy," I retorted, forgetting that less than ten minutes ago I'd sat quaking in my boots, thinking he was a cunning fiend.

"You just don't know, Grace," Jerry put in quickly.

"I do know," I said. "I saw the guy with the bandaged face go in the house, and I saw Roger come out with him. That doesn't necessarily mean . . ."

"Yeah?" Sandy cut in. "You think he just went in for a cup of tea with Miss Isabel? Look here, Grace—that bird was hired by somebody that knew all about Jerry's aircraft stock, and——"

"You don't actually think," I demanded heatedly, "that Roger sent that man after you and Jerry!"

I was wondering, perfectly coldly inside of me, why—as Sergeant Buck would put it—I had to stick my neck out at somebody else's funeral, and least of all Roger Doyle's. Except of course that it was Jerry's too.

"It's absurd," I said. "After all, he's a friend——"

"Oh yes?" Sandy said. "Then we'll take nothing but enemies, thanks. Fried, if you've got 'em."

I gave up. "Very well, angel," I said. "But allow me to add

84

that I think you're being a stubborn idiot—first class, front row."

He lighted a cigarette and shied the match in the empty fireplace, glowering like an angry bulldog.

Jerry tossed back her burnished head.

"Oh, Sandy, maybe . . . maybe she's right! Maybe he wasn't——"

He cut in shortly. "Okay. I know you're in love with the guy—have been since you were seven. All right, go ahead. Stick up for him. But don't come bawling back to me the next time you get it in the neck."

If I hadn't known he was her brother I'd have been more upset than I was. The taped knuckles on his hand denied practically all of it.

Jerry was up like a flash, her eyes sparking fire.

"What if I am in love with him!" she cried hotly. "It's my affair, isn't it? It doesn't hurt you!"

Sandy stared at her silently for a moment. Then he got up, took a quick step on the worn old bearskin rug and put his enormous long arms around her shoulders. "There, there!" he mumbled. "I'm a dirty hound. I didn't mean it. I just don't want it to hurt you, honey."

She clung to him a moment, her head buried in his arms, and pushed him away.

"I know it," she said. She hunted for a handkerchief and took his, and stood blinking back the tears. "It's just that if . . . if it wasn't as bad as it looks, it would——"

"Why in heaven's name don't you ask him what it's all about?" I demanded. "It's *so* simple."

That was a mistake. They both stiffened like the couple of red-haired proud young Tartars that they were. It was the old clan against the world. Roger had hurt them, sweet reasonableness was no part of the code. They'd rather hurt themselves than have Roger know how deeply he'd hurt them.

"Or see the man whose skull you cracked," I went on stubbornly. "He'll probably be delighted to talk if you can get him out on a country road."

I was definitely shocked, as soon as the words were out of my mouth, to hear myself talking so exactly like Sergeant Buck.

"Yeah," Sandy said. "But he's skipped. I ran him down this morning. Your taxi driver took him to a hotel on Vermont Avenue. I went around with my hand in my pocket and said I was the guy whose car hit him. They said he left at nine

85

this morning and came back in a hurry and checked out. He'd registered as Samuel Smith of New York City—name printed in block letters."

"Oh," I said.

Jerry touched my arm lightly. "Look!" she whispered. She was staring out through the curtains, her breath coming quickly between her parted lips. I turned. Across the street, standing in the handsome doorway of the original Candler house, was its present owner and occupant, Philander Doyle. He was speeding the parting guests with a large expansiveness that would have been a pleasure to watch if the parting guests had been anybody other than Colonel Primrose and his guard, philosopher and friend, Sergeant Phineas T. Buck.

I looked at Jerry. Her face was pale, her hand through my wool sleeve was icy cold.

Sandy's low whistle went shivering through the dead branches of my heart, making them tremble a little.

"Grace," he said abruptly,—"is this bird Primrose as good as they say he is?"

"He's better," I said. I didn't mean to sound as depressed or as resigned as I know I did. Then I remembered I hadn't told them all I'd learned.

"He's figured out, for instance, that whoever"—I couldn't bring myself to say 'Murdered'—"whoever it was last night, had it all planned so that the oil burner would come on at six this morning, when the house was full of gas, and blow the whole thing to bits."

They sat looking at me, their faces as blank as stone walls . . . and I suddenly remembered something else; what I'd heard through the flimsy wall of the tiny closet. I moistened my lips with a paralyzed tongue and forced myself to look away out the window.

Colonel Primrose and his sergeant were crossing the street directly below us.

"How . . . how does he know, Grace?" Jerry breathed, so softly that if my head hadn't been so close to hers I should never have heard her.

"The chronometer was set to go off at twelve and come on at six," I said. "I suppose he figures that if she planned to sleep till noon, as she'd written the maid, she wouldn't have had it go on much before."

She nodded. "She was terribly thrifty about a lot of things. She never had it on before eleven."

"Captain Fox turned the power switch off just three minutes to six," I said. I thought there was no use stopping now I'd begun. "It almost blew him and everybody around there to kingdom come."

We heard the heavy tread of feet on the steps outside and the doorbell far off in William's kitchen tinkle pleasantly.

"Well, well!" Sandy said grimly. He drew a deep breath. The telephone on the table by the bed buzzed loudly—urgently, it sounded to me, in spite of the fact that I know they're quite impersonal.

Sandy picked it up. "Just a minute," he said. "It's for you, Grace."

I took it. A cool aloof voice came from the other end—across the street.

"My dear . . . wasn't this the afternoon you were to have tea with me? Surely I haven't made a mistake? It's all ready and waiting. My brother will be *so* disappointed . . ."

I glanced at Jerry.

"I must have misunderstood, Miss Doyle," I said. "I'll be right along."

I put the phone down.

"I'm going to have tea with Miss Isabel," I said.

Jerry's eyes kindled.

"Maybe I can glean a little news from the trenches.—Any message for Roger?"

She shook her head. "Be careful, Grace!" she cried. I went out thinking she'd meant to be careful what I said to Roger. I'd got half-way down the stairs before I realized that that wasn't what she'd meant at all.

I crossed the hall. The library doors were closed. Colonel Primrose's overcoat and hat lay on the needlepoint bench, Sergeant Buck's hat and neatly folded coat were laid underneath the bench on the floor. It's amazing how rank will stick.

14

It was the great Philander Doyle himself who opened the handsome white door of the old Candler house. He took my hand in one of his and laid the other over it, patting it once or twice as if I were some way in a particularly bad spot and needed comforting. I suppose it was sort of the bedside manner of a lawyer whose most lucrative practice had once been divorce and alimony and breach of promise and little women who thought they'd had a rotten deal and wanted to cash in on it. Or such, at least, was the reputation that still clung to Philander Doyle like the vaguely malodorous miasma that rises from a cellar that isn't aired very frequently.

Of course, that might be really awfully unfair and prejudiced, I thought. Maybe it was just that Philander Doyle had from the beginning had an uncanny flair for publicity. Like some doctors who can't cure a stomach ache without making the front page, Philander Doyle couldn't take a case without its becoming instantly a *cause célèbre*. Perhaps, like the doctors who grub away doing the hard jobs without even getting paid for them, many lawyers looked askance at Philander Doyle as a grand tour de force. But many a woman whose mind was a complete blank while she filled her unfortunate husband's hide with lead from a pearl-handled revolver she just happened to have in her hand counted heavily on Philander Doyle. People actually said if she hadn't known she could count on him she wouldn't have bought the gun. However, be that as it may, he'd prospered under it, and the broad lovely rooms of the house that the Candlers had once owned showed it.

There wasn't a stick of mahogany or satinwood, from the Chippendale card table with the three feathers of a Prince of Wales inlaid in hollywood in its rich waxed surface to the petitpoint footstool with a box of candied cherries from the corner tea store on it in front of the gleaming old silvered fireirons, that any museum wouldn't have been delighted to have. The plump cupids in lovely pale pink and green and grey on the Aubusson carpet bore aloft the initials of a Queen of France in their rosy fingers. The Chinese Chippendale mirror above the Ming garniture on the carved roses of the pearwood mantel reflected the rainbow sparks from the Waterford lustre and the elaborately simple broken pediment of the doorway I was entering, with its carved rosettes and center pineapple. On the panelled walls hung a Watteau and a Reynolds, and a lovely Allan Ramsay of George III in wig and ermine so soft you could feel its warmth. On a low Chippendale table in front of the fire a silver tea service, so simple and lovely that I knew it must be early Baltimore, was set out on a broad balcony tray that made me simply green with covetousness.

Philander Doyle took my coat. I heard that awful key in my pocket clump against the Philadelphia Chippendale chair by the door.

"Sounds as if you're in the old iron trade, Mrs. Latham,"

he boomed, smiling. I tried to laugh, but I'm afraid I wasn't particularly convincing, because I saw something move behind his warm blue eyes that were certainly blue but not awfully warm, when you stopped to think about them. But it was only for a fraction of an instant.

"Sit here, Mrs. Latham. My sister will be down in a minute," he said cordially. "Let's not wait for her. She's just as apt to start mooning about upstairs and forget all about us as not."

He laughed with good-humored resignation, as if Miss Isabel and her vagaries were a sort of amusing cross he had to bear.

"You pour, will you? It's one of the little compensations of life, you know."

I didn't, but I sat down at the tea table and said, brightly, "Cream or lemon, Mr. Doyle?"

As he took the priceless Crown Derby teacup and balanced it precariously on his crossed enormous knee, his face changed like the decoration of a theatre from the mask of comedy to the mask of tragedy.

"It's pitiful about poor little Karen," he said slowly. And he made it sound so. I found myself suddenly rather moist-eyed, which I'd not been before, not even when I sat in her tiny glass house.

"I understand from my good friend Colonel Primrose that there's a question, not of how, but of—shall I say—the circumstances, of her death," he said. He hadn't looked at me. His soft blue eyes were fixed on the rosy cupids serving the French queen in the tapestry carpet.

"I must not drop one of these teacups," I thought. As I put down the one I had in my hand, the thin silver spoon clattered musically against the lovely porcelain.

"But I'm afraid our police methods are too clumsy to be of much use," he went on, as if he hadn't noticed. After a moment's silence, he said, "Karen was almost a daughter to me. I thought I was in love with her mother once. Not very seriously, because she already happened to be married to Lunt."

A dreamy tender smile of lost young love moved his lips nevertheless.

"Karen was like her—especially that last night."

I couldn't make out whether he meant the last night he'd seen her mother, or just last night when he'd seen Karen, until he said,—"With her curls on top of her exquisite little head, and that velvet gown. I kept thinking I must be dreaming.—And I was, I'm afraid, Mrs. Latham."

He looked at me and smiled—a whimsical kind of a smile that said, "Don't be too hard on a foolish old man, my dear."

"Colonel Primrose tells me you're an old friend of his," he went on.

I thought, "Ah—Colonel Primrose staking out signs to save my neck." I said, "Yes, I've known him a long time"—which wasn't true but seemed a justifiable stretching of a point under the circumstances.

Philander Doyle's eyes were fixed on me now with the utmost friendliness and even affection.

"I hope you're planning to stay on with little Jeremy until this . . . is over. Colonel Primrose said he was trying to persuade you to."

"The beast," I thought. I realized instantly that the Colonel was counting on me—as usual—as a decoy duck, and my safety was all a blind. Which wasn't a pun mixed with a metaphor, but just bitter truth.

"It may be a cruel thing to say, Mrs. Latham," Philander Doyle remarked, so telepathic that I blinked until he went on. "But my deepest concern in this terrible business is for my old friends across the street."

He looked at me gravely.

"You're a woman, my dear, and women have a God-given sense that men never approximate in this world. I want to help Jeremy. I believe the way I can help best is by you and I working together to keep our official friends from riding too roughshod. I'm a lawyer, you're a woman. Together, Mrs. Latham, we can do it."

For a moment I hesitated. The room, the tea, the man himself were so beguiling. Then I said, "I don't think Colonel Primrose would ride roughshod over anyone," which was a blatant lie. He'd ride roughshod over his own grandmother if the necessity arose, and I knew it only too well.

"I know," Mr. Doyle said. "Loyalty to one's friends is heaven's greatest boon. But after all, John Primrose is a policeman. His duty and yours and mine are very different things. You know that, don't you? I knew you did. A woman knows from her cradle that her part in life is defending the weak from the strong, protecting the defenseless from the iron hand of the blind goddess. It's something that not the law but the practice of the law has taught me, Mrs. Latham."

"You aren't implying that Jerry, or one of the other Candlers, did this awful thing—or that if they did they're to go

90

unpunished, are you, Mr. Doyle?" I asked. I was trying desperately to shake his siren's song out of my ears before I said too much.

"To the first, No—on my soul, No!" he said earnestly. "To the second—Yes. A million times Yes, Mrs. Latham."

Rich passion rose in his fabulous voice.

"Murder is something no man understands. How are we to judge what has gone before . . .? There are times no one would hesitate to take human life—if our homes, if everything we hold dear, were threatened. If your children were threatened, Mrs. Latham, you wouldn't stop and ponder any Critique of Pure Reason, any Ethic of Aristotle. You'd act. And what policeman has a right to say, 'She's got to hang by the neck until she's dead'?"

"Oh dear!" I thought. I could quite see myself shivering in a jury box, saying desperately, "Why shouldn't the little woman slay her husband?"

He smiled. "That's why I'm asking you . . . as a friend of my friends."

He held out his big warm hand.

"Is it a bargain, Mrs. Latham? You and I *versus* the State?"

My hand in his was cold as ice. He gave it back to me.

"The first thing we've got to know, then," he went on confidently, "is how much the police know—or think they know. I saw you over there after lunch."

I poured myself another cup of tea, feeling like a rabbit under a snow-covered hedge with a large, apparently quite friendly hound trying to coax me out. I knew I was a fool even to move a whisker, but I just couldn't sit and say nothing.

"They didn't let me in on much," I said. "Except that all Karen's plans for the next day were written down, so they decided she couldn't have been thinking of not being there herself."

He nodded.

"Karen, my dear Mrs. Latham," he said with a faintly ironic smile, "was the last person in the world to take her own life. I've known a good many suicides in my day. They killed themselves when they were at the bottom of the heap —not on top of it. Last night Karen was walking on air. She hadn't an idea Jerry would quietly hand over the stock. She thought she was going to have to make a fight for it. Moreover, if she'd ever contemplated suicide, it would have been the quintessence of the dramatic. She wouldn't have gone to any elaborate—if simple—arrangement to blow herself to bits, possibly . . . or risk burning herself to death if a spark from the electric icebox happened to ignite the gas before there was enough of it to blow up."

I said to myself, "Slowly, my girl." To Mr. Doyle I said, "That was . . . odd, wasn't it. I suppose it may have occurred to Captain Fox too."

"You mean to Primrose. I'm afraid Fox has too much faith in human nature," he said. "In fact, I must say it's unfortunate Primrose happened in. I understand he was on his way to Norfolk and heard it on his radio."

"That's what he told Captain Fox," I replied, and added —thinking he might as well have a token of my entire frankness, especially as he already knew it in some way—"actually he was just trying to save me. I telephoned him."

"You, Mrs. Latham?"

Philander Doyle raised his dramatic eyebrows ever so faintly and shook his head gravely. "Then it's doubly your duty to help save the pieces. Why, may I ask, did you ever do it, my dear young woman?"

I put down my teacup. I knew perfectly well that somehow I had to get away. I had less of a chance than if I actually were the rabbit under the hedge. I couldn't dig myself a hole in the floor to escape through. Whatever I said, not knowing how much he knew, would be just the wrong thing. But I didn't know how to get out the door into the dark street without letting him see I was terrified and utterly unequal to the combat.

Just then the front door burst open. Mr. Doyle looked up sharply. Roger Doyle was standing in the doorway under the carved broken pediment set with the white wood pineapple. His face was white and his eyes stormy.

"Dad!" he said. Then, as he saw me, his lips tightened to a line in his hard-set face. He gave me a curt nod and turned to his father again.

"Dad, I've got to talk to you."

Mr. Doyle's rich voice had the faintest inflection of reproof.

"I'm busy now, son."

"I know, Dad. But this is important. Grace won't mind waiting a minute. I'll walk over with her—I want to see her myself."

His father looked at him, the same odd cold movement behind his fine warm eyes that I'd seen when I came in.

92

"I'll be glad to wait," I said.

Philander Doyle glanced at me and back at his son, and got up with a deprecatory paternal smile.

"All right, my boy," he said. He gave me another kind of smile. "He doesn't realize yet that a pretty woman never waits.—I trust this one will."

I couldn't tell whether he realized I already had one eye on the door.

"People can't get rid of me," I said, trying to be gay, I suppose to cover up the situation that the tense young man, lean-jawed and dangerous-eyed, was creating from the doorway.

"The library's in the back, Mrs. Latham, if you hear me shout for help," Philander Doyle boomed jovially. And it struck me instantly that that didn't sound forced. He was actually pleased about something, though what it could be, with his son in the poisonous state he was in, was beyond me.

I heard their footsteps along the wide panelled hall, and a door close behind them. And then I did practically the most awful thing I ever did in my life. I got up and stood for a moment, looking around the room. I was absolutely alone—there wasn't even a Staffordshire spaniel or a China cat to see me. I slipped across the room to my coat on the chair, took the big old key to Karen's kitchen out of my pocket, and moved noiselessly back across the room to the mantel. I reached up and took down the center vase of the five-piece Ming garniture, and let the key slide gently down to the bottom. Then I put it back, my hands shaking as I suddenly thought that if I dropped it, I could never in the world scrape together enough money to pay the purchase price on a thing that was utterly irreplaceable.

I went back to my chair and sat down. Then I got up again, and went back and wiped the vase off neatly with my tea napkin, and settled down again. I had a sudden picture of myself flicking my hands off in precisely the way Karen had done the day she came from her questionable triumph over Jerry in Judge Candler's library; but for some reason or other I sat there feeling a lot more at ease inside myself than I had at any time before . . . and considering what I'd just done, than I had any right to feel if the wicked have uneasy hearts.

Finally, because it seemed to me that not even Philander Doyle would expect me to stay all night, I got up and put on my coat, and went out into the hall. I thought vaguely that maybe I'd see a servant and leave a message. But the hall was quite empty. Then, as I moved toward the door, I heard a sound on the elegant curving stairway.

I glanced up. Leaning over the mahogany hand rail, her full black silk skirt showing between the white spindles, was Miss Isabel Doyle. She came down, almost quickly, it seemed to me, and with one ear sort of cocked toward the library.

She held out her hand.

"I'm so happy you could come," she said, with aloof graciousness, as casually as if the whole proceeding hadn't been most irregular. "I'm sorry I couldn't get down, earlier, but I've been sorting some old things for the Leper Guild at the church."

"I had a very nice time," I said, edging closer to the door. From the end of the hall I could hear Roger's angry voice and his father's mellow one, but I couldn't make out their words.

Miss Isabel glanced back too. I thought I saw a worried line tremble at the corner of her mouth, but I probably didn't.

At any rate she turned back with her vague smile.

"My brother's a very unusual man," she said. "He always gets what he goes after—if not one way, then another."

There was a certain airy approval in her voice.

"I think it's most unfortunate that he dislikes Judge Candler so much."

I stared at her, literally open-mouthed.

"Oh, my dear, but he does, you know. He always has."

Her voice and manner were quite charming.

"I'm sure the whole business about Karen's stock was his idea, not hers. She really was too stupid to have ever thought of such a thing."

I had the odd feeling that I was quietly going mad. I moistened my lips.

"But . . . Karen was going to have the stock!" I exclaimed, not realizing—until later—that it must have sounded a complete non-sequitor.

Miss Isabel looked at me as if I'd said the butter tasted of fish, her eyebrows raised ever so slightly.

"But, my dear . . . don't you see that *that's* the point?"

15

I went back across the slippery street a very bewildered woman. For one thing, I was quite certain that inviting me to tea had been Philander Doyle's idea, not Miss Isabel's. And for another, that she had had a vague notion of what his purpose had been in asking me.

Whether she'd known it from the beginning, or had sorted it out with the garments that would certainly amuse the lepers if nothing else, I hadn't an idea. That she'd let slip an eternal truth when she said it was unfortunate that her brother disliked the Candlers so much, I was almost as certain as I was that it was dark and twenty minutes past six on a winter day . . . and I hadn't a doubt that her brother would have strangled her if he knew she'd said it.

Nevertheless, as I went up the Candlers' steps, with the pale yellow gas flames in their old wrought-iron standards glimmering feebly, I was still trying vainly to make sense out of her last remark: "But, my dear . . . don't you see *that's* the point?" What *was* the point, I wondered desperately? If it was Philander Doyle who was trying to frighten Jerry into returning Karen's stock by setting Mr. Samuel Smith of New York to dog her trail and her brother's, why should the fact that he'd succeeded be anything but a satisfaction to him? It was utterly beyond me.

I opened the door and went in. The warm smell of frying chicken from William's kitchen greeted my nostrils pleasantly. I glanced at the grospoint bench between the closed door of the library and the open one of the drawing room, and saw that Colonel Primrose and Sergeant Buck had gone. I had a little sinking feeling inside me, and realized I'd more or less counted on seeing one of them if not the other. I went on upstairs to my room. The fire had been replenished and the light on the bedside table was on. Beside it lay a folded piece of paper with William's long black thumbprint on it. I picked it up and opened it.

It said, "Dear Mrs. Latham—I'm staying in Alexandria at the George Mason Hotel.—John Primrose."

I crossed the room and dropped it in the fire. Whatever possible doubt I'd had that he hoped somebody would furnish him a fresh clue by slaughtering me had vanished. He could quite as easily have got rooms in the house next to the Doyles', on the corner, so he'd be near enough to hear me. I knew I was being unreasonable, of course, but that's never deterred me yet, and I couldn't let it now.

I washed my face in the cold water in the basin in the corner and changed my dress. As I was wondering vaguely what time the Candlers dined, I heard Sandy galloping down the

95

stairs. In a moment I heard Jerry's light footstep coming along the hall and stop, hearing me in my room. She tapped at the door and put her bright head inside. Then she came in, closed the door and stood leaning against it, her hands behind her on the tiny old-fashioned brass knob.

"Well—how was it?"

"Miss Isabel didn't show," I said. "I had a pleasant talk with the master."

I almost added "—mind," and stopped before I did.

"I suppose he's worried that his dear friends the Candlers may be involved in this unfortunate business," she said, with a faintly ironic inflection that somehow didn't go with her delicate ivory face and wide autumn eyes.

"That was what I gathered," I said.

She moved over to the bed and started taking off the big old counterpane.

"Roger was here again," she said, her voice muffled as she held the heavy woven cloth under her chin, folding it.

"Did you talk to him?"

She shook her head.

"My father opened the door. It was just as Colonel Primrose was leaving. I didn't know he was here till William came up. He said, 'Miss Jer'my, why you all treatin' Mr. Roger like he was scum,' and Sandy said, 'Because he is,' and William said he ought to be ashamed and that's all."

She put the counterpane on the window seat and folded back the blanket, moving as if something had died inside her.

"Did Roger talk to your father?"

She shook her head.

"You just throw scum out, don't you?"

"Listen, lamb," I said. "Sit down."

She slumped half down on the blanket chest, her eyes wide open, gazing into the fire.

"Roger's head over heels in love with you, Jerry," I said earnestly. "Don't you know that's why no girl has ever made any time with him? . . . and you know every new season's batch has a go at it."

She shook her head slowly.

"Then why all this Karen business? Mr. Doyle wouldn't have said . . ."

"Rot," I said rudely. "Why do you believe one thing he says and not the next? I don't believe for an instant that Roger and Karen had any understanding of the sort. If they did, it would only conceivably be because you'd turned him down

96

flat and he was trying to save things for you by marrying her
—but that doesn't make sense."

I looked at her. "—You didn't turn him down, did you,
darling?"

She caught her lower lip in her white little teeth and drew
a long breath.

"I told him I couldn't marry him unless his father and Miss
Isabel approved, and they wouldn't, of course."

"Why not?"

"Oh, lots of reasons."

Her eyes were fixed on the dark windowpane.

"What are they?"

"It doesn't have anything to do with me, really," she answered after a moment. "Miss Isabel has never forgiven Dad
for not marrying her. Mr. Doyle said he'd never let a daughter of Dad's benefit by the money he'd made sluicing out
drains while Dad stayed poor as a church mouse gathering
respectability and prestige instead of . . . money. At least
that's what Miss Isabel told me one afternoon at a tea at the
rector's. You can't believe anything she says, of course, unless she just lets it drop out of a clear sky without thinking."

I smiled. Which had she just been doing across the street,
I wondered—thinking, or just letting things drop?

"She's batty," I said.

"No, she's not, not by a jugful," Jerry said quickly. "She
just likes to get even with people when they aren't expecting
it. At least that's what Sandy thinks—and I do too."

She'd certainly got even with her brother then, I thought,
and in a big way . . . except that it didn't make sense.

"What did Roger say?" I asked.

"He said they didn't make any difference to us. I could take
in washing and he'd get a job with the W. P. A. He says he's
got a lot of political influence."

She smiled suddenly, more like her brother than herself.

"And what did you say?"

"I said I'd only think of marrying him on account of his
money, and anyway I had to keep house for Dad. William
won't live forever. He's getting so old now he spends half his
time praying. We couldn't afford a cook, if anything happened to him.—But this isn't important, Grace. I mean what
happens to me. It's . . . it's the other thing."

"I think what happens to you and Roger *is* important," I
said. "I don't think his father's money is, awfully. More than
that, no one will ever convince me that Roger had anything

97

to do with the man Sandy socked in the nose. Roger's over there now, closeted in the library with his father, looking as if he'd been through living torment. You're not being fair, not to at least let him say what's on his mind."

She leaned her head back against the foot of the high bed and closed her eyes.

"I . . . I know, Grace—but what can I do?" she said. "Don't you see, I can't let my father and Sandy down, not if I never see Roger again. I can't, I can't!"

"Look, my sweet," I said. "It's just about time you let your father and your brother start looking after themselves and begin listening to your own heart. Alexandria's full of women who let their father and their brothers keep them from marrying. Do you want to end your days like Miss Isabel, keeping house for Sandy, and have him marry some young snip when he's forty and you keep house for both of them? If you let them keep you from even talking to Roger, what do you think you'll do when they say, 'But Jerry, who'll cook now William's gone?'—I think female sacrifice is a beautiful thing . . . in nineteenth-century novels. I'm opposed to it as a working program. But of course if you *don't* love Roger——"

"But I *do*, Grace! I do!"

"Then for heaven's sake, act like it."

"What can I do? Father won't let him in the house. He hasn't said so—he never would . . . but let him try to come."

"Is your car out of gas?"

She hesitated, and shook her head.

"I can't . . . go running after him, Grace," she said.

"Well, you can have tea with me, and he can drop in, can't he?" I demanded.

A little smile lighted her face. "If I didn't know it, I suppose."

"All right," I said. "What about tomorrow at four?"

Her face went pale again.

"I've got to go to Karen's . . . funeral.—Oh, Grace, don't you see?"

Her voice sank to a frightened whisper.

"We're in a trap! He's part of it, no matter whether he wants to be or not! Can't you see?"

I think I was beginning to, as a matter of fact, just when the bell rang in the hall below. Jerry got up slowly, stepped to the mirror and dusted her eyes with my puff. She stood looking at herself for a long time. Then she turned around.

"It's funny to find you look just the same, isn't it?"

Judge Candler and Sandy were waiting in the library. We went silently in to dinner. Thinking of it now, I have no idea what we ate, except for dessert, which was apples baked in molasses with flour and butter till they were transparent gold, flavored with rum and served with thick yellow cream. I could never forget them. Yet it seems to me that the thirty minutes we spent at that long bare table, with the light from the tall candelabra at either end gleaming on the old silver epergne filled with polished red apples and clusters of raisins and nuts, was one of the longest and most disturbing half-hours I've ever spent. The silence, with old William's creaking shoes, was bad enough. Judge Candler's voice as he said the simple grace had faltered a little. The arms of his chair as he drew it in hit the table, a walnut rolled off the epergne onto the bare wood, so that I jumped at least a foot to begin with.

He didn't speak again, but sat there, his thick white-thatched head bent a little forward. William in his old black coat and white cotton gloves would stop each time he passed his chair, look at him and move sadly on. Jerry and Sandy kept casting secret sidelong glances at him and looking quickly away. Whether it was my knowing that Colonel Primrose had talked to him without my knowing what had been said that made his silence so alarming, or it may have been that it had some special quality of its own. Or it may have been that now I was back in the quiet house seated where I could see their young faces, strange and drawn in the candle-light, the brief conversation I'd overheard through the flimsy wallboard kept coming back to me again.

Outside the stiff icy branches of the old lilac trees touched the dark panes like fingers long dead. The wind whoooooed softly down the wide chimneys, frightening the sober yellow flame tips of the candles, making them tremble and try to flee from the black points that held their feet and brought them back strong again. I watched Jerry. She raised her fork to her lips and put it down again untouched. And then suddenly, when she couldn't stand it another instant, she pushed back her chair and stood steadying herself with her fingertips against the gleaming satin surface of the old table, her slim body shaking, her face as pale as the candlelight.

Her voice came in a quick heartbroken sob:

"Oh, Daddy, don't! Don't!" she cried. "Oh, I wish it had been me—you wouldn't have cared so much then!"

She turned and groped blindly out of the room. For a moment we were all too shocked to move, I think. Then Sandy pushed his chair back and went out after her.

I sat perfectly still looking at Judge Candler. Had he, I wondered, also been so much in love with Karen's mother that seeing her with her hair up in the black velvet dress had reminded him, as it had Philander Doyle . . . so that Jerry's mother, and Jerry, had become dim and unreal? He hadn't moved except to raise his head and look profoundly shocked but apparently unmoved at his daughter's outburst. It flashed through my mind, watching him, that never once had I seen him make the slightest gesture of affection toward her. From everything I'd seen he moved, an august person, through the house, accepting everything, giving nothing of himself—except to Karen Lunt. And yet, there must have been something to make her adore him so. I suppose that's what made me braver than the angels. I heard myself saying, with astonishing coolness, considering what I was saying and to whom:

"You don't deserve Jerry, Judge Candler."

His sombre eyes were still fixed, dumbfounded, on the door his children had fled through. He turned them slowly to mine, across the dark candle-lit table, and looked at me silently. Then he said, the timbre of his voice like the G string of an old violin, "I love my daughter very deeply, Mrs. Latham."

Dead fingers scratched at the windowpanes. The wind whooed down the chimney, the candlelights flickered so that his face was barely visible. But in that moment I saw what I hadn't ever thought to see there—anguish, and pain, and fear so naked and alone that my heart almost stopped beating.

He pushed his chair back and got up.

"Will you tell her that, Mrs. Latham?—I can't trust myself to speak to her now."

He moved across the room and stood a moment, his tall slender figure bent a little, by the empty hearth. "I'm afraid I've been blind, Mrs. Latham. Blind and . . . selfish. And now that I can see again, it's . . . too late."

"Good Lord," I thought, "—he thinks they killed her too."

I started to speak, and stopped. What could I say? A sear leaf from the old ivy on the chimney fell and scratched across the window. The Judge moved slowly out of the room like a man blinded not with selfishness but with sheer pain. I folded my napkin and just sat there.

Old William came in and set about moving the dessert plates, untouched except for mine, over to the serving table. I watched him not seeing anything very sharply, until he came back and stood by the judge's chair, his black face streaked with tears.

"It warn't none of them done it, Mis' Grace," he mumbled. "They was asleep in they beds. It warn't them took th' key off'n the board. It was somebody else done it. Judge he think it was them. It was me foun' th' key on th' groun' when th' fire engine was shootin' light ev'where. But don' you tell nobody. Mist' Pepperday, he call an' says they key done gone an' ain' Ah seen it no place. Ah tell him you got it, Ah ain' seen it since."

"Who do you think took it, William?" I asked.

The old man shifted his gaze.

"Tell th' truth, Mis' Grace, Mist' Pepperday done lef' that key here his self, when he was plumbin' for Mis' Karen. But Ah ain' tellin' him Ah know—he pride his self he don' nevuh make mistakes in de-tails. He know his self he lef' that key in Mis' Karen's seegar box she got painted an' fixed up pretendin' birds make a nes' in it. Ain' no use makin' nestes in seegar boxes. Ain' no use tellin' Mis' Karen that—ain' no use tellin' Mist' Pepperday he overlook a de-tail. They both knowed it already."

I said, "Oh."

"Then this mo'nin', Mist' Philander he come lookin' an say, 'Weeyum, didn' they use to be a key in that there box?' He don' miss *nothin'*. Ah figger he knowed that 'cause he messin' roun' when Mist' Pepperday do Mis' Karen's plumbin'. He say, 'You mis-took you' profession, Mist' Pepperday.' Mist' Pepperday he say, 'That's more'n anybody can say 'bout you, Mist' Doyle,'—snappin' lak a she turtle."

"You didn't tell him you gave it to me, did you?" I asked.

"Ah ain' give it to you then. Ah got it in mah own han's."

"When was Mr. Doyle looking for it?"

"When he come ovuh fust thing this mo'nin'."

"When the fire engines were there?"

"Not right fust, Mis' Grace. He nevuh come till they was workin' on pore Mis' Karen."

"After six?" I asked.

"Yes, *ma'am*. It was hittin' six when Capt'n Fox brung Mis' Karen out. 'Twas after that he come ovuh, him an' Mist' Roger."

"You don't say," I said.

"Ah do say. Ah seen 'em come, cross th' street."

"But the Judge, and Miss Jerry, and Mr. Sandy—they were down there, weren't they?"

"Mis' Jer'my, she was. Ain' nothin' woke up Mist' Sandy, ain' nevah since he bawn. Jedge he tryin' t' find his pants. Ah done had 'em all down in mah kitchen, goin' press 'em fust thing in th' mo'nin'. He shoutin', 'Weeyum, you fool niggah, wheah mah pants?' jus' lak he use' to when he was comin' up. Done mah soul good jus' hearin' him."

Somehow the picture of the dignified and distinguished figure of the Virginian jurist standing in the hall bellowing for his pants seemed to me very funny, and William beamed at me like an ancient black seraph.

"Then he shout, 'Tell Mis' Jer'my put some clothes on 'fore she go out theah!' But Ah couldn' fin' Mis' Jer'my, she gone."

16

I don't know what made me happen to glance up at the door at that moment. Perhaps my subconscious had heard something I wasn't conscious of. Yet why not, unless he'd crept in with the most extraordinary care, I can't imagine. It was the smaller-than-life-size figure of Mr. Pepperday. How long he'd been standing there I had no idea, except that it must have been some little time. He looked very severe, anyway, as if the sight of an old darkey and a white lady laughing about the Judge's trousers was undignified if not downright disreputable.

He screwed his spectacles into their niche on his beaked nose.

"I've come to inquire about a certain article," he said in his high prim treble—deciding, I suppose, that ignoring the whole scene he'd run in on was the better course for a man of any delicacy.

"Unfortunately, Mr. Pepperday," I said, "it's lost."

"The lostah the, bettah," William said darkly.

He and Mr. Pepperday seemed to have a subtle rapport that interested me, chiefly, I think, because I felt it without being able to define it in any way. They were curiously like the old Greek god whose name I've forgotten whose head had two faces. Though that was ridiculous, too, because anything with Mr. Pepperday's face on one side and old William's on the other would definitely not remotely resemble a Greek god.

"That depends, in my opinion, on how thoroughly it has been lost," Mr. Pepperday observed shrilly.

"Very thoroughly indeed, Mr. Pepperday," I said. "And since Colonel Primrose has already noticed it's gone from the board, I think it would be a mistake for it to be found and returned."

"He sure am smart, ain' he?" William said, with quite genuine enthusiasm. "He come out in mah kitchen this mo'nin' an' says, 'What's goin' on 'round heah, son? Gabriel goin' blow fo' you fus' thing you know. Bettah sta't prayin', and don' tell me no lies, or Ah'll bus' you irrega'dless."

"Oh, that's Serge'nt Buck, not Colonel Primrose, William," I said. If there had been any doubt, that last word would have clinched it.

"Mighty nice man, anyhow," William said. "Want to know, did Ah cook th' suppah ovah to Mis' Karen's. Said no girl nevah cook that there ham ovah in that there frigidary."

"You be careful of him all the same, William," I said. "Sergeant Buck is just as much of a siren in his way as Mr. Doyle is in his."

William shook his head. "No, ma'am—came jus' as quiet. Ask me who was th' young man Mis' Karen was sweet on."

"Did you tell him?"

"No, ma'am. Tell him Ah don' know. He's a foreign gennaman Ah ain' nevah seen 'fore; he come messin' 'roun' in th' kitchen lak he ain' nevah seen th' inside one 'fore, askin' what that clock runs th' oilburner was, callin' that hot watah tank a . . . a geezah."

I wondered.

" 'Course Ah tol' him. Seem *interested*. Ask don' we heat ouah watah. Ah took him down in th' cellah, showed him we ain' got no new-fangled apparatux to kill nobody in they sleep."

Mr. Pepperday, listening from the door, looked anxiously at his watch.

"Good night," he shrilled.

William picked up the Judge's napkin and folded it.

"Mr. Pepperday, he re-tahr at eight o'clock," he said, I suppose by way of explanation of the little man's abrupt departure.

"I know," I said. "By the way, did he show up at all this morning?"

"No, *ma'am*—Mr. Pepperday, he don' get up till half-past seb'n."

Mr. Pepperday then, no matter what might happen, was placed from eight, when he invariably retired, till seven-thirty, when he invariably arose. It was unfortunate, I thought, that all the rest of us weren't as methodical.

I watched the old darkey move around, snuffing the candles with a pair of silver snuffers. He polished off the satin-smooth old table and took up his tray.

"Good night, Miss," he said.

He waited for me to precede him into the empty hall, and switched out the single electric light overhead. I heard him padding slowly back to his kitchen. Poor Mr. Geoffrey Mc-Clure, I thought. I've always suspected that what Sergeant Buck gleaned backstairs was what made his Colonel so omniscient in the drawing room, and I was sure of it now. Heaven knew what else William had told him, in the secure conviction that he was not telling him anything. Then I paused with my hand on the stair rail. Or *had* he, I wondered? He was certainly nobody's fool, even if he did have the old Negro's suspicion of "apparatux." Nevertheless . . .

I went slowly up to my room. The clock on the landing pulled its old joints together to boom out Mr. Pepperday's bedtime. Somewhere in the dark recesses of the quiet house Mrs. Harris raised a plaintive meow. Sandy's voice raised suddenly: "Why doesn't somebody strangle that damned cat?" I listened. Mrs. Harris didn't make another peep. Jerry's level voice said, "You'd better pull yourself together, darling."

"I'm sorry!" Sandy said. "But every time she squeaks I can see——"

"Sandy! Stop it—stop it!"

If I'd had my coat I think I'd have slipped out of the front door and gone home. But I didn't, and I didn't care about freezing to death on my way back to Georgetown. Then as I went on up the stairs the telephone rang. I heard Sandy say, "Just a minute," and then he opened the door and shouted for me.

I went on in. It was Colonel Primrose.

"Look, my dear. What about your bringing Miss Jerry around for a confidential chat? Not here——"

"The police station?" I asked acridly.

He chuckled. "No, to Fox's house. He's not there. I don't expect you to take my word for it. Bring the Melton pack and nose him out if you like."

"I'll see," I said. I turned to Jerry. "Colonel Primrose wants to talk to you.—I *know*, Sandy." He was glowering angrily. "But you can't keep her incommunicado and you might as well face it. You might as well have Colonel Primrose see her with me as have Captain Fox have to get at her officially."

"I'll be glad to see him," Jerry said quietly.

I turned back to the phone and said, "All right." He gave me a number in St. Asaph's Street, and I put the phone down.

Sandy and Jerry were standing looking at each other. She turned abruptly and went out into the hall.

"Make him pull the old punches, Grace," Sandy said. "She's not as elastic as she looks."

No one would have thought her the least elastic as she joined me downstairs a minute later. She was pale gold and brittle as spun sugar in her short brown beaver jacket and little brown velvet hat perched on the back of her copper head. But she smiled back at Sandy standing in the dim light of the open door. We got in my car. I would have given a great deal to know what was going on in her mind as we drove slowly through the dark silent street to the gleaming white little clapboard house with its three rows of tiny windows looking out like bright eyes through the dead winter branches of the big maple tree in the sidewalk.

Colonel Primrose opened the door. "Mrs. Fox has taken the children to the movies," he said. I listened. There was no sound in the house except the scratching of the big good-natured dog in front of the fireplace.

Jerry took off her jacket, sat down on a stool by him and scratched his head, his long tail knocking noisily on the hearth. She looked at Colonel Primrose, her golden eyes as open as the sky, and smiled a little. He sat down beside me on the davenport and put down his cigar. I looked around the room. It was a pleasant chintzy sort of place, with school books on the big table, a businesslike radio and miniature broadcasting set beside it. Captain Fox's leather slippers poked their worn noses out from under an armchair, his pipe was on the smoking stand close by. Mrs. Fox's knitting bag and a basket with socks in it and a darning egg were on a low table beside the couch. Somehow my heart rose a little.

"I want to know all about this business of the aircraft

105

stock you hold, Miss Jerry," Colonel Primrose said. He wasn't trying to be casual, or kind, and I saw Jerry relax a little.

"It's quite simple, Colonel Primrose," she said. "When Karen's father died, he was supposed to be a rich man. He'd appointed my father her guardian without bond. They'd had a long correspondence about her future. When Father took everything over he found Mr. Lunt had left very little, actually. There was some real estate in what they call a 'blighted area' in Baltimore, some gold mining stock in Nevada, where it cost more to get the gold than it was worth, even with new chemical methods, and one hundred shares of aircraft stock, at one hundred dollars a share."

I was proud of her cool straightforward voice and her steady unwavering eyes meeting his.

"There wasn't much insurance, and what there was was invalidated by a suicide clause. We weren't wealthy. My father got what money he could out of everything he could sell—to keep Karen on at Briar Hill, which he'd promised Mr. and Mrs. Lunt he'd do. He tried to sell the aircraft stock, but it wasn't worth a thousand dollars, much less ten thousand. Still he kept her at Briar Hill. When he found he'd have to take her out because he just couldn't pay the bills, he went to Mr. Doyle, who'd been a friend of her parents too, and got him to take the aircraft stock, which still wasn't worth anything, at its face value as an act of friendship."

There was no trace of bitterness in her voice as she spoke Philander Doyle's name.

"Then Mr. Doyle got in a jam. It was just before he moved back down here and bought the old house. By that time the five thousand dollars had been more than spent on Karen, but Father had a salary from the bench then, so it didn't matter—very much . . . not to him. Mr. Doyle brought the stock around, and asked Father to take it back. He had to have ready cash. Father took it, at the price Mr. Doyle had paid. Then he got very ill."

She hesitated and went on.

"He was terribly alarmed about all of us then.—The doctors said he couldn't live six months. He arranged with Mr. Doyle to take Karen over and keep her at Briar Hill, and then he scraped together everything he could lay his hands on—even collected a few of his old unpaid fees—and put everything in an irrevocable trust for me and my younger brother Billy, with Mr. Doyle as guardian ad litem. He left

106

Sandy the house, with instructions to sell the furniture only when he had to keep us going. The aircraft stock was listed at five hundred dollars then, but with everything he had he got the trust up to $20,000, and he had $5000 insurance. Then . . . he didn't die, we wouldn't let him die. And . . . after a while everything went on the same. Karen stayed at Briar Hill, flunking a year or two. Billy went to public school, I went to Miss Ebury's in Charlottesville, Sandy went to George Washington instead of Princeton."

"That was . . . ?" Colonel Primrose said.

"Five years ago. And then, two years ago, with all the war scare and armament, somebody took the company our stock was in and put it on its feet. And the stock went way up."

Colonel Primrose nodded.

"Did Karen know that?"

"Oh, yes, of course," Jerry answered quickly. "She'd finished school, finally, and she'd gone abroad and come back and was living with us. All she had was twenty-five dollars a month from a trust her great-aunt had left her. Father was still taking care of her, as he'd promised her father and mother he'd do till she married. She knew about the stock. She said several times it showed there was a God, because Father was getting back the money he'd spent on her, and didn't it serve Mr. Doyle right."

Colonel Primrose touched the grey column of ash of his cigar on the side of the metal tray. "Nothing was said about it belonging to her?"

"Nothing at all, ever, except last year when she decided to do over the carriage house and live by herself, and the estimate was terrific. She said, 'But darling—I haven't cost a whole hundred thousand, and that's the morning quotation on your stock.' I guess I looked blank, because she put her arm around me and said 'I was joking, you baby—but it'll be so much better for all of us if I have a place of my own. I'll try to cut it down.' But she didn't, and Father said to me, 'But we don't want to be selfish, Jeremy.'—The idea that it was hers, or that she had any claim to it, except through our good will never was suggested, even."

"When did it first come up?" Colonel Primrose asked.

Jerry looked at me. "It was the night I stopped by your house on my way home from the office, Grace."

"What office?" Colonel Primrose asked.

"Where my job is," Jerry said. She said it as if he ought

107

naturally to have known she had one. "You see the stock doesn't pay but two per cent, and my kid brother's at St. Paul's, and Karen's house costs more to keep up than we'd planned."

"I see," Colonel Primrose said. He blew out a rather ironical trail of blue smoke. "Go on."

"That's all, really."

"But you haven't answered my question. What day was it you were at Mrs. Latham's?"

"It seems years ago now." She looked across at me. "I guess it was Monday night. This is Friday, isn't it? Karen came in after dinner and stayed in the library a long time with Father. Sandy and I were jittery, because that usually meant an awful wallop of some sort. Then when she'd gone he called us down and said he was going to let her have the stock. She wanted to marry a young man who hadn't any money, and . . . oh, a lot of things. We were appalled, of course, but he said after all we didn't want to profit by her . . . her misfortune, was the way he put it."

She bent down and rubbed the dog's ears.

"I guess I lost my temper. I said a lot of things I'm sorry I said, now."

She didn't look up at him.

"Father said he was sorry I was being unpleasant, because I'd have to sign over my rights before the trust could be absolved, because I was twenty-one. I had a birthday three weeks ago."

Colonel Primrose looked at her, his cigar suspended in mid-air. I'm sure he hadn't thought she was eighteen.

"I hadn't realized that, of course. I asked him how Billy—he's fifteen—could agree to give up his share. He said Mr. Doyle as guardian would do that. I said Mr. Doyle could, but I wouldn't. Nothing could ever make me do it. I guess I said a lot more I needn't have said. But I was . . . furious. It meant . . . so much, you see."

Colonel Primrose nodded.

"And Sandy?"

"He felt the same way about it," Jerry said quietly. "After all, we'd sacrificed a lot ourselves—if that doesn't sound too noble, because we weren't ever that. We used to gripe horribly to ourselves about what we'd do if it weren't for Briar Hill."

She smiled suddenly, and some way the fact that she could made the "gripe" not terribly important.

108

"Anyway, I'd got my back up, and I went to see Mr. Doyle. He said he thought I was perfectly right. If Father insisted, and he would insist—he knew him well enough to know that—he'd have to sign over Billy's rights, but he felt it was my duty to keep Father from making an unselfish fool of himself. After all, the Lunts had run through a big fortune in a few years, and if my father had sold the stock to any broker Karen couldn't have gone around and got it back. He said he was glad there was one Candler who had a vague instinct of self-preservation. What if Father got sick again and what if the next telephone pole got Sandy instead of vice versa? What would Billy do, and old William, and half a dozen ancient cousins and all the rest of it? He said everything that was exactly what I'd thought myself."

I looked at Colonel Primrose. His sparkling black parrot's eyes were resting very intently on her, and the expression on his usually bland countenance was not very pleasant.

"And then?" he said.

"I told Father I wouldn't think of it.—And then, last night, I changed my mind."

"Why?"

"Several reasons."

Colonel Primrose shook his head politely.

"Now look, my dear," he said. "Let's not be unreasonable. Karen Lunt was murdered last night in perfectly cold blood. I don't think, at this moment, that you had any hand in it, and I don't want to think it. I think Mrs. Latham will tell you that I have a lot of admiration for you. I don't want to see all this glaring in the headlines—which it will do if Captain Fox is in duty bound to ferret out what you're trying to hide."

"That's the reason I decided to give her the stock," Jerry said quietly. "—Headlines."

"What made you think there'd be any?"

She was silent, her little chin set, her dark eyes smoldering.

"You might as well tell him," I said. "He'll find it out anyway."

She nodded after a minute.

"I didn't go to the office yesterday morning," she said. "I was too upset. I did go back around four. A man was waiting for me in the lobby. He followed me up in the elevator and got out with me, and said, 'Just a minute, Miss Candler. I've been instructed to look into the management of Miss Karen

109

Lunt's estate. I think you'll see the wisdom of returning her stock to her. It won't look so well for your father if we have to take it to court.' That's all he said. He got in the elevator as it stopped on the way down. I was just stunned. Mr. Doyle had said she hadn't a legal or moral leg to stand on, that she was just trying to get something for nothing.

She stopped again. Colonel Primrose waited, watching the smoldering anger rising in her flushed cheeks.

"I didn't go home right away," she said. "I went out and walked around a while, trying to . . . to cool off, I suppose. Then when I did go home Sandy came in. The same man had caught him when he was coming out of the office and said about the same thing, I guess."

"And what did Sandy do?" Colonel Primrose asked.

She hesitated.

"I hope he beat him up?"

"He did," Jerry said. "But we were both scared—not of him but what was behind it. We both know that if it never got to court even, where Father could go on the witness stand and explain a fight between a man in public life and his orphaned ward; it would make a grand story—especially if anyone wanted a story."

"Especially just at this time," Colonel Primrose put in. She looked at him gratefully, and nodded her copper head.

"We decided—Sandy and I—not to tell Father. I don't think he'd have believed us if we had. Anyway, we were sick of the filthy business—it wasn't worth having Dad's name ruined. No one would ever have stopped to see that the orphaned ward living in an old stable on her guardian's place was a lot better off than the people living in the colonial mansion with poor old William expanded into a retinue of liveried servants."

Colonel Primrose chuckled.

"Then we were going to Karen's for supper. I didn't want to go, but Sandy said I had to. We didn't know whether she was planning to serve us a summons with the soup or not. So Sandy went over early. I got dressed and went down just as Mr. Pepperday, who's a notary, came, and Mr. Doyle as Billy's guardian. He told Father he thought it was a mistake, and then it started all over again."

She hesitated.

"Somehow, at home, and seeing Karen's little house so beautifully lit up and ours so dark, I began to think I'd dreamed the man in the elevator. Just then you came in,

110

Grace. Then I don't know what it was. It seemed to me Mr. Doyle was sort of on the qui vive, but still I didn't think it was anything except that he wanted to get it over with and get some food."

She hesitated again.

"Until he made a sort of speech that I couldn't tell about —whether it was supposed to hurt my pride and goad me into signing, or just what. And then, all of a sudden, it struck me like a flash that he really didn't want me to sign it . . . and not because of us at all, but . . . well, I didn't know. And then it all came back—the man, and lots of things. And I saw it—whatever it was—just as a whole set-up in which I'd acted exactly as anyone knew I'd act. So I . . . I asked Father for his pen, but before I could take it Mr. Doyle had grabbed the paper and thrown it in the fire. I knew then that that was what he'd been on edge about, that he'd been ready all the time to do just that. Only Grace's coming had made it a little less smooth than he'd planned."

She smoothed back her hair with one trembling hand and moistened her lips with the tip of her tongue.

"It was too late then," she said evenly, "because Mr. Pepperday has to go to bed at eight o'clock if the heavens fall. I didn't want to make a scene. Father, of course, hadn't the faintest notion what was going on in my mind—or in Sandy's and mine earlier. Then we went out. Sandy'd got worried and come back, afraid I'd gone berserk again. And then, as we went over to Karen's house, we looked back and saw that man again—who'd spoken to me by the elevator— and he was coming out of the Doyles'."

Colonel Primrose looked steadily at her. "Are you sure? It must have been pretty dark by that time?"

She nodded unhappily—and so did I for that matter.

"He'd got his head all bandaged up. Anyway, we both recognized him in the headlights of the taxi he was getting in."

Colonel Primrose nodded. "Go on."

"Well, we went to Karen's. Sandy wanted to go back and finish the job he'd started when the man talked to him, but I wouldn't let him."

—No mention, of course, I thought, that he wanted to include Roger Doyle in that program. Roger might have been in Baghdad for all of us.

"I knew the minute I got inside Karen's house that this was part of the same show. The people there—except one man I'd never seen at Karen's before. They were exactly the

111

sort of people that if the point came up, could hurt Father the worst, with the best intentions in the world, and for the public good—so they'd think."

Colonel Primrose nodded again, with a scarcely perceptible sidelong glance at me.

"So in the first moment I could, when I knew everybody would have to hear, I told Karen I was giving her back her stock in the morning."

Colonel Primrose looked steadily at her for a moment.

"And thereby," he said, very placidly, "quietly signed her death warrant."

She looked at him, her wide thoughtful eyes very steady.

"I've been wondering if I didn't," she said. Her voice was leaden, as if it weighed too much to lift past her lips. "And yet I can't figure just why. I never meant to. I was . . . well, like the boy with my finger in the dike, trying to keep it from going out, while all those people were there, trying to . . ."

She finished with a hopeless shrug of her slim shoulders. Colonel Primrose looked at her oddly. I had the sickening feeling that the analogy of the Dutch boy had been horribly unfortunate. He knew the burghers would come and relieve him. Had Jerry known death—or murder—was coming to relieve her? It was such a little step for Colonel Primrose to take . . . and I knew he was precisely the man to take it.

17

Colonel Primrose got to his feet.

"My advice to you, my dear," he said gently, "is to go home and try to forget it. And don't worry."

Jerry reached for her jacket.

"I'm not worrying, about myself," she said. "It's just that everything I tried to keep from happening is so horribly much worse, now."

"Not if we can prevent it," he said quietly. He helped her on with her jacket. She went quickly out into the hall and opened the door. Colonel Primrose picked up my coat. I heard Jerry go quickly down the steps and open my car door.

"I think perhaps we may be able to get somewhere with Mr. Philander Doyle, now," Colonel Primrose remarked. "Unless of course Buck has decided he's a blackguard and takes matters in his own hands."

I looked about in a perfectly involuntary movement.

"Buck? Is he here?"

Colonel Primrose smiled.

"Of course. I assumed you'd know he wouldn't allow me in an empty house with two women.—He's in the kitchen."

The dog on the hearth, hearing a magic word, pricked up his ears and looked around.

"Well, I hope Mrs. Fox left the dishes," I said, philosophically. "Did he tell you, by the way, all the things he gleaned out of old William?"

"About the foreign gennaman?"

I nodded.

"I knew that before," he said. "I saw Mr. McClure after I talked with the judge. He's in a state of petrifaction—about his family and his job on the one hand, and Karen on the other. He's really knocked in a heap. I gather he was actually pretty much in love with her. That note was to him, of course. But you knew that, didn't you?"

I've long ago given up allowing him the satisfaction of "Elementary, my dear Watson." I just nodded.

"That's how I found out about the stock business," he went on. "Apparently Karen thought that if she got the stock back, they could get married. So did he, I imagine."

I looked quite blank.

"No," I said. "He thought it was dishonorable . . ."

I couldn't stop in time, and Colonel Primrose, one hand on the door knob, looked at me, his brows lifting a little.

"I hoped I'd get *something* out of you, sooner or later, Mrs. Latham," he said, very blandly. "Buck! Go out and tell Miss Candler to wait a minute, please."

Sergeant Buck's great granite form appeared from behind the swinging kitchen door and passed through the narrow hall with the agility of an out-sized elephant. He cast me one glance *en passant,* but he didn't say anything. There was a slightly brassy flush on his dead pan, as if he'd been raiding the icebox when his chief called, and I saw him wipe his mouth vigorously with his hand as he went out the door.

"Come back here and tell me about it," Colonel Primrose said. His voice was pleasantly suave, but I caught a faint clank of the mailed fist just the same. As a matter of fact, my concern for Geoffrey McClure had waned a good deal in my rising concern for Jerry and Sandy . . . and for Jerry and Roger. It's hard for any American, I suppose, to see the European point of view about marriage, in spite of the enormous sense it makes. If he'd said "I love you, Karen—blast

113

the foreign service and my family and my mouldy sisters," I'd probably never have abandoned him as instantly as I did. But I rationalized it, of course. What, I thought, if by some chance the things William had said had a deeper significance than the mere curiosity of an Englishman about American plumbing? What if Colonel Primrose was right, that he was so entangled with Karen, and the pull from the other side was so great, that he knew that while he had an even chance to escape the gallows he hadn't a ghost of one to escape the altar?

"Sit down, Mrs. Latham," Colonel Primrose said, most politely. "Tell me all about it."

I sat down again.

"It's quite simple, really," I said. "I broke a shoulder strap when Jerry told Karen she was giving her the stock."

"Surprised, I take it?" he said.

"No, not terribly—not at that. If you'd seen her after Mr. Doyle threw the paper in the fire you'd have known something like it was going to happen. It was just that Miss Isabel, who hadn't seen her then, and who evidently—from what she told me today—didn't think the stock was very important, dropped her fork and a potato ball. Somebody else picked up the fork, and I reached down too abruptly to rescue the potato ball from its niche in a purple-velvet bowknot on her skirt. As soon as people started moving about so I could get upstairs without too much publicity, I slipped up. I was in the bathroom, and that's when I heard him saying it was dishonorable, that he adored her and what not, but he had his family and his job and his future, and so on."

Colonel Primrose took another cigar out of his vest pocket and unwrapped its cellophane jacket. He bit the end off and sat there, looking meditatively into the fireplace.

"Yes?" I inquired politely, after I'd sat waiting three minutes by the alarm clock on top of the piano.

"I'm just trying to put it together," he said. "I shouldn't have thought the stock business disturbed him. That scene may have continued later."

"He went home before we did," I said.

"He could have come back, I suppose?"

I hadn't thought of that. There was certainly nothing to stop him.

"Oh well," Colonel Primrose said, "we'll see."

I started to get up.

"One other point, Mrs. Latham. Did Jerry, or Sandy, or

you, recognize the man with the battered face?"

I shook my head.

"Sandy traced him through my taxi driver to a hotel in Vermont Street. His name was Samuel Smith in block letters from New York. He left hurriedly at ten o'clock."

"Would the papers have had the story then, I wonder?"

"I wouldn't know," I said.

He got up.

"There are several other things we've got to find out. The laboratory across the river, by the way, reports that Karen was pretty full of codeine. The sleeping pills upstairs are one of the barbiturates."

I stopped halfway to the door. "You mean, she was———"

"Oh no. She was just sound asleep when the gas went on."

I stood stock still. Gradually I became aware of myself in the hall mirror, my mouth slightly open, looking as blank as the opposite wall. Colonel Primrose's snapping black eyes were fixed intently on my face.

"Come clean, Mrs. Latham," he said.

"It just struck me," I answered slowly. "She drank a big glass of milk while she was showing me her kitchen. It was on the sink on a little silver salver. She said it was her tonic and downed it like a man. She could have taken most anything in it then, without knowing it."

He looked at me thoughtfully.

"So that she probably then sat up waiting for the cat to come in—or waiting too for the hesitant Mr. McClure—and dozed off," he said. "Neat, if you ask me."

We went on out and down the steps and across to my car. Sergeant Buck, having delivered his message apparently, was doing sentry up and down the block. Hearing the door close he came back, his enormous square bulk shrinking a little as the headlights of my car reduced his looming wooden figure to reality.

"Good night," Colonel Primrose said through the window. "Tell your brother, Miss Jerry, that I'll be around to see him in the morning."

I switched on the motor. My tires whirred around in the icy shallow gutter, gripped finally, and we moved off.

"Let's go somewhere and get a cup of coffee," Jerry said, her voice muffled there in the dark. "We won't see anybody we know at Pete's in Royal Street."

That wasn't, as it turned out, precisely the case. We went in there and sat at a clean white-enamelled-top table in a golden-oak booth festooned with fly-specked paper flowers, with paper napkins in a patent container and a sugar bowl that picked up a lump as you raised the lid, and ordered coffee. The Greek proprietor, apparently an old friend of Jerry's, brought it himself.

"How's the Judge, ma'am?" he inquired.

"Fine, thanks," Jerry smiled wanly. "How're the youngsters?"

"Okay," he beamed. "Okay. My little kid in school now. Doin' *fine*."

He went back behind the counter, where the mirrored wall was stocked with cartons of appalling cakes and pies and festooned packages of salted nuts.

Jerry, looking like a pale ghost under the arc lights glaring overhead, sat staring down at her coffee cup, watching the cream form a tight film on the top. After a moment she took her spoon, skimmed it off slowly, looked at it and put it down on the table.

"Is that . . . Roger?" I inquired.

She looked up at me, a twisted little smile on her lips.

"As far as I'm concerned, I guess."

"What is it now?" I asked, not as patiently as I might have.

"Nothing. It's just that it all came to me while I was talking to Colonel Primrose. And afterwards, sitting out there in the dark in the car."

"Not, I trust, that Roger had any hand in all this," I said.

She picked up the thick cup, sipped at it and put it down again.

"He couldn't have helped *knowing*, Grace. He's in his father's office, and he lives at home. He's no baby. Why was he so bent on my giving back the stock if he didn't?"

"Suppose he did, Jerry!" I said. "Assuming the very worst —after all, Philander Doyle is his father, and a very good one to him as far as I can see. He's devoted to him. He's given him everything in the world. No matter what he did, wouldn't you expect Roger to be loyal to him? He might try to get around him, because he's in love with you—but you'd hardly expect him to denounce his father to the housetops, would you?"

"Why not—if he was doing something horrible?" Her eyes caught fire from her voice.

"Oh, don't be a child, Jerry," I said. "What if it was Sandy, or—I'll admit it's preposterous, but just for example—your father, or even William, who turned off Karen's pilot light,

116

and you knew it—would you have told Colonel Primrose to-night?"

"Of course not," she breathed.

Then I saw her eyes go blank and the color that had come into her face drain out again. She was staring past me at the mirror behind the soda fountain near the door. I turned around. A man was sitting hunched up on a high stool there, his hat pulled down over his eyes, his overcoat collar turned up around his neck. I didn't recognize him, not till my own eyes moved from his back to the mirror. Even then I don't think I recognized the white haggard face and burning eyes as Roger Doyle's for at least ten seconds.

18

The waitress pushed a glass across the counter. He raised it, and as he did his eyes met Jerry's in the mirrored wall. He stared, shook his head like a man in a daze, and looked again. Then he put his glass down, turned around slowly, slid down off the stool and came toward us. I looked at Jerry. Her wide-open eyes were glued to his face, moving as he moved.

I slid over in the booth. "Sit down, Roger," I said.

He put his hat on the table and sat down, looking across at Jerry. "If this were only some place else," I thought. A less suitable site for a meeting of the sort I could hardly imagine.

"Look, Jerry," he said at last, his voice grating like wind in the cornhusks. "I'm . . . I'm sorry about everything. I know it sounds phony, but I'd . . . like you to know I didn't know what was going on. I don't really expect you to believe it. I don't suppose you'll believe I meant everything I said yesterday morning. But that's true too, every word of it and a lot more. I can't say. Honestly, Jerry!"

Her face, that had opened with a sort of anguished tenderness, looking at his haggard face, closed up again.

"Then why did you try to make me do as she wanted?" she asked. The sparks kindled in her eyes again. "You did know . . . something!"

He looked around at me despairingly, and back at her. "I thought that would end it, Jerry. There wasn't anything else I could do . . . except marry her. I'd even have done that, to save all this."

Her eyes really flashed fire then.

117

"Then why didn't you tell me—instead of sending that man around?"

"I didn't send him around, Jerry. I'm telling you I didn't know anything about him. My God, do you think I'm a——"

"Yes, I do!" Jerry cried.

Somebody put a nickel in the electric phonograph, and its merciful blaring proceeded to drown out all thought or other sound within a mile. Two youthful jitterbugs performing in front of it absorbed the proprietor and his black-eyed waitress, drawing them and a couple of taxi-drivers away from our end of the narrow restaurant.

"We saw you—Sandy and Grace and I—coming out of your house with him, just last night!"

His jaw relaxed drunkenly as if she'd slapped his face.

"Deny that if you can!"

"Perhaps if you'd give him a chance to explain," I remarked peaceably—with the usual lot of the peacemaker. Jerry turned on me instantly. "—You've always been on his side!"

"Glad somebody is," Roger put in. He'd got hold of himself again at a moment when I thought his Irish was up and he was going to pick up his hat and walk out, telling her to go to the devil.

"Listen, Jerry—if you'll keep your shirt on a minute," he said earnestly. "He came to see my father. I didn't know he was the guy. He said he'd slipped and got hit by a taxi. He's done a lot of . . ."

I thought he was going to say "dirty work," and I think he was, at first, because he hesitated and said, "—work for my father in the past. I didn't know he was in on this—not till you just said so. I thought he was just mooching. I gave him a ten-spot and told him to scram, we were going to a party."

While he was talking I could see something working behind his voice . . . something quite different going on in his mind.

Jerry came back, womanlike, to her point.

"But you *knew* . . . all the time you were . . . talking to me yesterday and knew your father was pitting me against Karen, so she could . . . so she could ruin my father!"

His lean jaw hardened.

"You could have told me! You could have said, 'You've got to outwit them,' instead of pretending it was because you loved me and the money didn't matter! It was your fa-

118

ther you were trying to save, not me! It didn't matter about me! Well, you can just go back and see what you can do to save him now!"

He stared at her, white-lipped and taut, and got up, his fingers clenched in his hat brim to keep from shaking. "Good night," he said shortly.

As he strode out I heard the waitress say, "Hey—you forgot to . . ."

"Okay, Okay," the Greek proprietor said. "You shut up."

I looked at Jerry. Her face was as white as death.

"Oh, Grace!" she whispered. "I didn't mean it—I didn't, really!"

"It's too bad," I said. "Because nobody could possibly have guessed it. Let's go."

I signalled the waitress. "How much was his drink? I'll pay for it."

"A nickel," she said. "Fifteen cents altogether."

We didn't speak on the way back to Chatham Street. Jerry sat huddled in a silent miserable little heap in the corner of the seat. I had to give her a poke when we stopped in front of her house. I looked across the street at the other house. The windows of the first two stories were lighted behind their drawn Venetian blinds. Karen's house lay dark and still, white against the trampled dirt-stained snow. It didn't seem credible that twenty-four hours ago it had been lighted up like a Christmas tree, as my taxi driver had said, and full of gaiety and warmth . . . and with death standing unseen at the door, his grim invisible reflection looking back with all the others from the mirrored walls.

We went up the steps and opened the door quietly. Sandy and his father were in the library. I could hear their voices through the closed door. Jerry didn't stop. She went quickly up the stairs, I following, on tiptoe not to disturb them and bring Sandy out to read in one swift glance at her stricken face something quite erroneous. At the top of the stairs Jerry stopped and put her hand on my arm.

"Call him up, Grace. I want to . . . to talk to him," she whispered.

We went into her father's room. I looked in the phone book and gave the operator the number.

It was Philander Doyle's rich prismatic voice at the other end.

"Is Roger there?" I asked. "It's Mrs. Latham, Mr. Doyle."

"You don't have to tell me, my dear lady," he boomed

pleasantly "Roger isn't here. Won't I do? I'm much more entertaining than he is, right now."

"I'm sure of that," I said.

"Then what about lunch with me tomorrow? We can compare notes."

I thought quickly.

"All right," I said.

"In town, then. Do you like shrimps?"

"Love them," I lied. "—Especially with curry."

"Shall we meet at"—he named a well-known seafood place on Connecticut Avenue. "—At one, shall we say?"

I put down the phone. Jerry was sitting on the steps beside the high old bed, looking at me, all the misery in the world in her proud pale-ivory little face.

"I guess I'll go to bed," she said. "Good night."

I couldn't, somehow, bear to tell her I'd heard Roger's voice perfectly distinct, saying, "I'm not here, if it's for me, Dad."

I undressed in front of the fire in my room and climbed up onto the four-poster and put out my light. I wouldn't, I'm afraid, have made a very good Spartan, even if I'd escaped being left, as a female infant, in the mountains for the wolves to devour. I couldn't bring myself, in the pleasant warmth of the room, to put up a window and let the cold sub-freezing air inside—especially as I knew I'd lie awake for hours, the last twenty-four of them trampling sleep to bits as they went back and forth through my mind, a minute by minute kaleidoscope of doubt and suspicion.

I must have been more exhausted, however, than I'd realized, for when I was aware again, the fire had died, the house was as silent as the grave and the grandfather clock on the stairs boomed once, twice and was still. The room was stuffy now too. I lay there in the pitch darkness, trying to decide whether after all fresh air wasn't just a doctor's racket to make people get pneumonia. Nevertheless, I pushed back the covers, slipped out of my warm bed onto the needlepoint steps and groped over to the window. And I stopped dead.

Through the stark black branches of the trees Karen's little house lay like a pale ghost. For a moment I thought I must be tenanting it with one, because the round disc of light I'd seen moving in it was gone. Then I saw it again, this time in the kitchen, through the little window where Mrs. Harris had sat, the gas seeping out into her mottled fur pressed against the tiny triangular hole in one pane. Then it

moved, the disc of yellow light, up the wall across the refrig-
erator and on, so that without seeing it I could remember
that next it must hit the storage tank and the hot-water
heater beneath it, and then the pilot light.

I could see it in my mind's eye rest there, and move again
to the power switch, and then across the open panel to the
chronometer by the door . . . and it wasn't entirely in my
mind, because the white paint of the opposite wall reflected
the glow, and moved as the light moved. I stood there breathlessly a long time. The light moved back into the mirrored
front room and disappeared, and reappeared upstairs, first
in the front room and then in the bath. Then it came out
again and down . . . and I saw the kitchen door open
slowly.

I closed my eyes. If whoever it was came up the crape
myrtle path to the house, I didn't want to see him. If he
passed through to the front, on the other hand, I did. I
moved back a step so that the door and the path were
blocked from my sight, leaving only the front part of the
little building. Then I waited, hours it seemed to me, my
heart quite still, knowing that in a moment I would hear steps
downstairs.

And then quite abruptly a dark figure appeared against
the window I'd broken with the brick from the path, and
came on toward the front, shadowy in the darkness. I lost it
for a moment; then I heard a faint meow and saw the ball
of light strike the ground out in the cobblestone gutter. The
little black figure of Mrs. Harris was galvanized in it for an
instant; then I saw the light shift and something—a piece of
ice, I thought—strike her. She let out one yowl and fled back
to the house. I slipped to the front window. The ball of light
struck the Doyles' steps and went out . . . and framed for
an instant against the white door I saw Philander Doyle.
Then the door closed quietly behind him.

There were no lights in his house, not even in the ellipti-
cal fanlight over the door.

I stood at the window for a moment, my breath caught
in my throat. And then I saw another figure move out from
behind a tree in front of the Doyle house, and stand there,
quite motionless, for a long time. It went up the steps too,
then, and for a moment Roger Doyle's lean frame was silhouetted against the white door as his father's had been. As
he went in the fanlight gleamed brightly for an instant.

I stared out there for a moment, wondering, my breath

121

coming too quickly, why Roger Doyle had been watching his father. Then I raised the window a little and crept back into bed.

19

We were just finishing breakfast the next morning when William announced Colonel Primrose to see Mr. Sandy.

Sandy's coffee cup half-way to the table stopped so abruptly that it slopped a little, and spattered on his empty plate. Judge Candler glanced at him with a surprise that wasn't, I thought, as mild as it seemed.

"It's my fault," Jerry said. "I was supposed to prepare you."

Sandy folded his napkin and pushed back his chair.

"Excuse me, sir?" he said.

His father nodded. Sandy's pleasant ugly face was disturbed. He looked across the table at his sister. They hadn't, I decided, had a chance for a post mortem on her interview with Colonel Primrose at Captain Fox's house. Her sleepless eyes must therefore have been rather more alarming to him than they might have been if he'd known about the later session at the Greek's. He crossed the dining room to the door.

"Tell the Colonel I'd like to see him before he goes, Sandy," Judge Candler said. "And close the door, please."

He waited until Sandy had gone out, and then, without turning his head, he said "William."

The old darkey behind him jumped practically a foot. "Yes, *suh*," he said. His old eyes rolled around like a couple of apoplectic billiard balls, and his face was suddenly more like dirty putty than polished ebony. I couldn't tell whether it was the tone of his master's voice or a conscience streaked with guilt, but William obviously smelled trouble in the air.

"Yes, suh, Jedge," he said. There was an ingratiating softness in his voice as he came reluctantly around and stood a little back, between Judge Candler's chair and Jerry's. The noise I heard may not have been his knees quaking together, but it certainly sounded like it.

"William," Judge Candler said, still without looking up. "The key to the carriage house is missing from the board in my office."

" 'Deed, suh? Tch, tch, tch!" William said sympathetically.

Judge Candler turned then and looked steadily at him.

"Where is it?" he asked.

Williams eyes bulged.

" 'Deed an' Ah don' know, suh, an' that's the Lawd's truth. Did you as' Mr. Pepperday, suh?"

His old frame was bent forward, his voice as gentle as sunshine.

"Mr. Pepperday doesn't know either," Judge Candler said calmly. He looked at the old darkey steadily from under his white tufted brows. "You were over at Miss Karen's all that afternoon?"

" 'Deed an' Ah was, suh . . . but Ah nevah touch none of th' apparatux. Ah cook th' ham ovah heah. Ah dished up, Ah wash th' dishes an' put 'em away. Ah give Miz' Harris her milk in her saucer, Ah fix Miz' Karen's milk an' lef' it on the sink, an' Ah come home an' said mah prayers an' went to bed. An' moreovah, suh, Ah don' know th' whereabouts of that ol' key."

Judge Candler turned back to his plate.

"I want that key on my table by noon today, William," he said quietly. "—Is that clear?"

"It certainly is *clear,* jedge," William said, with a pleased smile. "Clear *an'* plain. But Ah got to *re*-peat mahself, suh. Ah don' know th' whereabouts where it *is.*"

"Then I'll expect you to find out before noon," Judge Candler said evenly. "That's all."

"Yas, *suh.*"

When the door closed behind him Judge Candler turned to Jerry.

"Do you know where that key is, Jeremy?" he asked.

"No, sir," she said. "And I'm sure William hasn't got it. There's one hanging over the kitchen sink, if he wanted it. We had three made when we had March Wind. I gave Karen one. We kept one here, and there's one in the office."

I just sat there. It seemed a bit awkward to speak up and say, "I wonder if that could possibly be the key I planted in the Ming vase on the Doyles' mantel," so I held my peace. It was rather dubious ethically, no doubt, but sound socially, and possibly a stroke of genius criminologically.

Judge Candler pushed back his chair and got up, standing there tall and distinguished, his eyes sombre and alive . . . an impressive figure, but vaguely terrifying, in some way. I seemed to sense, all of a sudden, the same feeling of trouble brewing that I thought William had done. And Jerry sensed it too. I felt, without seeing it happen, that she'd gone quite still, as if to protect herself, the way a little lizard does when danger is near him on a sun-baked wall. And then it came. As Judge Candler cleared his throat I recognized Mr. Pepperday's great original.

"I'm going to make a very special request of you, Jeremy," he said. His sombre eyes turned to his daughter.

"Yes, Dad," she said softly.

"I shan't explain. I shan't, as you know, make any attempt to check on you. I shall merely ask you to give me your word, in front of Mrs. Latham, so she will understand and not unwittingly lead you to break it, that you will not again, under any circumstances, whatsoever, see Roger Doyle."

She sat as still as alabaster, and as pale, her eyes fixed on her father's. Then they moved slowly to mine. Only her pulse in her throat betrayed her. Her face was as expressionless as a death mask. She looked back at her father.

"I'm sorry, Dad," she said at last, and very calmly. "I can't promise that, because I'm going to see him the first moment I can . . . to tell him that I do want to marry him—if he still wants me."

Her autumn eyes raised to her father's were frank and unflinching. Judge Candler looked down at her, a strange spasm of pain contracting the muscles of his lean jaw as she spoke. He hadn't, I'm sure, the least idea that things had gone so far.

For a moment he stood there in a sort of stunned silence. I picked up my cup and took a sobering sip of stone-cold coffee, and put it down again, wondering dismally how long this extraordinary calm would hold before the storm broke. Knowing Jerry and suspecting her father, it already seemed superhuman.

Judge Candler's face tightened the way Sandy's had when he first heard about the man's calling up Jerry.

"I . . . think you'll understand that that's entirely out of the question, Jeremy," he said quietly. "Roger has betrayed his friends."

"Only to be loyal to his own father, sir," Jerry said. I could see the fire kindling in her eyes. "He tried to persuade me to give Karen back her stock, the way you wanted me to."

Her eyes were flashing now, the color flaming in her cheeks. She started to rise, and settled back in her chair.

"I'm sorry, Dad," she said, controlling her tongue with perfectly superb determination. "But it just happens that I love Roger . . . and he loves me. It wouldn't be fair to either of us . . ."

Her voice broke a little.

"You *must* see that . . . you must have loved *some-body* when you were young! Can't you try to remember?"

I caught my breath. I couldn't for a moment understand the expression in her father's eyes as she said that she loved Roger and he loved her. It couldn't possibly, I thought, be that he was a man who couldn't bear the thought of his only girl being in love; that didn't make sense. And the expression was gone when she finished.

"I remember very clearly, Jeremy. But there are other things in life."

"What are they?"

"Honor is one of them. Decency another."

"And Roger has both!"

"Roger has neither."

Judge Candler's voice was cold as blue steel.

"He *couldn't* tell you he loved you—with Karen's body not yet in its grave!"

I stared open-mouthed at him as I realized what he'd said, and as he went on.

"Roger murdered Karen. I'm as convinced of that as I am that you're sitting in that chair. I haven't spoken, because of someone else. It's up to you whether I shall speak now."

She sat motionless, looking up at him, her lips parted, her face so pale that I thought her heart must have died.

"Karen was afraid of Roger. He was with her, alone, last night after you all had left."

But Jerry hadn't heard any more. Suddenly she flashed to her feet, her eyes blazing into her father's, her head high.

"I don't believe it!" she cried. "I'll call Colonel Primrose! You can tell him that, if you dare! He'll know it isn't true!"

She thrust her chair back and ran to the door.

"Jerry!" I cried. "Don't—*don't!"*

And it was I who stopped her, not her father, towering with controlled anger at the end of the table. Roger Doyle's black figure, watching, last night, from behind the tree while his father went through the little carriage house, room by room, burned in my brain.

Her hand on the doorknob dropped to her side as she turned, her eyes dazed and aghast. *"Grace,"* she whispered. "You don't . . . not *you?"*

"I don't know, Jerry," I answered breathlessly. "But wait a minute, *please!"*

"Promise me you'll not see Roger Doyle again, Jeremy," her father said quietly. He'd not moved.

She leaned back against the door and closed her eyes. Then she moistened her lips, opened her eyes slowly and looked back at him.

"I'm going up to my room, Father. I'll let you know."

The door opened, and closed. I didn't look at Judge Candler, but I knew he still hadn't moved. Then he sat down suddenly and put his forehead in his hand, his elbow on the table. We just sat there silently for a minute. My hands, clasped tightly together in my lap, were like blocks of ice. I couldn't have spoken even if I'd known anything to say. Then he raised his head.

"He doesn't love her, Mrs. Latham," he said quietly. "He's using her for his own protection."

All I could do was shake my head.

"You don't know the Doyles, Mrs. Latham."

His voice was controlled and even, and it had a dogged iron conviction in it that I knew I could never move or change.

"If you . . . know Roger killed her, why *don't* you tell Colonel Primrose?" I got out. "Surely you won't become an accessory after the fact on Roger's account, will you?"

"Not on Roger's, no," he said. He looked down the long polished table, his eyes sombre, his face suddenly drawn and ill. "Jeremy asked if I remembered being in love," he said, so quietly that I could hardly hear him. "I was very deeply in love with one woman, Mrs. Latham. She was not in love with me. I was devoted to the children's mother, but I was not in love with her. I was hotheaded like Jeremy—I married to show I didn't give a damn . . . That's why I'd never denounce Roger Doyle except to save my own daughter."

I took another sip of icy coffee, nearly choking on it, completely mystified I may say. Yet I couldn't very well ask him to explain. I had the feeling, anyway, that he wasn't really talking to me. I said nothing and waited.

"Karen knew she was in danger," he said, after some time, his voice stern again. "I should have gone in."

"You——"

"I went to my office from Karen's to make out another transfer for Jeremy to sign before she changed her mind again," he said. "When I came back the lights were still on. I thought the guests were still there, and thought I would go in again. As I passed the window I saw Roger sitting there, alone with her. She was asleep, Mrs. Latham—with a glass

126

of milk in her hand, on the arm of the small sofa. I saw Roger take it from her and go out to the kitchen. I saw that everyone else was gone, so I came along home. As I was putting up my window I saw Roger go up the steps of his own house, look back, take out his watch and look at it, and go in, after looking back at the carriage house again."

I stared across the table at him, moistening my own dry lips.

"In view of Karen's expressed fear of him, and his determination to marry her, in spite of the fact she'd told him she was in love with another man, I think you'll see the strength of my——"

"But . . . it's so appallingly circumstantial, Judge Candler!" I cried.

"All evidence of murder is circumstantial, Mrs. Latham. The murderer seldom calls in eye-witnesses to his crime."

"I . . . I know," I said. "But surely no jury——"

"Very likely," he interrupted. "—Not with his father defending him, at any rate, Mrs. Latham."

He got up.

"I know what my decision involves . . . and the effect of it on my own future. That is beside the point. You told me the other day that I didn't deserve Jeremy. I would make any sacrifice to keep her from the step she wants to take. Some day she'll fall in love with a man worthy of her.—I wish you'd go to her now. I know the struggle she's having."

I got up too. I didn't know anything to say. If it hadn't been for the conversation I'd overheard between his own children, struggling in my own mind against what he'd told me of Roger, I might have been able to say something. There was still the picture of Roger, waiting out there to go inside after his father had gone upstairs in the dark. There was the picture of Philander Doyle moving from room to room. Did he suspect Roger? Was that why he'd crept over there in the shadow of the night, to still a doubt in his own mind? Or to affirm it?

I suddenly remembered I was going to see him at lunch, and wondered what Judge Candler would think of that.

"I'm lunching with Mr. Doyle today," I said at the door. "I hope you don't think I'm being disloyal to you and Jerry."

He looked at me, his face unmoved.

"You are a free agent, Mrs. Latham."

It was certainly one way to put it. I went out and closed the door. William was hovering in the entry door as I started upstairs. He came padding out, looking around like the third conspirator in an old melodrama.

"Mist' Philander call up. Said would you min' havin' lunch to his house 'stead of down town, Mis' Grace."

"Thanks, William," I said. "And William—about that——".

He looked at me so blankly that I stopped.

"'Deed an' Ah don' know what you goin' t'say, Mis' Grace . . . but Ah wouldn't know what you was talkin' 'bout if you did."

He padded off, and came back a few steps.

"Ah jus' nevah pay no 'tention to th' Jedge when his stomach's bad," he said, and went away again.

I went upstairs and into my room, and stopped. Jerry was there, sitting on the low stool in front of the fire. She didn't look up. I closed the door, sat down beside her and patted her shoulder. After a long time she got up, went over to the mirror and brushed my feather puff over her face. She came back and sat down, looking at me silently.

"Well?" I said. I was glad she wasn't crying. She seemed superhumanly calm.

"What would you do?" she asked.

"I don't know," I said. Then I said, "Do you know any reason, absolutely and irrevocably, that he *didn't* do it?"

Her eyes, steadily on mine, didn't change.

"You mean do I know who *did* do it?" she asked.

"Something of the sort."

She looked away. "No," she said shortly.

There was a knock at the door just then and William put his head in.

"Mis' Grace, Cunnel Primrose say he like to see you—whethuh you busy or not.—Soun' like an invite-tation to th' White House."

I thought, as I got up, that it might have been as mandatory but it wasn't as agreeable by a long shot, not just then. Still I went downstairs. William stayed to talk with his mistress. I heard his soothing, "Chile, don' you let 'em get you . . ." before I was out of earshot. I went on down, thinking he'd be a far better comforter than I was.

The library door was open. The Judge was sitting in his chair, nothing in his face to indicate the scene in the dining room. Sandy was standing at the fireplace, not the least disturbed as far as I could see, and Colonel Primrose was sitting in the chair by the fire. He got up and shook hands with me.

128

"How's the arm?"

"Fine, thanks."

Beyond having William change the bandages before breakfast I'd forgotten about it entirely.

"I wanted you to hear the report Captain Fox got this morning," he said. "I understand you're lunching with Mr. Doyle. I thought he might want to know what was going on, and I shan't have time to see him."

I doubt if he even thought he was fooling me. For an instant I did think he might just be gratifying the curiosity he knew I'd have, but I abandoned that, suspecting bitterly that I was merely being unobtrusively coached for my rôle of decoy duck again.

"The gas company has figured from the last meter reading, which was four days ago, and the normal consumption over the last eight months, that the burner was on between four and five hours," he went on. "I won't go into the cubic feet involved. That would make it coming on between one and two o'clock, since it was turned off at the main by the fire department about a quarter to six. They don't pretend it's an accurate estimate. However, the post mortem puts Karen's death roughly between four-thirty and five-thirty. The gas must have been going at full tilt, of course, for two or three hours before then.

"We also have reason to believe," he continued, "that it was never intended the circumstances of the crime should be discovered. The maid says the chronometer governing the oilburner was normally set for eleven in the morning. Karen Lunt seldom got up before noon, and the maid, who comes at 11:30, always complained that the house was cold when she arrived to close the windows. The chronometer yesterday morning, however, had been set for six o'clock—at which time Miss Lunt was dead and the house so full of gas that the flame of the burner, if it had gone on, would have sent it sky-high in a second."

I couldn't bear to look at Judge Candler.

"You can see, of course, that if Mrs. Latham hadn't gone down when she did, nothing would ever have been discovered."

His black eyes moved from one of us to the other.

"Miss Lunt had taken—was given, rather, we think—enough of an opiate to keep her soundly asleep for several hours. She was in the habit of drinking a half-pint of milk, sometimes more, before she went to bed. Although the glass

129

she'd drunk from was in the sink and full of water, and the tap had been left dripping, traces of codeine were found in it. A number of fingerprints were found on the chromium-plated lever, one more distinct than the others. A milk bottle was found with the same print; there was a trace of it on the handle of the icebox, though it's badly blurred by a succession of people apparently sampling the ham some time later."

"Do you . . . know whose fingerprints they are, Colonel Primrose?"

I thought I could hear in Judge Candler's voice the same dogged undercurrent I'd heard before.

Colonel Primrose hesitated for the fraction of an instant.

"That's part of the usual police routine, Judge Candler," he said. "You'll all be asked to allow your fingerprints to be taken some time today."

He went on imperturbably.

"Of course there is no evidence of robbery, or any similar tangible motive. It would seem, therefore, that the intangible motives—revenge, hate, love, fear, self-protection, perhaps the prevention, in this case, of some act on Miss Lunt's part—are what we have to consider. It's in the routine business of sifting those over that we've come across the aircraft stock at one time in Miss Lunt's estate and now in Miss Candler's trust."

Judge Candler spoke quietly. "I should like to explain——"

"I shall ask you to, a little later," Colonel Primrose interrupted suavely. "At the moment, I have two explanations that jibe in all details, and a young man at the Securities Commission is verifying the essential facts this morning. I'm more interested, at present, in . . . other things.

"For instance: the key to the carriage house, which I understand normally hangs on the board in your office, sir. It is missing. Mr. Pepperday can't account for it. He had no idea that it was gone, he says, until this morning."

He looked inquiringly at Judge Candler.

"I can't help you there, I'm afraid, sir. Mr. Pepperday called my attention to it last evening, when he came for the mail."

"You don't recall seeing it, or not seeing it, at any time, recently?"

Judge Candler shook his head. "No. I do not."

"But . . . if this was all set, and Karen given a drug in her milk, it was somebody who wouldn't need a key?" Sandy put in.

There was a flicker in Colonel Primrose's eyes, deceptively innocent as a lamb's.

"You mean the murderer must have been at the party?"

Sandy nodded.

"Not necessarily. It's true it was all carefully planned by someone who was very familiar with the working of Miss Lunt's utilities . . . and her habits. The milk, however, comes in from the outside. She takes a pint and a half a day. The pint was used in the kitchen and for the cat, the half pint was always kept for her to drink before she went to bed."

His parrot eyes rested steadily on Sandy.

"The milk was left on her front step around six o'clock in the morning, the company says. It doesn't get light, nowadays, until eight, by which time it's stood there two hours. It would be extremely simple for some one to exchange a doctored bottle for the one there and slip away unnoticed.—The idea of the drug, of course, was simply to make sure she'd sleep soundly when she went to bed. She apparently stayed up to let in the cat and dropped asleep on the sofa . . . the result being the same."

I kept my eyes steadfastly on the old carpet.

"It's interesting, too, in that connection," Colonel Primrose continued calmly, "to notice that all the milk bottles around the place—the maid or Miss Lunt was careless about putting them out—are from the same distributor . . . with the exception of that last half-pint bottle. We know it's the last because the maid identifies it and her prints on it are clearer.—Do you happen to know what dairy you use?"

"If you'll pull the bell there, Mrs. Latham," Judge Candler said deliberately, "William can tell us."

"Never mind," Colonel Primrose said. "We can check that later."

I think by this time I had a clear idea of what the victims of the Inquisition felt like with water dripping slowly, drop by drop, hour after hour, on the top of their skulls. Or even oil—because Colonel Primrose's voice was suaver than water, even if it didn't take him hour after hour to drop all those unbearable bits on our heads.

"And just one other thing," he went on politely, "and then I'll have to go.—Did Miss Lunt's cat spend much time here . . . normally?"

The room was completely silent, for a long moment. Then, before anyone could speak, he got to his feet.

131

"William probably knows more about that than you do," he said calmly. He moved to the door.

"I must get along. I'm afraid you'll see me around a good deal, for a day or so. Good morning . . . and thank you, sir."

The three of us sat there when he'd gone—myself, at least, perfectly dumbfounded. Then Sandy shook himself and said everything there was to be said. He said, "Gosh!"

20

I went out, as soon as I could move, and Sandy followed me.

"Where's Jerry?" he asked as we went up the stairs.

"I left her in my room," I said.

He looked at me inquiringly. "Dad doing the heavy father again?"

"About Roger," I answered.

His jaw tightened. I stopped on the landing. "Look," I said. "You make me sick."

"Not as sick as he makes me," he retorted stubbornly.

"Look, Sandy," I said earnestly. "We ran into him last night . . . by the sheerest accident, believe me. He didn't know anything about your Mr. Samuel Smith of the Broken Head."

"Yes?" he said. "Who'd he think he was—the Female Stranger?"

I knew he was referring to the most romantic incident in old Alexandria's glamorous past. A girl—a lady—was brought to Gatsby's Tavern late one night, over a hundred years ago, from a ship that had just come in from the Indies. She was ill with typhoid fever. No one but the doctor and an old nurse and her husband saw her lovely face; and she died and was buried, no one but her husband knowing her name.

I said, "Probably," and pushed open my door. Jerry was gone. I turned back to Sandy.

"Look, darling," I said. "—Whatever you think of Roger Doyle, Jerry's head over heels in love with him. It doesn't matter to her, at the moment, if he's one of Miss Isabel's lepers, or is hanged, drawn and quartered in the market place tomorrow. She *loves* him . . . and that's the kind of girl she is. Now for heaven's sake quit chucking your weight about, and try to give her some sort of break!"

He stood there, glowering and resentful, his ugly red-thatched face a field of the most conflicting emotions. Then he shrugged his shoulders.

"Okay, lady."

He turned and went along the hall. I saw him stop a moment, tap on her door and push it open. I heard him say "Come on, snap out of it, honey chile," as the door closed.

The tall clock in the entrance hall of the house across the street struck one as the maid opened the door.

"Mr. Doyle's in the library, miss," she said, taking my coat and galoshes. She pointed to the polished mahogany door at the end of the handsome panelled hall. It opened as I approached and Philander Doyle held out his big warm hand, booming cordially.

"This *is* a pleasure, my dear young lady. Come in. Will you have a cocktail or sherry?"

"Sherry, thanks," I said. He took a crystal decanter off the lowboy by the door and poured a glass of pale amber liquid. I sat down in a green leather Williamsburg wing chair by the fire. Mr. Doyle crossed the deep-piled Sarouk rug and handed the glass to me, his twinkling blue eyes on mine.

Mr. Philander Doyle's library, I reflected, was the kind of place I'd give my head to have, if I didn't also have to have the neat rows of elegantly matched, handsomely bound, gold-tooled sets that I'm sure no one ever took down except to dust. Their color, however, I had to admit, was perfect, in their mahogany cases reaching almost to the high ceiling. In the carved overmantel hung a Trumbull of the first Chief Justice, flanked by a pair of heavy silver candlesticks that looked as if they'd come from the Hearst Collection. At one side of the square room, facing the door, so that when he sat there Philander Doyle was against a magnificently panelled wall under a fur-collared portrait of Thomas Jefferson, was a broad walnut desk. It was the only thing in the room that wasn't, in one way or another, a collector's piece, from the Queen Anne walnut chairs to the heavy gold curtains looped up at windows, overlooking the walled garden that had at one time stretched down to the Candlers' tobacco warehouse and wharf on the Potomac.

Mr. Doyle's imposing bulk moved back across the heavenly wines and blues and yellows of the old rug to the door. He smiled at me as he turned the big key in the shining brass lock.

"Privacy, my dear lady, is practically the only thing in the
133

world you can't buy," he said. "Certainly not in this house."

He came back and sat down behind his desk, and drew up another chair. "You're too far away," he said, waving to it.

I came over and sat down, putting my glass on the desk.

He leaned back and drew open a long drawer in front of him. I started a little in spite of myself. Besides the papers in it were two things, one of which I certainly shouldn't have expected to see there. It was a small cylindrical green bottle about an inch in diameter and three inches long, with a black composition screw cap. It was empty . . . but it had typed on its white label "Codeine—one or two tablets when necessary." Below that was the familiar printed druggist's label: "Not to be refilled without prescription."

The other object I wasn't so surprised at, or so interested in, except as an indication of the kind of shadow a man with Philander Doyle's clientele must constantly walk in. It was a small blue-steel revolver, and it had an ugly cylinder fixed to its muzzle that even I, knowing as little of firearms as I do, recognized must be a silencer. After all, Colonel Primrose hadn't taken me through Mr. Hoover's museum at the Department of Justice quite for nothing.

Mr. Doyle shuffled it off a little sheaf of papers, took them out, and closed the drawer.

"Now then," he remarked, putting them on the green-tooled leather blotting pad in front of him. "I was talking to your friend the Colonel last night. He told me a number of things that I found extraordinarily interesting."

I glanced at the papers on the pad. At the top of the top one was written in large dramatic hand, "Judge Candler." Below it I could see five sub-headings. The first, which was the only one I had a chance to see, said one word: "Motive."

I picked up my glass and took the last sip of smooth dry wine, and set it down again. I tried to keep my breath from coming more rapidly as I wondered if Mr. Philander Doyle's intentions weren't rapidly becoming plain.

"Planning to hang Judge Candler?" I asked, knowing he knew I must have seen it, and thinking he probably had wanted me to.

"No—not hang him," he said coolly. "Not by the neck, at least."

"You don't really like him at all, do you?" I said, as casually as I could.

He looked at me, a curious smile in his big very handsome face.

134

"You know, it's an odd thing, Mrs. Latham," he replied slowly—"—and interesting too . . . to me, anyway, knowing people as I do, and not having many illusions, I'm afraid, about Homo sapiens, and none at all about Philander Doyle. —But Peyton Candler has had me down since the day I first met him."

He was looking very steadily at me, across the corner of the walnut desk, something moving curiously in those extraordinary and—I saw now—very cold blue eyes.

"He was five, and I was six. He had on a white broadcloth sailor suit and a straw hat. I had on a ragged cap and a pair of somebody's cast-off knickerbockers with the knee torn out and the seat patched. He was with a colored nurse on his way to Sunday school. I was with my gang of tunnel town toughs on my way to wash the glasses in my father's saloon on lower King Street. I knocked him and his white suit and his sailor hat into a mud puddle. He got up. He didn't cry; he picked up his hat and tried to brush the mud out of his eyes, and went back home and got cleaned up and went on to Sunday school. I stood looking after him a minute. Then I chased the gang home and went to the saloon, knowing I'd been licked. That's the whole story."

I looked at him, sitting there in his fabulous room, one of the most successful men in the world in his field, and took a deep breath.

"In college I had all the money I needed," he went on, with the most good-humored urbanity. "He didn't have a nickel. He belonged to the best clubs—I didn't. I had the better brain. I gave the valedictory. He made whatever oration it was by popular vote. Girls took everything I gave them, and they'd cut a date with me to go for a walk and eat a bag of peanuts with him. Then my turn came. He fell in love, and I double-crossed him . . . and then he married the only girl, not that I'd been in love with, but that I wanted to marry. I made money hand over fist, he didn't have enough to keep the rain out of the attic—and the first thing I knew he was a judge in the state's highest court. I was invited to talk to conventions in Atlantic City, he addressed the bar associations. I had a son; he had two sons and a daughter and Karen. I came back here. I bought his old family home and his antique furniture, and the Walpole Club dined across the street. I pay the best wages in town, and there isn't a nigger who wouldn't leave me and go work for him for nothing. Today a chorus girl murders an angel and runs to me, and the Sunday supplements have my picture plastered all over them . . . and when they look for a man in Washington they go to Peyton Candler."

He looked at me with a smile compounded of whimsical and ironic deprecation.

"And the truth is, Mrs. Latham, that I can't take it."

"I see," I said. "Is that why you . . . persuaded poor Karen to sue him for her stock?"

"Poor Karen, as you call her, couldn't take it either," he said pleasantly.

"Did she know why she was doing it?"

He looked at me as if a little surprised at my innocence.

"She was doing it for a good fat roll, my dear—so she could marry her Englishman," he said. "—She didn't really believe Jerry'd give the stock up, and she knew she hadn't any legal grounds for demanding it."

"And . . . when Jerry decided to give it up, she double-crossed you, I suppose?"

"I'm afraid she . . . would have," he answered.

"But surely, even if you'd sued . . ."

"Oh, I wasn't going to sue. I was to . . ."

He stopped, looking steadily at me again.

"—I was to defend."

I stared at him in complete horror, utterly staggered. The opportunity he'd have had, I thought!

"And we'd have won, obviously. But the . . . ."

He shrugged his shoulders, his blue eyes twinkling very engagingly.

"The damage would have been done?" I said.

He laughed.

I sat there, just staring at him for a moment. Then I looked down at the paper in front of him. "And now that that's failed?"

"I'm afraid I've lost again," he said. There was a kind of frank expansive charm in his whole manner. "You see, my dear Mrs. Latham, I have just one moral principle—never deceive yourself. I've watched Philander Doyle year after year, literally appalled at what is and has been the motivating force in everything he's done since the Sunday morning he shoved Peyton Candler in his white monkey suit in the mud in Cameron Street.—Unto thine own self be true, Mrs. Latham . . . and thou canst then be false to any man."

I suppose it shows a definite weakening of my own moral fibre that I didn't get up, excoriate Mr. Philander Doyle with indignant wrath and sail out. But I didn't. I was completely fascinated, and when, just then, the luncheon gong sounded musically through the house, I was quite ready and even eager to go and eat his tainted food.

He got up, went to the door and unlocked it. I saw, behind him against the bookshelves, a delicate wrought-iron standard holding a double panel of glass in which was framed a sheet of an old yellow crumble-edged newspaper.

"What's that?" I asked.

He smiled. "That, my dear lady, is just more of the same."

I looked as puzzled, I suppose, as I felt. He stepped aside and pulled it out where I could read it. It was the Alexandria *Gazette* for November, 1798, and it had nothing in it that I could see but lists of sales of Negroes and ship ladings from the mother country. Then I saw a marked paragraph. It was headed "Sheriff's Sale."

"By virtue of the writ of fieri facias issued for the Court of Common Pleas for the County of Fairfax directed and delivered to me, I have levied and taken the goods and chattels and tenements of Ramsay Candler which I shall expose to sale as the law directs on Saturday the 10th day of February at 10 o'clock in the forenoon in the town of Alexandria. December 10th 1798. John P. Doyle, Sheriff."

I stared at it, and then at Philander Doyle. I'd known, of course, that there were a lot of Irish in early Alexandria, but I hadn't known . . .

As he laughed his great booming laugh my blood fairly curdled.

"A cavalier gentleman's debts of honor, Mrs. Latham. . . . Oddly enough, I don't think any of the Candlers have ever been particularly amused by that."

"It is odd, isn't it?" I said.

He laughed again. "What about some lunch?"

He took my elbow in his warm big hand. I really needed steering. The cumulative effect of his urbanity, covering, as it had covered for years, his hatred and envy of the man across the street, literally staggered me.

We crossed the hall to the elegantly appointed dining room where the suddenly gay winter sun shone on the small center portion of a gorgeous Chippendale banquet table. The end pieces were against the panelled walls on either side of the door, two vast silver punch bowls filled with yellow mimosa on their waxed and polished tops. The table was set for four. As we stood there the slim colored girl in burgundy

137

silk uniform and frilled coffee-dipped cap and apron came in with a tall silver pitcher and stood waiting in the doorway.

"Is my sister coming down?" Mr. Doyle said.

"Yes, of course, my dear." Miss Isabel's voice floated down the stairway outside, and then she came in, in a green rig too antiquated even for Red Cross flood relief. "My dear—this is *so* nice! I do hope I'm not late, Philander."

Her brother, who I thought had stared a little in spite of himself as she came in, smiled affectionately.

"No later than usual, Isabel.—Where's Roger?"

"Oh," Miss Isabel said. "Didn't Rosie tell you?—Or didn't I tell Rosie?" she added vaguely. "Captain Fox called him up. He's down at the police station."

Philander Doyle's polished urbanity disappeared so abruptly that I caught my breath.

"What for, Isabel?" he demanded curtly. "For God's sake, try to pull yourself together! When did he go?"

"Oh, it's been half an hour, anyway . . . or maybe that was when a man named Smith called. He wanted to talk to you. Anyway, my dear, he left. I mean Roger left, or rather Mr. Smith. And said not to worry you."

Her brother's hand gripped the ladder back of the leather upholstered Chippendale chair.

"For *God's* sake, Isabel!" he began angrily. He controlled himself and broke off, as I just stared openly at him. "Ring the bell!" he ordered curtly.

Miss Isabel fished around with her foot under the table and found it at last. The maid appeared in the doorway.

"Have the boy get my car over here, Rosie," Mr. Doyle said. "As quick as possible. Tell him I mean quick!"

She ran out.

"I think you're being absurd, dear," Miss Isabel said, still in her coolly detached tones. "You know your heart can't stand these violent scenes, and your soup's getting stone cold."

Mr. Doyle gave her one glance and turned to me, more disturbed than I could ever have imagined he could be.

"Excuse me, please, Mrs. Latham," he said shortly, and hurried out of the room.

"Don't forget your overcoat," Miss Isabel called. The front door slammed immediately afterward, so violently that the ice in the glasses clinked, and the silver handle-rings of the punch bowls. Miss Isabel took a sip of her soup and put down her spoon.

"I'm sure Roger has nothing to fear from the police," she remarked. "Just because my brother spends most of his time with people he says the police use rubber hose on, he thinks it can happen in a civilized community. Please, my dear— your soup."

I picked up my spoon. It clattered against the rim of the fine porcelain in spite of all the control I was trying to exercise.

"Are you going to the services for Karen?" she asked sociably.

"I'd rather not. It depends on Jerry," I said.

"Jerry's a very sweet girl, I've always thought," she observed. "Poor Karen. You know, my dear, I think it's just as well we *don't* know what Providence has in store for us, I really do. Don't you?"

"Unless we could stop it by knowing," I said.

"Oh, of course," she replied vaguely.

"Did you really want Roger to marry her, Miss Doyle?" I asked.

She looked at me with her aloof slightly raised eyebrow manner and said, "Well, of course, you know Karen was a very worldly woman. I think perhaps she'd have been very good for Roger . . . for a while. I don't, of course, think divorce is the most pleasant thing in the world. But my brother could have arranged it without any difficulty, and he's always paid very liberally for Roger's education. I think it would have been . . . well, perhaps *experience* is the word I'm looking for."

It seemed to me perhaps a very *worldly* view of marriage. I think that was the word I was looking for.

"Of course," Miss Isabel said, "I'm really a very formal person. I find Jerry a little too impulsive. It's true she comes of very nice people. Karen's mother, I believe, came from rather plain people."

This, I thought, from the sister of the little boy who'd shoved Peyton Candler's monkey suit into the mud. I took a leg off the baby broiled chicken on my plate and separated the tender meat from the bone.

"Was Roger in love with Karen, Miss Doyle?" I asked.

"I think it's awfully difficult to say about young men, my dear. Possibly Roger is too like his father to fall very deeply in love with anyone. Tell me about your trip abroad last summer, won't you?"

As I hadn't been abroad last summer, it was a little difficult, but the implication was clear enough. I said, "Your house is lovely, Miss Doyle."

She looked at me, and then glanced about at the simply priceless objects so beautifully arranged against the panelled walls, exactly as if she'd not really noticed them before.

"Oh, yes . . . of course," she said vaguely. "But, you know, I don't care much for it. I always think it belongs to the Candlers, really. Are you interested in the work the Leper Guild is doing?"

We managed some way to finish lunch without mentioning the late unpleasantness again. After lunch we went across to the drawing room for coffee. I glanced up at the Ming vase under the mirror on the carved mantelpiece. Miss Doyle handed me a tiny eggshell cup of coffee and poured herself one. As she put down the silver pot the maid Rosie appeared in the doorway.

"You said you wanted to speak to th' laundryman, Mis' Isabel," she said.

Miss Doyle looked a little startled. "Oh, did I, Rosie?"

"Yes, ma'am. 'Bout Mist' Doyle's shirt that didn' come back."

"Oh, of course. Excuse me a moment, Mrs. Latham."

I waited until her footsteps had faded. Then I put down my coffee cup and got up quickly. With these present complications, the last thing in the world I wanted to do was complicate them any more. If the key was found in Roger's house now that his fingerprints were no doubt in the files of the F. B. I. it wouldn't, to put it mildly, be a point in his favor.

I slipped quietly to the mantel, and then, with one eye in the mirror and both ears on the doors, I took down the priceless vase and thrust my hand inside . . . and stood there, my heart a frozen lump in the pit of my stomach. The key was gone.

21

Before I could do anything more than get the vase back on the mantel, my hands shaking violently, I heard a key in the latch. I got back to my chair and picked up my coffee cup, and was sipping the last of it when Philander Doyle came in. Roger was not with him. He stopped in the doorway, took a sort of sharp hold of himself and came in. He bent over the coffee tray, poured a cup of coffee and drained it, poured another and drained that. Then he sat down heavily, his great head dropped forward a little, the veins on his forehead swelling dangerously, his breath coming in stertorous waves.

When he looked over at me after an instant his eyes had lost their Irish twinkle. They were glazed with anxiety and . . . fear.

"I made two mistakes, Mrs. Latham," he said heavily. "I didn't know Jeremy was in love with my son. I didn't know he was in love with her."

"Both are bitterly true, Mr. Doyle," I said.

He nodded, his big hands clasping and unclasping the arms of the chair.

"So . . . why don't you call off your dogs?"

He got up abruptly, his massive form towering above the low table.

"Not now."

His voice vibrated through the room, tinkling the Waterford lustres of their thin sudden music.

"Not now."

He went out of the room down the hall. I heard the library door close sharply.

Miss Isabel came in from the dining room.

"Has my brother come?"

I nodded.

"Oh, dear!" she said. "I told them not to save his lunch. The laundryman's eating it. I'll go tell them to fry him an egg. Or do you think he'd rather have it poached?"

"Neither," I said. But she was gone.

I hurried out the door, my galoshes in my hand. Just as I got down the steps I heard a heavy familiar tread. I turned around. Sergeant Buck was coming from the kitchen. I stopped abruptly.

"Nice day, ma'am," he said stiffly, out of the corner of his mouth. He touched his hat and walked off toward Prince Street.

I pushed my hair back from my forehead with a trembling hand. His wide granite figure was even wider in the midriff than it normally was. From the bulging pockets of his dark overcoat I saw protruding the open mouths of a pair of empty milk bottles.

I fastened my coat collar around my throat, suddenly unbearably cold. Then I hurried across the street and up the Candlers' steps.

We didn't, fortunately, Jerry and I, have to go to the funeral. Or unfortunately, perhaps, for I think the only reason Judge Candler let his daughter off was that she might see Roger Doyle there. We sat, she and I, up in my room, saying nothing. I couldn't tell her, not possibly, all or any of the things Philander Doyle had said to me, and she couldn't—I imagined—tell me what Sandy had told her. So we just sat . . . or I did. She moved around the room, sitting first in the window overlooking Karen's white lovely little house, and then moving as she became aware of it to the other window, and coming away from it quickly, seeing Roger's house across the street.

At last, when I'd begun to think both of us would go mad if something didn't happen, she stopped her aimless pacing and stood by the bed, her hand grasping the mahogany post.

"Grace," she said.

I looked up. Her eyes were aching, as torn and anguished as her voice.

"Yes, Jerry," I said.

"I . . . I gave Father my word . . . not to see Roger any more."

I looked down into the fire. I didn't know whether I was glad, or whether I was sorry, or whether actually I wasn't too numb to feel at all.

"Oh, Grace!" she cried. "Can't we go to your house? I can't stay here. I can't! I hate it! I'll *die!*"

She collapsed in a sudden sobbing heap at my knees, her slim body shaking convulsively.

"Oh, of course you can't!" I said, wondering why I hadn't known it, seeing her face as her father and Sandy and William had gone out the door and closed it on the two of us, alone in the desolate old house. "Let's go, now. I'll leave a note for Sandy. Go get your things."

Lilac let us in my door in Georgetown, her face, I think, the pleasantest thing I'd seen for ages. If she was glad to see me, however, I'd never have guessed it. She took my bags and Jerry's and plodded up the stairs, and came down again, her old eyes following Jerry, angry and resentful. Finally she went off to her kitchen, muttering, and came back bringing her a glass of milk with an egg and sherry in it. She stood over her till she'd drunk half of it, and handed it back until she'd finished it to the last drop. Then she stoked up the fire and went out again, grumbling darkly to Sheila, my Irish setter, who'd more or less subsided after her first storm of welcome in the middle of the hall. I got up and closed the door, Jerry settled in the corner of the sofa and stared unseeing into the fire.

Even time passes. I sat there after we'd finished dinner, going over in my mind that extraordinary recitation of Philander Doyle's and his extraordinary conduct when he learned about Roger. And I don't know when it first seeped up through the morass that constituted my mind just then and leaped into sharp and clear form: what if Philander Doyle had killed Karen himself? What if his problem was a dual one now . . . protecting himself on the one hand, saving his son on the other? I shook my head. He hadn't wanted Karen murdered. He very much wanted her alive, to bring suit against Judge Candler, so that in defending him he could do the worst in his very considerable power to ruin his name. The evidence that the Judge had sold him the stock and he'd sold it back would have to come from him. He could have found a hundred ways to distort a perfectly simple and honest act into a dreadfully unscrupulous act. And what if he found that by underestimating Jerry's intelligence, or her intuition, he'd overstepped himself? What if he'd then got the idea of involving his old friend in a murder case . . . and again underestimated Jerry and Sandy's deep suspicion of him, probably of much longer standing than I'd realized?

I stopped abruptly at that. In that case he'd never have set the chronometer to blow Karen's carriage house to bits and all his plans with it. Unless, I thought . . .

The doorbell rang, and I heard Lilac going out to open it. I knew she wouldn't let anyone in, having explained carefully to her that we weren't at home, absolutely. "Not *nobody*," she'd repeated firmly, for once in complete agreement with me on a subject. But I'd over- or under-estimated her—I don't know which—for the door into the living room burst open violently and there inside it stood Roger Doyle.

Jerry flashed into life at the end of the sofa, her eyes wide, lips parted, staring at him . . . but only for about a part of a split second. Then she was in his arms in the middle of the room, though I couldn't for the life of me have told how either of them got there. She clung to him, and his arms were practically smothering her and his lips against hers.

I looked away. "What will the Judge say to *me*," I thought ironically, "bringing her here where she can see him, to break her word?"

Then all of a sudden she struggled free. "Oh, I can't, I mustn't see you, darling!"

She tore loose and flew out the door and upstairs. He took a leap after her.

"Roger!" I said sharply. I needn't have bothered; Lilac's solid black form blocked the door. The Navy line couldn't have gone through there without bloodshed.

He turned and looked at me.

"Sit down," I said. "She promised her father she wouldn't see you. It'll make it hell for her if she breaks her word."

"But what in God's name, Grace . . ."

"Just sit down, darling," I said. "And take it easy. I'll be glad to explain."

He sat down, or rather flung himself down on the ottoman in front of the fire. "Let's have it, fast."

"It's quite simple," I said, with admirable composure. "Her father thinks you murdered Karen Lunt."

"He's not the only one, apparently," he said. "Does she think so?"

"She doesn't," I replied. "But if she did—and if you did—she doesn't care. She just doesn't want them to hang you, is all."

"Good God!" he groaned. He dropped his head in his hands and sat there literally tearing at his hair. Then he managed to pull himself together to the extent of being able to pace wildly about the room.

"I just got out of that damned police station," he said. "I tried to call her up. William said he wasn't allowed to tell anybody you'd taken her home with you."

He grinned suddenly.

"William will be permanently in the dog house now," I observed. "And so will the rest of us."

"I don't care if I can keep out of the White House."— Which is what the colored people call Alexandria's painted brick jail in St. Asaph's Street.

"What happened?" I asked. "Did you see Colonel Primrose?"

He nodded.

"Fox, mostly. It seems my fingerprints are all over the place, and I was in love with her, and she was giving me the air for this McClure."

"Oh," I said. "Is that why you did it?"

He nodded. "It's what that human monolith with the lantern jaw calls a 'cream pashunell.' "

144

"And what did you say?"

"What could I? I told them I'd been trying to see one or the other to tell them I went back after Jerry gave me the gate and talked to her. She was okay then and there wasn't any gas that I could smell. But none of 'em had time to listen and I don't have influence enough to rate an extra."

"Judge Candler saw you through the blind," I said.

He stared at me. "So that's it."

I shook my head. "I don't think he told them. It was the price of his keeping still on that and something else that Jerry promised not to see you."

"What else?" he demanded blankly.

I was in it now, and there seemed no point in stopping.

"Karen," I said. "She was afraid of you."

He sat there speechless for a minute, staring stupidly at me. "Afraid of . . . *me?* Well, for God's sake."

Then his eyes lighted suddenly. "Look—that's the line she tried to wangle a dot out of the Judge with. What a girl!"

I watched him with more interest, I may say, than I'd ever done before. He sat there, shaking his head back and forth, completely flabbergasted. Then he looked up suddenly, a new alarm in his blue eyes. "Grace—Jerry didn't fall for that, did she? If she did I'm going upstairs and beat the . . ."

"I don't think she knows all," I replied, sardonically.

"Look," he said. "I'm going to tell you about this. Maybe it'll sound phony to you, too, but it's God's truth. I went back to tell Karen if she'd lay off, I'd give her half of everything Dad left me. He's . . . he's got a rotten heart, and he drives himself like a bull. She was sitting on that little sofa, sort of half asleep. I tried to talk to her. She said, 'You know about a bird in the hand, darling? Go get me a glass of milk, I've got to stay up till that damned cat comes in and tomorrow I'm going to send for the S.P.C.A.'

"I went out to the kitchen. There was a glass on the sink that had had milk in it. I got a bottle out of the icebox, poured some in the glass and took it in to her. She drank it and said, 'Go away, Roger. I want to write a letter, and I'm sleepy.' She rolled her head back and closed her eyes. I thought, of course, she was putting on an act—she always did. I took the glass, took it out to the sink, filled it with water and came back. She woke up and yawned and said, 'Lord, I'm sleepy. I wish you'd go home, and if you see Mrs. Harris tell her to hurry.'

"I tried to make her talk sense. She just shook her head.

145

She said, 'Darling, if your father found out about it, he'd leave his money to the Salvation Army. Neither of us would get a thin dime. I'll take my stock, thanks. Close the door quietly, dear.' So I gave up and went home. I didn't see the cat."

"—And you stopped on your front steps," I said, "looked back at her place, and looked at your watch. Judge Candler saw you."

He looked blank for a minute. "Did I?" Then he said,

"Oh yeah, I know. I was wondering whether she'd go to sleep with the heat off and freeze. I had some idea of going back and making her go to bed. Actually I thought she was half-tight, though I hadn't seen her take a drink."

"Have you told Colonel Primrose this?" I asked.

"I tried to, but with a couple of invisible dicks watching me through that trick mirror Fox has got rigged up behind the first aid kit and that bird Buck with a couple of milk bottles sticking out of his pockets, it didn't sound so hot even to me. I couldn't tell 'em the reason I wasn't in love with Karen was I'd never seen any girl but Jerry since we came back and she used to ride by with that red hair of hers on the tail end of that old spavined hack they had in the stall behind the carriage house."

"They'd have been sure you killed her, then."

He nodded.

"Well, anyway," I said, "you go home. You know Jerry loves you, if that's any comfort. And for heaven's sake try to call off your father. He's after Judge Candler's blood, and you're the only one can stop him."

He looked at me with suddenly ageing eyes.

"It's funny how he hates him," he said. "I don't suppose Jerry'd . . ."

He got up and stood looking down into the fire, not finishing the sentence. Then he turned to me.

"I don't suppose you could give her a note, could you?"

"I couldn't, but Lilac's down in the kitchen," I said.

His face brightened. He went over to the desk, pulled out a piece of paper and sat a minute chewing his pencil. Then he grinned and wrote like mad for a few minutes, got up, grabbed his hat and went out. I heard him a moment later shout "Goodbye!" up the stairs and heard the door slam. When I went up to bed Jerry was sleeping like an angel.

I woke up the next morning startled—as soon as I got consciousness—almost out of my wits. Lilac was tiptoeing about the room as quietly as a large black cat stalking a mouse, not a mutter or grumble to be heard out of her. When she ran up the Venetian blind with a positively velvet hand I couldn't stand it any longer.

"Lilac!" I said. "What *is* the matter?"

She peered around the bedpost at me, rolling her old eyes.

"Hush-sh-sh!" she whispered. "Don' you wake up that chile, she's sleepin' lak a lamb."

She tipped about, gathering my scattered belongings. "Look lak 'bout all she needin' was a little sleep an' su'thin in her stummick and Mist' Roguh. Pore baby, Ah tol' her ain' nobody t' look out for her 'cept herself."

She put my tray on my lap and even poured me a cup of coffee, tiptoed back to the door and said, darkly and sotto voce, "Don' let me hear yo' bangin' 'roun' droppin' things."

She closed the door noiselessly, and I didn't even hear her going down the stairs. It was wonderful . . . the first really peaceful morning I'd had since she and Julius, the man she calls her husband, got the last of their periodic so-called divorces. I sat there, lulled by the unaccustomed serenity to a leisurely roseate frame of mind I seldom face my breakfast with.

Perhaps that was my mistake. At any rate, I'd just unfolded the paper and glanced at the headlines when the telephone on the table beside my bed jangled. I picked it up with as little qualm as the people you read about who take a bite of watermelon at a church picnic and find too late that one black seed was a hornet. Although I should have known, I suppose, the minute I heard Colonel Primrose's voice.

"Listen, my dear," he said abruptly. "I'm calling you, so you can prepare Jerry for a shock.—Philander Doyle has just been found in his library, shot through the head. Fox has arrested Roger . . . —Are you there?"

"I wish I weren't," I managed to say.

22

I've never been quite sure how I got through the ordeal of "preparing" Jerry . . . or rather the ordeal of preparing myself to prepare her. As I look back on it it seems to me that that was infinitely worse than what actually followed. She was sitting up in bed with a deep blue maribou jacket on that an aunt of the children's had given me for a summer evening wrap. It was marvellous with her sleep-rumpled copper curls and pale good face and autumn eyes. The smile she raised to me as I came in faded so abruptly that I knew I must be more alarmed myself than I'd thought. She put down the cup of chocolate in her hand. I remembered noticing that the hardly-touched breakfast Lilac had managed to get on her tray would have kept a Welsh miner and family for a week.

"What's . . . the matter, Grace?" she said softly. "Had Dad found out . . ."

I shook my head.

"Listen, Jerry," I said. "Philander Doyle was shot dead last night. They've arrested Roger."

She looked at me silently, her firm little Cavalier jaw relaxing a little under that blow. Then her eyes moved to the piece of my notepaper propped against the silver sugar basin on her tray. Without a word she reached out to the bedside table, took up a card of matches, struck one, picked up Roger's note, held it while the flame licked it up, dropped it in her empty cereal dish, and watched it roll into a black crisp heap and die. Then she moved the tray down to the foot of the bed and slipped out.

"Let's go down, as soon as we can. I've got to see him," she said quickly. "Hurry, Grace."

I looked at the mess of carbon in the dish. I could see Roger at the desk, grinning suddenly and writing like mad, and I could guess that what had seemed funny when he wrote could easily be anything but funny now, and that Jerry was frightened . . . more frightened, I imagine, than she'd ever been in her life before.

We crossed the Memorial bridge less than half an hour later. Arlington gleamed like a Grecian temple in its dark snow-patched niche in the hills in front of us. In the mirror over my windshield the Lincoln Memorial receded and was gone as we turned left along the highway. Across the river, blue as the sky, Washington lay in the sun, a fabulous city of white, the Monument and the Capitol dome gleaming brilliantly. Jerry didn't speak at all as we went the eight miles to Alexandria at considerably more than the allotted fifty-five miles an hour. We turned off at the post office and sped down to Chatham Street, the patrolman on the corner waving us through, and drew up in front of the Candlers' house. The melting snow dripped from the eaves and the leafless branches of the trees in a hurrying alarming obligato to fear. Across the street the Doyle house stood out clean and lovely for a moment . . . until the cars and the black-overcoated men coming in and out made it horrible, some way; a house without a soul.

Jerry hesitated.

"You better go in and see Sandy," I said. "I'll be in in a moment."

She nodded, got out and ran up the stairs. I went across the street. Sergeant Buck was standing in the doorway. He turned his viscid fish-grey eyes on me and said, out of the corner of that wide slit in his granite façade, "Captain Fox wants to see you, ma'am.—Let her come in," he added to the detective on the steps.

"Is Roger here?" I asked, stopping on the threshold.

Sergeant Buck turned his head and spat neatly over the brass-tipped railing.

"In the jug," he said.

I don't know why things said out of the corner of the human mouth—if Sergeant Buck's can really be called that—sound so dreadfully more sinister than if said normally. The impression I got was that Roger not only was there but had every possible chance of rotting there . . . which I believe is the accepted opinion of the process that goes on in jails. I hurried along the panelled hall to where I saw Colonel Primrose with Captain Fox and two men I hadn't seen before.

From out in the kitchen I could hear Rosie and somebody else wailing loudly.

"Somebody go turn those damn yowling niggers off," Captain Fox rapped out, and one of the men started out and stopped when Sergeant Buck got to the dining room door first.

Colonel Primrose's face was very grim, and his eyes as he looked at me were snapping black. I stepped over beside him, and caught one glimpse, before I turned away, of the library, and the blood-spattered desk in front of Philander Doyle's empty chair under the fur-collared portrait of Thomas Jefferson.

On the desk still, on the side away from the chair, as if whoever had shot him as he sat there had just laid the gun down and walked off, leaving it smoking there, was the revolver I'd seen in his drawer the day before. As my eyes moved away in sick horror, they saw, strewed over that magnificent rug, literally thousands of bits of broken glass. Then I saw that the doors of the mahogany bookcase were shattered, jagged pieces left hanging down and jutting up like grotesque transparent stalactites and stalagmites. The green tooled binding of one book was ripped where the bullet had struck and buried itself. In front of the bookcase, still standing there but empty except for jagged bits of glass still holding in its iron rim, was the stand that had held the glassed page from the Alexandria *Gazette* of December 10, 1798. Otherwise, as far as I could tell, the room was undisturbed.

As I turned away I saw that Colonel Primrose was looking intently. I turned still farther toward the drawing room. My mouth tasted as if I'd drunk a tremendous draft of water from the Dismal Swamp . . . but something inside of me had quickened in spite of it. For it wasn't Roger Doyle, I was perfectly certain, who'd destroyed the framed fragment of the old newsprint. I could have sworn to that, just as a matter of common sense. For he might not have thought it was amusing as his father did, and he might easily have been ashamed of having it there; but he was certainly used to it by now. It wouldn't have had any significance to him . . . not enough, anyway, to risk rousing the neighborhood to destroy.

Colonel Primrose followed me into the drawing room and stood there, looking out across the street through the tilted slats of the blinds.

"It must have made a fearful clatter," I remarked.

He nodded.

"What happened? And when?"

"What you saw there, in the first place," he said. "He was killed between ten and eleven last night."

Roger, I thought, had left my place around half-past nine. From the last part of our conversation, and I supposed from the burned note to Jerry, he'd certainly been coming straight back to his father.

"He wasn't found till this morning, however," Colonel Primrose said. "The maid found the key to the library door thrown out in the snow at the side of the service walk. It's been melting rapidly since midnight, which is how she happened to see it. She thought Doyle had dropped it. She picked it up and unlocked the library door, planning to dust in there first thing. She called Roger and he called the police."

"Why did you arrest him?"

He shook his head. "That was Fox."

He looked at me with a sardonic twist to his lips. "Judge Candler called Fox last night. After Roger saw Jerry."

"Oh," I said. "How did he find it out?"

"He heard William telling him where she was. He then heard William and your Lilac congratulating each other over the phone . . . on true love finding a way. So he called Fox."

"You already knew, I suppose," I said.

"Fox didn't know Karen had lived in fear of the boy."

"Baloney," I said.

He chuckled. "Why, Mrs. Latham! You surprise me."

"Well, isn't it?" I demanded.

"*I'd* think so," he said seriously. "But Karen never batted her eyes at me. She was completely astigmatic, you know, but she wouldn't wear glasses to spoil her looks. That's what gave her that beautiful blank stare."

I reflected that it was also why she hadn't seen me the day she came triumphantly flicking her palms together out of Judge Candler's library.

"Which might explain why, even if she'd gone into the kitchen," he went on, "she wouldn't have noticed the pilot light off or the chronometer reading changed or the plug out of the ice-box."

"But about Roger," I insisted.

"Well, this business of his going home and standing on the doorstep looking at his watch, and the business of none of the Doyles appearing across the street until after the deadline for the explosion, is going to take some explaining."

I looked at him blankly.

"Doyle said it was because they couldn't find the keys to any of the outside doors in time."

"Where were they?"

"Nobody seemed to know but Mr. Doyle. He found them after Roger had climbed out a back window . . . or so he said."

"Wasn't he there till after six?"

Colonel Primrose shrugged.

"Nobody was checking on them with a stopwatch, in what William calls 'excitement times.' I doubt if we'd have noticed it, probably, except that Mr. Doyle seemed to feel it needed explanation."

"And last night?" I asked.

"Roger came home. The maid who sleeps in heard him and his father having a violent row. She also heard the crash of glass, but she was too scared to take her head out from under the covers. She didn't hear a shot. The revolver was equipped with a silencer, however. She wouldn't hear it

151

through these walls."

"What does Roger say?"

"He admits the quarrel. He went out immediately afterward and went down to the wharf at the foot of Prince Street, and just sat there throwing stones in the Potomac. When he came back he went to the library door to talk to his father again, but it was locked, as it frequently is, apparently, and his father didn't answer. He assumed either Doyle didn't want to talk to him or had gone out. He went upstairs and waited a while, and finally decided to turn in and sleep on it. He didn't hear anything."

"And Miss Isabel?"

"She's upstairs—you might go up in a while and talk to her. She's so upset about her brother they haven't told her about Roger yet."

"Didn't she hear the glass breaking?"

"She was at a meeting of the Leper Guild of her church," Colonel Primrose said. "She didn't get home till late. She found the front door open and thought they'd had a burglary until she'd spent half an hour looking in closets and drawers. She waked the maid, who told her Roger and his father had had a quarrel. She then assumed her brother had locked himself in the library or gone out, leaving the door unlocked, or that Roger, who'd never had a quarrel with his father before, had been so upset that he left it open."

"She admitted they'd quarrelled?"

He shook his head with a quick chuckle.

"Heavens, no. Even when Fox told her the maid had told him about it, she said, 'But, Captain Fox, you know what colored people *are!*' She said Roger always left doors open and so did her brother. As a matter of fact, the door *was* open. A neighbor noticed it. He's in the oil business, so I suppose he thought it wouldn't hurt if the burner had to work a little to keep up with the thermostat. It also happens he doesn't like Miss Doyle. His chickens kept getting over her fence, she gave him three notices and had them flung back the fourth time with their necks wrung. Doyle paid up but there was still hard feeling. Miss Isabel insisted on going to jail instead."

He chuckled again.

"Miss Isabel, by the way, electrified—I put it mildly—the members of the Leper Guild last night by remarking, not entirely out of a clear sky because they were all buzzing about it, that she knew quite well who murdered Karen Lunt, but

152

that her brother considered it an improper subject for discussion."

I gasped. "Have you asked her——"

There was a little flicker in his sparkling black eyes.

"Fox did. His wife was at the meeting. She looked quite surprised, he said, and asked him if he had to depend on women to do his police work for him. She'd definitely regarded it as not her duty, especially since he'd acted in the extraordinary way he had about the chickens next door. Anyway, she realized now she'd made a mistake."

"In other words, she'd thought it was her brother?"

"Fox asked her that too. She said she thought that under the circumstances it was a question nobody with any breeding could ask, and she'd always thought his wife a very charming little woman. She'd only met her casually, but that was her impression."

All I could think of was that it really sounded exactly like her. "So . . . where are you now?" I asked.

"I'm chiefly interested, personally," he said, "in a sheaf of papers that were flung into the fire there in the library last night and weren't entirely burned.—Doyle apparently spent his last evening making out cases against everybody in town."

I looked at him too quickly.

"You know about that?"

"Only . . . one," I said. "Were there others?"

He nodded. "Only the tops where they were clipped together weren't burned. There were apparently statements of a case against Sandy, Jerry, William, Pepperday, McClure, and a fellow named Smith in quotation marks. Their names and 'I. Motive' were all we rescued."

"Wasn't there——" I stopped abruptly.

"Wasn't there what?" he asked, after waiting for me to go on.

"Nothing," I said.

"You mean, wasn't Judge Candler's name there?" he asked, with a smile. "The answer is No. Which, as you haven't said, is very strange, because everything the man said, without saying it at all, pointed that way."

` He didn't need those black X-ray eyes of his to read the question that flashed through my mind. Had Judge Candler himself . . .

"I think it's unlikely he would have left anything at all, if he'd taken it," he said quite calmly, as if I'd really asked it.

153

"It's a possibility, of course. On the other hand, whoever put the lot of them in the fire undoubtedly expected them to burn completely. The Judge's statement may still be around somewhere—waiting future use. I expect it would be the most patiently worked out of the lot. It might be exceedingly damning."

I looked intently at him. "Don't be absurd, Colonel Primrose," I said. "You can't believe . . ."

"My dear, I can believe anything."

"Well, I can't."

"Unfortunately," he said with a smile.

"But you surely don't think Roger did it?"

"I think he's in a tight spot," he said soberly. "I have great respect for Judge Candler. That doesn't blind me to the fact that he could be an implacable enemy. He's taken a lot from Philander Doyle. He adored Karen. I think he's even more deeply devoted to his daughter. If he were convinced—and I think he is—that Roger killed Karen . . . then I think Roger will need more than his father, even if he wasn't dead and could defend, to get him off. The fact that he's in love with Jerry of course makes it worse, if anything."

"I didn't ask you that," I protested. "I know all that as well as you do. I asked you if *you* think he's guilty."

He stood looking at the ash on his cigar.

"No," he said, absently. "I don't think so."

Then he looked up at me intently.

"There's one thing that interests me very much, Mrs. Latham."

"What's that?" I asked . . . too eagerly, I'm afraid, because he smiled faintly.

"That cat," he said.

I stopped to think a minute. "What's she done now?"

"She came across the street, last night, into the hall. You can see her tracks if you look at that waxed floor in the right light. She came in as far as the library door, and she went back again.—In other words, it's quite probable that she followed a friend over, and back. She's not a familiar in this house, and she's lonesome."

He was watching me with a veiled scrutiny that wasn't particularly comforting, since I couldn't keep the other morning, or the other evening, out of my mind.

"It's even occurred to me, Mrs. Latham," he went on calmly, "that she may have been following someone the other morning—the morning you let her in—to the Candler house. She was cold, she couldn't get in her own house, and she recognized some friend."

My heart sank inside me.

"Well," he said, dismissing that abruptly, "I just throw it out. I see it's occurred to you too. Why don't you go up and see Miss Isabel?"

I nodded. "Shall I tell her Roger's in jail?"

"Let's see if I can't get him out, first," he said, and smiled as he saw my face brighten. "Don't count heavily on it. By the way—do you know what was in that glass in the wrought-iron frame in there?"

I nodded.

"What?"

"I'm not going to tell you," I said. "And anyway, I've always thought your wife was a very charming little woman."

He smiled again, and I left instantly as I saw Sergeant Buck's own wrought-iron frame miraculously in the doorway.

23

Miss Isabel Doyle's room was oddly bare, compared with the rest of that house. It had a few pieces of old furniture in it, but not the same kind that were downstairs by any manner of means. Nor were there any pictures like the ones downstairs. There were a couple of undistinguished water colors, and a pencil sketch of herself when she was a really very lovely young girl. Otherwise nothing but photographs, rather absurd looking now that hair styles for women and collar and hair styles for men have changed so much.

Miss Isabel herself was sitting in an old hickory rocker staring into the empty fireplace. She'd been writing, and she put down her pen as I came in and looked up. There was a little stack of letters on the table at her elbow, stamped with the old pink two-cent Washington stamp. Even the paper of the envelopes looked old, like the clothes she always wore. She looked up at me with a haggard dreadful face.

"They've arrested Roger, haven't they?" she asked.

I nodded.

"They wouldn't tell me, but I heard it over the radio." She pointed to the little set on a table by the window.

"Oh, they can't think he did anything so dreadful!" she whispered. "He loved his father, and my brother worshipped him. He was so worried, that's all. He thought they were going to accuse Roger. Oh, why did I go out last night! It's all so useless! I told him I didn't want to go, but he made me."

"Why, Miss Doyle?" I asked.

"He was expecting someone to come. He didn't want me here for fear I'd say something."

"Who . . . was it?" I knew it really wasn't my place to be asking her such questions, but I couldn't help it.

"It doesn't matter, my dear," she replied, with a return of her usual vague manner.

"I should think it mattered a lot, for Roger," I said.

"Oh, no, no. It's too absurd for them to do this. They can't keep Roger. Captain Fox is a very nice man. I know his wife. She's a lovely woman."

"But that isn't going to help Roger, Miss Doyle," I protested gently.

"But Roger is in love with Jeremy, my dear—you don't understand."

I said, "I certainly don't," after some thought.

"Well, you will eventually," she said. "I know Roger would rather have me leave him there than . . . do anything to hurt her."

Then she did relapse, entirely, into her social manner.

"And anyway, you know, my dear, the cells at the police station are really *quite* nice. Captain Fox showed them to the Women's Club one day. They keep sheets, even, for the better class of prisoners, if they think they won't tear them up, and I'm sure Roger wouldn't think of it, he's always been used to sheets."

There was a tap on the door. Miss Isabel jumped. The little stack of letters on the edge of the table fell off onto the floor. I started to reach down for them. She stopped me quickly.

"See who's there, will you, my dear? I really don't feel like seeing anyone."

She bent down herself to pick up the letters, but not before I saw that each of them—every one—was addressed to Peyton Candler.

I went to the door. It was the colored maid Rosie with a brown earthenware pot of tea and some toast on a silver tray.

"Tell Miss Isabel Ah done what she tol' me," she whispered, handing me the tray, "an' there weren't no more."

I closed the door.

"Rosie says to tell you she did what you told her," I said, putting the tray down on her table, "and that there weren't any more."

The letters were nowhere in sight. Miss Isabel closed her eyes for a moment.

"I'm so glad!" she whispered. Then she opened her eyes and looked at me. "Did my brother happen to show you the old copy of the *Gazette* he had?" she asked, in a tone of purely polite conversation.

"Yes," I said.

"You're very fond of Jeremy, aren't you, my dear?" she asked then, without the slightest indication that the subject had been abruptly abandoned.

I nodded.

"I think it would be awfully nice if the papers don't get hold of that," she remarked. "My brother had an unusual sense of humor. I think it would distress Roger too."

"Did it . . . amuse you?" I asked, brazenly.

"I'd forgotten about it, my dear. And of course, we had no idea Roger was in love with the child. They'd grown up together. I can see now that the police might say my brother's feeling about Judge Candler had eaten into Roger's heart. But that's nonsense, Mrs. Latham. I think my brother was really fond of the Candler children."

There was one point that genuinely puzzled me, and I thought I might as well bring it up now as ever. "How does it happen, Miss Doyle, that Judge Candler never seemed to know Mr. Doyle felt the way he did about him?"

"My dear," she said, "Peyton's a child in many ways. Look at the way Karen had him fooled. And my brother had a fine sense of people, he really had. The only trouble was, he didn't realize that there's an end to all things . . ."

She looked terribly distressed again, so much so that I could have slain myself for bringing the point up.

"My dear," she went on then, "there's one thing that must be done, it must really. I don't want the police to know who came here last night."

As I simply couldn't tell her about the cat, I just sat there.

"Do you think you could mail a letter for me—without their finding it out, and without yourself reading the address . . . even by chance?"

For a moment I almost told her that I'd already—quite by chance—seen the address, but I couldn't bear to do it, some way. I nodded. "I'll do my best," I said.

She got up and turned her back to me. When she turned again she had a small brown paper bag in her hand, the kind you get things in in a department store. She gave it to me.

"Put it in your pocket. They won't search you, will they?"

"They'd better not try," I said. I put it in my pocket. "—Do you think it's wise?" I asked.

She nodded, in her vague way. Then she went to the door and stood there, listening. She came back and put her hand lightly on my arm.

"I loved my brother very dearly, Mrs. Latham," she said. "I promised him I'd never communicate with certain people again. I'm only breaking that promise for Roger."

"All right," I said. I hadn't, of course, the faintest notion of what she meant.

She kissed my cheek.

"Will you ask Captain Fox if Rosie can take Roger his lunch?"

I nodded and went out. As I came down the stairs the hall was empty. Roger, I thought, could jolly well eat jail bread and water for lunch. I didn't want Colonel Primrose's black snapping parrot eyes X-raying my pocket and stopping me well before I got out. I hurried, as quickly as I could without appearing to, out the front door and down the steps, and crossed the street. I got in my car. As I turned on the motor the Candlers' door opened and Mr. Pepperday came out, Mrs. Harris after him, rubbing against his legs. He shooed her back and came down the steps.

"May I give you a lift," I asked.

He stopped, looked at me penetratingly, screwed his spectacles back up on his nose, and said shrilly, "Thank you very kindly, miss." He got in the car and sat very primly, both little feet on the floor, one brown wool-gloved hand holding his green baize bag on his lap, the other clutching the window ledge. If he'd had another hand to hold his hat on with I'm sure he would have used it. I moved off slowly, got up at last to a dashing twenty, and crept around the corner into Duke Street.

"Have you been with Judge Candler long?" I asked, more by way of getting his mind off the hazards of modern locomotion than anything else.

"Fifty years, man and boy," he said briefly. "With the Colonel and the Judge."

"How is he taking Mr. Doyle's death?" I asked, as we crossed King Street.

Mr. Pepperday, to my shocked surprise, cackled suddenly for all the world like an amused bantam rooster.

"With . . . fortitude," he said, in his high treble. "Yes, I

158

think I may say with fortitude."

He cackled again, and as I couldn't think of anything to say offhand, we went on in silence. I drew up in front of the Judge's office, and looked back at the police station. Poor Roger, I thought. I hoped he was taking his misfortunes with fortitude. I opened the door for Mr. Pepperday. He clambered out as if he thought I was very likely to start up before he got to the sidewalk.

It seemed to reassure him that I didn't, for he turned back after he'd sprung clear and said, "You'll be interested to know, miss, that the key has been returned."

I was so startled that I moved my foot off the clutch and stalled my engine.

"The importance of the key," he went on, with a kind of shrill stiffness, "was not to establish any possible connection between . . . this office and Miss Lunt's house."

If he thought he had cleared anything up in my mind, he was quite wrong. I stared at him. Was it the Candlers he was trying to protect . . . or was it himself?

"A great many people come in and out of the office.—But I shouldn't want the police to think we'd been negligent in protecting our tenant."

He lifted his hat. "Good morning, miss. I'm going to my dinner. I have it at eleven-thirty every day. I find being regular in my habits is a great comfort."

"Do you always retire at eight o'clock?" I asked.

"Invariably, miss. In my opinion people only get into trouble, staying up after the time nature appointed for them to retire."

They certainly had the last few days, I thought, getting started again. I drove across King Street to Duke Street, turned right and slowed down in front of the handsome new post office on the corner. I got out, hurried up the broad steps and in the door, and went across to the letter chute. And just as I put my hand in my pocket and pulled out Miss Isabel's paper bag of letters, I felt a large cold shadow across me.

I turned to find myself staring at the enormous roughhewn façade of Sergeant Phineas T. Buck. My stricken eyes travelled up the frozen vastness and quailed under the viscid fishy glint pinioning me against the chute.

"The Colonel wants them letters, ma'am," Sergeant Buck said, out of the corner of his mouth.

I was afraid he hadn't seen the signs that said "No spitting," but he had because he didn't.

"He . . . can't have them," I said, more than a little appalled at my temerity.

"Sure he can," Sergeant Buck said.

"It's tampering with the mails," I retorted.

"Irregardless of that, ma'am, hand 'em over," he said. His cold grey eyes glinted again. His patience, I saw, was very rapidly coming to an end.

"No," I said firmly; and as I did his great ham of a hand shot out and took them quite simply out of my astonished grasp. He put them in his inside pocket and looked down at me.

"No hard feeling, ma'am," he said.

"Oh, perish the thought," I managed to answer, with what I intended to be fine irony. It was a flower wasted on that barren mountainside.

He looked at me almost kindly, and said, "The Colonel will sure appreciate your corporation, ma'am." It may, of course, have been an even finer irony on his part, quite wasted on me. He turned smartly and marched out the door, not quite saluting as he left me, and broke into a double-quick as he went down the stairs.

I went to the window and saw him get into Colonel Primrose's car and drive off. He must have been following me, I reflected, from the moment I'd left the house.

I drove slowly back down Prince Street toward the river, a prey, as novelists used to put it, to mixed emotions. Whether my annoyance at Colonel Primrose's low cunning was the greater, or at my own abysmal stupidity for not guessing what he'd do sooner than he guessed what I or perhaps Miss Isabel would do, I couldn't tell. In either case it was considerably greater than my vague fears for the possible consequences.

As I crossed Royal Street and continued on Fairfax, I saw again, just pausing a moment to see if traffic was clear before he put his hand on his hat and scurried across, the grotesque little figure of the methodical Mr. Pepperday. I touched my horn, scaring him half out of his wits, and came to a stop, holding my door open.

"May I give you another lift?" I asked.

He cleared his throat, after he'd got over his initial alarm.

"No, thank you, miss," he piped. "—Unless you'd be so kind as to drop me at my own door."

"I'd be happy to do even that," I said. He clambered nervously in and settled himself, the way people from the country used to do on the roller coaster at Coney Island.

"Just along to Franklin Street, if you please," he said.

"I just had some letters Miss Doyle gave me to post to Judge Candler stolen from me in the post office," I remarked. . . . for what possible reason or purpose I have not the foggiest idea.

The effect was startling. Mr. Pepperday turned as if he had been stuck with a sharp pin, and looked at me with the most extraordinary and comical alarm.

"If you can stop, miss, will you let me out at once?" he shrilled hastily. "I forgot something at the office."

As I was carefully going at a perilous twenty-two, I managed to stop immediately. "Shall I take you back?" I asked. His distress was increasing so rapidly that I was a little uneasy.

"If you please, miss!" he said.

He was so disturbed that he forgot to clutch the window ledge. And not another word did he say until I'd stopped at the cobbled curb across the street from his office.

"I thank you kindly, miss," he said then, struggling with the window lever. I reached across him and opened the door, and he was out and across the street like a minute elderly cat out of an oven, without a glance to the right or left, in spite of the fact that a big orange oil truck couldn't have been more than thirty feet from him.

"Extraordinary little person," I thought to myself. He was fumbling through his greatcoat, if so small an object can be called that, for his key. I saw him find it at last, jab it in the lock, throw the door open and scoot inside, banging the door shut behind him. I waited, but he didn't come out again, and in a minute or so I saw his hand reach out and remove the sign "Out for Lunch" from the window cut in the old door. I was too near the police station to stay around any longer, so I let out the clutch and moved off.

I couldn't tell, really, whether my desire not to go sprang from my curiosity about little Mr. Pepperday or from a deep-seated reluctance to return to the Candler house and have the door remain quietly closed in my face. Nevertheless, I couldn't, it seemed to me, leave Jerry indefinitely to bear the brunt of the Judge's wrath alone. I went along till I came to Chatham Street, going over in my mind just what I'd do if William couldn't let me in, and what I'd say to the Judge if he did. The first seemed very much the pleasanter alternative to look forward to.

I stopped in front of the house and glanced across the

street. Colonel Primrose was standing in the Doyles' door. Behind him was his man with the iron mask. On neither of their faces could I detect anything that remotely resembled a sense of shame, though Colonel Primrose did have the grace to turn his back while I got out of the car and went up the steps and pulled the old brass bell set in the brick beside the door frame. I stood there, hours it seemed to me, before I heard old William's feet padding slowly along the hall. His face as he opened the door had lost all its shine. He looked precisely like a piece of mahogany that had been waxed but not polished. He held the door open, rolling his eyes ominously toward the library.

My heart, already low, sank another notch. I gave him my coat and tried to give him a reassuring smile. It was a definite failure, I'm afraid, because he shook his head mournfully.

"Ah nevah went fo' t' do it, Mis' Grace," he whispered.

The library door was open, and Judge Candler was standing facing the fire, his hands clasped behind his back. He turned as I came in, inclined his head coldly, and turned back. Jerry, pale but calm, was sitting on the edge of his desk, and Sandy was there, sort of torn between the two of them and his own deep resentment toward the one-time friend his sister loved, and looking more distraught than I'd ever seen him.

Jerry got up quickly as I came in, her eyes brightening.

"Tell him we didn't go just so I could see Roger, Grace!" she cried passionately. "Tell him I . . . I didn't talk to him!"

"She didn't say a word to him, Judge Candler," I said. "It's entirely my fault, and my maid's. I didn't impress on her as much as I should have that she wasn't to let Roger in. Neither Jerry nor I had the faintest idea he'd know we'd left this house."

He turned slowly.

"I don't doubt your word, Jeremy," he said quietly.

"Then why . . . why did you——"

"I did doubt it last night—It's my own wisdom I doubt now, Jeremy."

Her eyes widened as she stared at him.

"I . . . want you to know, my dear, that your happiness means a great deal to me."

He spoke very slowly, hesitating between words. He'd never, I imagine, been a demonstrative man, and now the effort to speak, to try to make her understand him, was almost greater than he could manage.

162

"I . . . don't want to be unjust, least of all to you," he went on painfully. "I've suffered two great blows. The fact that you and Sandy have seen more clearly than I, for years past, and that you've borne, so loyally, all the brunt of my blindness . . . makes it even more difficult for me to face myself."

There was nothing but pity and devotion in Jerry's face now as she looked at him across the old rug.

"I can only ask your pardon," Judge Candler said steadily. "—I can do a little more for you, Jeremy. Sandy has told me the circumstances of Philander Doyle's death. I can testify that he was alive after his quarrel with Roger, and after Roger left the house."

"Dad!" Jerry cried.

"I talked to Philander Doyle myself, after Roger had gone," he said. "He was shot after I left him. I heard the crashing of glass after I'd returned to this house. I have sent for Colonel Primrose to tell him so."

Jerry's face had gone as pale as wax again.

"But . . . Dad!" she cried. Her voice was tense with alarm. "You mustn't tell them you were there! Don't you see?"

I thought something like a smile lighted Judge Candler's eyes, as he turned away for an instant.

"If it would save your love for you," he said quietly, "I'd be happy now to say I shot Philander Doyle myself. I think I could plead self-defence—quite literally."

Jerry went quickly across the room, and put her hand out timidly to touch his arm. He turned around and looked down into her upturned eyes. Then he raised his hands slowly and took her pointed little face and burnished-copper hair in them.

"I love you very deeply, my dear," he said gently.

The tears rolled down her face as she flung her arms around her father's neck. I looked at Sandy, he looked at me. We went out together.

For a moment he didn't speak. Then a grin appeared on his ugly red-headed face.

"Affecting domestic scene in the last act," he said. "—I hope, I hope, I hope . . ."

24

I picked up my coat that William had laid on the needle-point bench and put it on.

"Where are you going?" Sandy demanded. His big face looked as dismayed and long-eared as a spaniel's when everyone appears to be departing with no provision made for him.

"I'm going to leave you people to a quiet day at home," I said, "and see if I can manage the same."

"Oh gosh, don't go. That convoy of the Colonel's gives me the creeps, and they'll be steaming up any minute."

"That's *just* what I figured, darling," I said, pleasantly.

"Come on, then," he said. "Let's both go and get a sandwich some place, and give Jerry and the old man a chance to smoke the pipe of peace before the massacre starts."

"All right," I said. I knew Colonel Primrose would see us go out, and if he wanted Sandy there was nothing to stop Sergeant Buck from coming along and getting him.

We went down the steps and got in the car. I glanced across the street. Neither of them, the Colonel or his Sergeant, was visible, but that, as I knew, meant less than nothing, or perhaps a great deal more. We turned out Washington Street onto the Mount Vernon Highway, Sandy staring glumly ahead of him, and stopped at the last hot-dog stand that decorates the landscape there.

"Grace," Sandy said suddenly. "Honestly, what do you make of all this?"

"Who, me?" I said. "Darling, I wish I knew. I'm completely bogged. At the moment I'm taking even money on Mrs. Harris."

He scowled. "Seriously."

"Well," I said . . . and just as I opened my mouth I saw a strangely familiar car go past and slow up quickly, and I could see the dead pan of my friend the Sergeant glance casually over at us. Sandy looked over at him too, his face darkening.

"It's just that he can't bear to see a man in the clutches of a widow," I said easily, but somehow I didn't go on with what I'd been going to say. "I guess we'd better go back," I said instead.

Sergeant Buck's car spun around in the road and drove in in front of us. He got out, slammed his door, and came over.

"The Colonel wants to see you, ma'am," he said. He signalled the boy. "—Two cheese on rye."

He turned back to me. "He says meet him at the Anchorage. Come on, Mr. Candler. You can go back with me after you've et."

I think Sandy was on the point of declining impolitely.

164

I nudged him and said—out of the side of *my* mouth—"Go on, you idiot!" He got out, scowling, with the hamburgers we'd ordered. I backed out and turned. When I looked around he and Buck were getting in the other car.

Colonel Primrose got up as I came into the lovely old hall of the Anchorage in Queen Street. He smiled in a cheerful and peculiarly offensive way.

"I hope you didn't mind."

"A lot of good it would have done me if I did," I replied amiably. "It *does* just happen that I don't care about spending a night in jail, even if they do have sheets for the better class of prisoners.—What if I didn't qualify?"

He sat down opposite me. "I've ordered your lunch."

"Thanks," I said.

He smiled. "Don't be annoyed. I'm sorry about this morning, but you see I had to have those letters. Nobody would tell me anything. I couldn't just keep on guessing, could I?"

"No—but you could have quit and gone back to Georgetown. We've really missed you."

"If you'd stayed there, I wouldn't have left in the first place," he answered, with a faint smile.

"I'll admit the original error was mine," I said. "But you could have gone home when I wanted you to."

"I think now I might have," he agreed. "I . . . didn't know what was happening, you see.—Now that I do, I think perhaps I'm sorry I didn't."

I stared at him open-mouthed.

"You mean . . . you know——?"

He nodded slowly. "Yes, I know.—I've often heard people at the F.B.I. say they didn't care how many gangsters shot each other up, so long as they let laymen alone. I think that applies to people like . . . well, could we say Philander Doyle, anyway?"

"But not Karen Lunt?"

He shrugged.

"She knew what she was doing. Maybe she got pretty much what she deserved. She was ruthless and egocentric and amoral. In any other place in the social scale I'd shudder to think what she could have been. She double-crossed the Candlers, who'd taken care of her since she was a child, she double-crossed Philander Doyle . . . not with any desire to save Judge Candler, just to get what she wanted the quickest and easiest way."

165

"You do think she knew what Mr. Doyle was doing?" I asked.

"Oh, definitely. It was his idea, she elaborated on it in her own way. She played a neater game than he did, just because she was a woman and had Candler buffaloed. And they both found out what the whole history of man points out, from time to time—that the worm turns."

He stopped me before I could speak.

"There's just one thing I want you to do," he said seriously. "You can't help or hinder anything at this point. I'm going to ask you just to take it for granted that I do know who killed those two people. I want you to tell me, in detail, everything you remember about four things. One: the interview you barged in on at the Candlers' before the party. Two: the party, and everything you noticed at it. Three: the saga of Mrs. Harris the Siamese cat. And four: your interview with Philander Doyle before lunch. I know now, incidentally, about the copy of the *Gazette* that was shot out of the frame in the iron standard.—He had a pile of photostated copies in his dresser drawer. So begin at the beginning, my dear. I won't interrupt—or I'll try not to."

I hesitated. I wouldn't, since the business at the post office, have trusted him between me and the gatepost. He gave me a faintly sardonic smile.

"Fox and Buck and I have been busy as a lot of moles, Mrs. Latham. I don't think there's anything we haven't turned up. I'm only asking you to tell me about those things to find out the extenuating circumstances—which I'm sure exist. Believe me, my dear."

I suppose I was a fool, but I did believe him, some way. I sat there, telling him everything, including even the pad of snow and ice on the drugget inside the garden entry at the Candlers' house. I told him about Philander Doyle's 2 A.M. inspection of Karen's carriage house, and Roger's watching him from behind the tree.

When I'd finished he nodded soberly. Then, without a word, he pushed his chair back, paid the bill and helped me on with my coat.

"The Judge asked me to come and see him this morning," he said as we got into my car. "I gather he wanted to tell me he'd been over to see Doyle last night."

"Not entirely," I said. "He wanted mostly to tell you he'd seen Roger leave the house before he talked to Mr. Doyle. That was to atone for his calling Captain Fox last night."

I looked at him as I shifted into high.

"It was the same person, wasn't it, who . . . killed them?"

He nodded.

"Was it because Mr. Doyle knew who had killed Karen——?"

He shook his head. "No. He was killed for exactly the same reason that Karen Lunt was."

William opened the door when we got back, his face still greyer, as if the wax had quite dried by now without ever being polished and had left a thick film over the shining mahogany. His hands shook as he took my coat. Colonel Primrose waited for me by the library door. I stopped on the threshold. Mrs. Harris was standing there in front of me, one dainty yellow-tipped paw raised tentatively, looking around. She arched her back and walked in, her tail high, rather like a well-drilled debutante making an entrance, stopped in front of Mr. Pepperday, meowed gently, jumped up into his lap and settled down on his green baize bag. I looked around the room. Roger was there, sitting beside his aunt. Miss Isabel had apparently discarded all of her outlandish rigs, and was quite decently dressed in quite normal clothes.

Judge Candler rose from behind his desk as I came in. Sandy was balanced on a footstool in front of the fire, close to Jerry . . . both of them quite pale, each in a different way. I noticed Sergeant Buck standing there, a menacing cross between the guard of a peculiarly vicious road gang, the beadle of a French cathedral and the Great Pyramid of Cheops if they'd all been run through a grinder and then smelted by Krupp. Captain Fox was not there.

Then I heard William turn the heavy key in the front door and put the chain on. He slipped in behind Colonel Primrose and closed the library door, and stood there until Jerry nodded to a chair. I don't think his pounding knees would have held him upright very long. My own were pretty watery, certainly, as I sat down by Jerry, and my hand, as she reached for it and held it like a frightened child, was as cold as hers.

Colonel Primrose sat down by Judge Candler's desk. I saw on it the letters I'd got from Miss Isabel, the stamps uncancelled, that Buck, I supposed, had brought to him. Beside them was another pile. The stamps on them were cancelled, and I could read the red letters of the post office notation: "Return to Sender."

"I asked you to come here because it seemed simpler this

way," Colonel Primrose said. "What motivated Karen Lunt's death and Philander Doyle's is, of course, known to all of you. It was done simply—and entirely—to prevent Judge Candler's being dragged through the public prints at a moment when his unblemished reputation stood him in greater stead even than his knowledge of the law . . . at a moment when, as we all understand, any allegation, no matter how unjust, could do him a cruel wrong."

Judge Candler's fingers beat a soft tattoo on his desk, Mr. Pepperday's did the same on the arm of his chair.

"I suppose you all realize, too, that the great driving force in the life of Philander Doyle was his single-minded desire to . . . get even with his lifelong friend, by fair means or foul. That that had become an obsession with him . . . and that, from Mr. Doyle's point of view, he was on the eve of his greatest failure, because his friend was on the eve of his greatest success. I am not, of course, telling any of you anything you haven't been aware of . . . for a longer or shorter time."

He turned to Sandy.

"You knew, I believe, Mr. Candler, that a plan to ruin your father was on foot? When Miss Lunt was found dead . . ."

"I . . . yes," Sandy said quietly. "But I . . . I couldn't figure it out. When I saw that chronometer, and saw it was all set for six o'clock, when the house would be full of gas, that beat me. It seemed to have gone all haywire."

I gaped at him, remembering so well hearing him through the flimsy boards of the little closet in my room, and Jerry saying, "—So now we have a murder on our hands." I could remember sitting on the blanket chest there, my head going round in dizzy dreadful circles.

Colonel Primrose looked steadily down at the little man bolt upright in his chair, with his green baize bag and Mrs. Harris in his lap.

"You knew all the circumstances of Karen's relations with the Candlers, Mr. Pepperday," he said quietly. "You knew better than anyone else the mechanism of her hot-water system. You had as nearly perfect an alibi as it's possible to have in your well-known methodical habits. You had access to Karen Lunt's cottage. You have been a devoted friend to three generations of Candlers. Mrs. Harris the cat follows you in preference to anyone else in this house.—I wish to apologize to you for thinking for some time that you were the man we were looking for."

Mr. Pepperday blinked, open-mouthed, stroking Mrs. Harris's café-au-lait back mechanically with trembling fingers, too shocked to speak.

Colonel Primrose turned back to the rest of us.

"Murder was no part, of course, of Philander Doyle's scheme of action against your father. That was quite another idea altogether. Some other person had planned, at the same time that Philander Doyle was planning, to remove Karen Lunt, and to do it in such a way that it would have all the appearance of an accident.—And in a way, because she upset all that, Mrs. Latham is responsible for Philander Doyle's death."

Jerry's hand on mine steadied it.

"For with Miss Lunt gone, there would have been no one to bring—at just the crucial moment, from Mr. Doyle's point of view—a quite fictitious suit against Judge Candler. As it turned out, however, Mr. Doyle was left not with a dubious lawsuit that would have needed a good deal of hocus-pocus even to get into court—though to get it into the newspapers was, of course, the primary idea—but with a first-rate murder charge . . . something better than he had ever dreamed of, requiring nothing at all that would compromise him in the least.

"He made, however, as he told Mrs. Latham here, two substantial mistakes. He thought it was the pride that he'd touched in Miss Jerry that had made her decide to give back the aircraft stock——"

"But it wasn't!" Jerry cried. "It was because I saw I was acting exactly as he'd planned for me to act! I——"

Colonel Primrose smiled a little.

"It didn't occur to Mr. Doyle," he said placidly, "that a twenty-one-year-old girl would see through him. And his other mistake was that he hadn't realized that his son's desire to protect a girl he loved could be greater than his devotion to him."

The room was as silent as the grave as he stopped for a moment.

"And that's why Roger Doyle," he went on quietly, "went back to the party in the carriage house, after everybody had gone. That's why he gave Karen Lunt that glass of milk. That's why he came home, after he'd done it, and——"

Jerry's hand in mine unclasped slowly, relaxing as a dead hand relaxes. I stared at Colonel Primrose, my heart seemingly quite still inside me, my lips dry.

Then, not suddenly or abruptly at all, but quite normally, as if it were a drawing room gathering where there's been rather a longer lull in the conversation than was socially desirable, I heard a cool and well-bred and vaguely aloof voice.

"Well, *really*, Colonel Primrose," Miss Isabel Doyle said. "It's absurd to say that Roger killed his father. He did no such thing. I know perfectly well who did it.—Because, don't you see, I did it myself?"

25

If the men from Mars had dropped into that frozen and speechless room by the millions, utter and complete devastation could not have been more awful. Sitting there by the fire, quite breathless, Jerry's hand gripping mine with a sudden convulsive tightness, I couldn't bear to look at a single face. Then my eyes were drawn by some terrible fascination to Roger Doyle's. He hadn't moved a muscle; but I could see the cold perspiration standing in beads on his white forehead.

I heard Colonel Primrose's quiet voice.

"Yes, I know you did, Miss Doyle," he said, and there was a gentleness and pity in his tone that sent another colder chill to my heart. "You did it because . . . it was the only way you knew to save a man who meant more to you than your brother."

"Than all the world," said Miss Doyle.

She hadn't taken her eyes, quite steady under her slightly-raised brows, from Colonel Primrose. I didn't dare look at Judge Candler, but I heard his chair creak suddenly as he moved under the impact of that cool, perfectly calm declaration.

"—You wrote those letters," Colonel Primrose said, pointing to the table in front of Judge Candler. "They were never answered. The others Peyton Candler, a young man, wrote to you. They were returned to the sender . . . so that each of you believed the other was unfaithful. Your brother, as he told Mrs. Latham, in double-crossing his friend, kept him from marrying the woman he loved."

Miss Isabel Doyle looked vaguely surprised.

"Oh, but I'm quite sure he never thought of it that way, Colonel Primrose," she said quickly. "He thought I'd marry someone in New York, you know. He always had the house

170

quite full of eligible young men."

Her voice was as aloof and charmingly detached as ever.

"You don't understand him, really. He was devoted to me. He gave me everything in the world to make up for what he'd done. Really."

I saw Colonel Primrose's glance rest for just an instant on her dowdy clothes, her cheap shoes and cheaper bag. She flushed as if he had caught her off guard. I thought of that barren room, of the awful old cast-off garments she wore.

"You see," she said coolly, "I just never accepted the things he wanted me to have. He wanted me to be stylish and smart. I wouldn't, just to annoy him. He understood it perfectly. He'd try to bargain with me. If I wanted something, I'd try to hide it from him. Just as I wanted Roger to marry Jerry, but if I'd said so . . . That's why I pretended I thought it would be lovely if he married Karen. It was all kind of a game."

I tried to stop the ache in my throat, to move my icy and paralyzed hands, as I stared at her. It was so utterly incredible, her quietly checkmating all his grandeur by simply refusing to be part of it, hiding what she felt under the mask of aloof vacuity so that he couldn't guess her heart.

"And the framed copy of the *Gazette*, Miss Doyle?" Colonel Primrose asked. "You've broken that often, haven't you? So that the maid didn't get up when she heard the crash of glass?"

"Oh, yes," Miss Isabel said calmly. "But he always had more. He had hundreds of them made."

"And . . . when you shot him——"

"Oh, but I didn't want to," she said quickly. "I was really very fond of him. I implored him to stop. You see, he read me the case he'd constructed against Judge Candler. It was damning, it was horrible, really! You see, he'd been watching, ever since Karen moved into the carriage house. He watched that night. Early in the morning he saw Judge Candler coming in his garden door. He'd seen him come out, and walk down toward her house just before . . . but he could forget that, he said, to make it look . . . too horrible."

Judge Candler sat erect, motionless.

"It *was* you," Colonel Primrose asked calmly, "that the cat followed to this house?"

Judge Candler nodded.

"Would you mind very much . . . explaining?"

"Perhaps I should have done so earlier," Judge Candler

said. His voice was slow and firm, and controlled with a painful effort. "I woke and saw Karen's lights still on. I was disturbed, because of the scene earlier in the evening."

He didn't look at Roger.

"I got up and went part way down there. I saw the cat at the window, and I saw Karen, sitting as she had been on the sofa. I realized, of course, that she was not a child . . . that she had a right to her private life. I knew she hadn't the same idea of the conventions that . . . I have—and that four o'clock was not as late to her as it is to me. I came back, without going any closer, not wanting to know—I presume —what might have hurt me very much to know. I knew the cat came with me. I thought she'd go back again for Karen to let her in. I didn't smell gas, but I haven't a sensitive nose. And I didn't go close to the house."

He hadn't looked at Miss Isabel, and he sat there now, his head bowed.

Colonel Primrose nodded. "—He read you his case against Judge Candler?"

Miss Isabel's voice sounded even cooler and more vague, after Judge Candler's firm tones with their undercurrent of pain.

"I knew of course that nothing could stop him then, not Roger and Jerry, no one. So I told him I'd turned on Karen's gas, and why. You see, I did that when I went in the kitchen as we were all leaving. I'd already unhooked the icebox and set the chronometer earlier in the evening when I helped cook dinner. I knew she was quite blind and wouldn't notice. Then I left the water running upstairs when I got my wraps. I went in the kitchen again when I was pretending to look for a cat and flicked the pilot light off."

She looked about the room, explaining all of it to us quite simply.

"I told him that. He said he knew it, but that if I tried to say it on the stand he would have me put away until it was over, because everyone thought I was crazy anyway. I was desperate, I really was. I told him I couldn't allow it, not possibly. I said I would even kill him to stop it, just as I had her . . . though I really didn't know how I could do it."

She hesitated for an instant and went on.

"He laughed. He said I wouldn't dare. Then he opened a drawer in front of him and took out the revolver he'd taken away from a man who'd come to shoot him once. He looked at it to see if it was loaded, snapped it shut and pushed it across the table to me. He said, 'All right, I dare you to shoot, my dear.'

"I picked it up, and I shot him.

"Then I shot the *Gazette* out of the frame, and laid his revolver down, and tore off the sheet he'd read with the case against Judge Candler on it, and burned it, and put the others in the fire too. Then I locked the library door and threw the key outside."

Miss Isabel paused. Roger Doyle reached over without a word, took her hand and held it in both his own, not looking at her, his eyes closed.

"You see, Judge Candler had been there," she went on softly. "My brother told me that, but I didn't think anyone else would know it. I went out for a walk, leaving the door open. When I came back I waked the maid and we looked under all the beds. Then I went to my room. I didn't know till she told me that Roger had been in and that he and my brother had quarrelled. You see, I didn't mean to point the guilt to anyone else."

Colonel Primrose looked at her for a long time, the same expression in his black eyes.

"How long have you had those letters, Miss Doyle?" he asked gently.

"Oh, I found them last fall, when we were housecleaning. —And I'd begged him not to come down here! But he said I needn't worry. He said, 'Surely, my dear, you don't remember that, do you?' He thought it was rather amusing. He said, 'Don't go making a fool of yourself, Isabel, Peyton's forgotten all that a long, long time ago. He's been a widower for years, he's known for years it wasn't you that jilted him. He could have come for you if he'd wanted you. But you're such a scarecrow he wouldn't even recognize you if he saw you.'

"And of course I knew men forget, and women—if they don't marry—don't forget. I was afraid I would make a fool of myself. That's why I didn't ever see him, it wasn't till Roger began to think Jerry was old enough to marry that I put my pride in my pocket and began coming here. And it wasn't till the other day, when I first taxed him with being behind Karen, that he admitted Peyton had never known.— And even if it was too late, and I was an old scarecrow, I still . . . wanted him to know. It was very foolish of me."

When she got up I saw the tears in her eyes for the first time.

"You see, I only wanted to save Peyton . . . and his chil-

173

dren. The rest didn't matter. And knowing my brother, I knew there wasn't any other way. And I'm really very sorry!"

She smiled in that vague way of hers, only rather as if she was tired, desperately tired, now it was all over.

"Only, you see, Colonel Primrose, if you arrested me now, everything would have to come out, everything I did it for would be lost."

Her voice was not pleading in the least, only casual and charming and matter-of-fact.

"So, I think, if you'll excuse me, I'll go home for a few moments."

I suppose we all knew there was one more step she'd known from the beginning she would have to take . . . and yet it seemed as if no one in the room could move, that all of us were just frozen where we were. Then Roger Doyle sprang to his feet and caught her in his arms, trying desperately to speak. She raised her lips and kissed him.

"Forgive me, Roger," she whispered, trying to release his hold.

"Please!" Her voice caught ever so little. "Please make him let me go!"

Then abruptly she wrenched herself loose and with a quick motion brought her hand to her mouth. She turned back to all of us. "I'm so sorry, I preferred going home!" she said.

Judge Candler had pushed back his chair and was across the room. She smiled as he caught her in his arms, and she died.

I have no clear idea of much that happened after that, nor do I want to have one, except that I don't know what any of us would have done if it hadn't been for Sergeant Buck and Mr. Pepperday, and William, and Colonel Primrose. I know that a little later, when Sandy and Jerry and I were still in the shabby lovely drawing room, with the library door closed, we were still too stunned to talk. The door opened as we just sat there, and Roger came in. He closed it behind him, and he stood there, with Jerry across the room by me, the two of them just looking at each other. Then Sandy got to his feet and crossed the room to him, and held out his hand.

"I'm sorry!" he mumbled awkwardly.

Roger gripped it silently.

Then Sandy said, with a sort of twisted attempt to be himself again, "I guess I was fifty kinds of a damn fool. If it'll help any, you can have her . . . if you'll take her away in a plain van."

He nodded toward his sister. And I looked out the window. I couldn't bear the way those two met and clung to each other.

Sandy came over beside me and stood, his back to them too. A cardinal sitting on a dead branch of the lilac tree opened his throat and sang.

"That means a change of weather, according to William," he said, a little shakily. "And that being the case, Mrs. Latham—what about you and me having a colossal drink?"

Colonel John Primrose pressed the trigger of the syphon and shot his glass full of soda, and came back and sat down in the wing chair by the fire in my garden sitting room in Georgetown.

"It's just as well it broke when it did," he said. "I hear the Judge's name is being sent to the Senate this week. She left a note, and since everybody has always thought she was half-cracked anyway, nobody seems to have been surprised."

"—Do you think she was?" I asked.

"By no means. She was the sanest person I ever knew," he said. "A lot saner than her brother, whose sanity nobody ever questioned. She had too mordant a sense of humor to be otherwise. Oddly, the thing that worried her was that Roger and Jerry would sell the house and furniture, feeling they couldn't live there."

"But they've decided to close it for a few years and go back if they can," I said. "That's what she asked them to do."

We sat there for a few moments. Then I said, "What made you think it was her?"

"I didn't," he said. "Not for some time. I thought it was the Judge. I thought he'd finally seen through Miss Karen and simply decided to execute her—judicially. When I learned, then, that Roger was the only Doyle to show across the street—having climbed out of a window—before six o'clock, and inasmuch as Karen's death was the last thing in the world that Doyle wanted, everything pointed at once to his sister. The half-pint bottle was from a dairy that both the Candlers and Doyles used, by the way. It was very simple, and exactly the kind of thing a woman would think of, not a man.

175

"And *where* did you get Judge Candler's letters?" I demanded.

He chuckled.

"I'm . . . not quite sure," he said. "I remember Buck was greatly interested in Mr. Pepperday's clocklike routine. Of course, I'd reprimand him severely if I had to think he made an unlawful entry."

"Oh, I'm sure you would," I said.

"And by the way," he went on, "how *did* that key get over to the Doyles'?"

"I haven't an idea," I said, unblushingly. "How did it get back to the office?"

"I suspect Mr. Doyle just left it in the back door the night he had a look around," he answered. "William found it."

"Dear me," I said. I didn't see any point in telling him what I'd realized that night, that Philander Doyle had heard that key hit against the chair, in my coat pocket, and must have guessed. After all, the center vase in a garniture mantel is a pretty obvious place to hide an embarrassing object. I must really have been very transparent indeed to Mr. Doyle.

"If it had been found in the Doyle house," he said, with the faintest smile, "it could easily have hanged Roger. Except of course for Miss Doyle."

I skipped it. "I wonder," I said, "what might have happened if I hadn't called you in?"

He shrugged. "Who can tell, Mrs. Latham? I wouldn't have seen the water color of the Isabel D. I mightn't have healed an old wound in Judge Candler's heart that may make the ones Karen and his old friend dealt him less hard to bear. Roger and Jerry mightn't be on their way south. I mightn't ever have found out that you thought of me the minute you were scared out of your wits. You know, my dear——"

A black object that was my Lilac appeared in the door.

"Th' Sergeant, he down stairs, ma'am. He want to know, *is* th' Cunnel comin', or is he not?"

"Oh, I'm sure he is, immediately," I said.

"As a matter of fact, Lilac," Colonel Primrose said, blandly, "you may present my compliments to the Sergeant, and tell him that I say he can go to hell.—And sweeten this up a little, please."

"Yas, *suh*," Lilac said. "Ah sho' will—an' with *pleasure*."